Advance Prais

"*Retribution* is a complex and deeply moving work. It is a saga of love, courage, determination, and acceptance, in which three generations of women confront political upheaval and subsequent repression, find strength and consolation in their friends, lovers, and family, and link together their lives in Chile and Canada, two countries whose histories have become increasingly inter-twined. Carmen Rodríguez brings a warm, human, yet realistic voice to the tragedy of the Pinochet coup d'état and the inspiring resilience of the Chilean people."

Hugh Hazelton, author and winner of the 2006 Governor General's Award for Translation

"...[T]he important story of family, love, political repression, and resistance in this novel of the Pinochet dictatorship and its repercus-sions in the lives of people and the nation."

Amy K. Kaminsky, author of *After Exile*

"The retribution attained in Carmen Rodriguez' novel is neither vengeful nor violent, but a beautifully human way of countering the world's evil. Rodriguez' direct and often poetic language, rich in vivid detail, conveys the growth from innocence to aware-ness of a mother and daughter, Soledad and Sol... The novel's themes—political divisions within families, social transforma-tion, torture, betrayal, class consciousness—are rare in Canadian fiction, and the book is a valuable gift to this country's literature."

Cynthia Flood, author of *The English Stories*

-Continued-

Retribution

Retribution

a novel

Carmen Rodríguez

Women's Press Literary

Toronto

Retribution
Carmen Rodríguez

First Published in 2011 by
Women's Press Literary, an imprint of Three O'Clock Press Inc.
180 Bloor St. West, Suite 801
Toronto, Ontario M5S2V6
www.threeoclockpress.com

Every reasonable effort has been made to identify copyright holders. Three O'Clock Press would be pleased to have any errors or omissions brought to its attention.

Three O'Clock Press gratefully acknowledges financial support for our publishing activities from the Ontario Arts Council, and the Government of Canada through the Canada Book Fund. We acknowledge the support of the Canada Council for the Arts which last year invested $20.1 million in writing and publishing throughout Canada.

Library and Archives Canada Cataloguing in Publication

Rodríguez, Carmen, 1948-
    Retribution / Carmen Rodríguez.

ISBN 978-0-9866388-1-7

    I. Title.

PS8585.O373R48 2011 C813'.54 C2011-905656-9

Poem excerpt from: Peri Rossi, Christina. "XXIV." *State of Exile*. San Francisco: City Lights Books, 2008.

Cover Photo: Copyright © http://www.istockphoto.com/stock-photo-15378522-dark-sunset.php
Cover Design: Sarah Hope Wayne
Printed and bound in Canada by Transcontinental

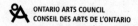   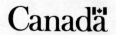

For the essential ones: Armando and Carmen, my parents; Choche and Nelson, my brothers; Carmen and Alejandra, my daughters; Ted (Lalo), my son; Finn and Santiago, my grandsons; and Alan, my partner in life.

Es seguro que nuestra venganza será el amor
poder amar, todavía
poder amar, a pesar de todo

For sure our revenge will be love
to be able to love, still
to be able to love, in spite of everything

Cristina Peri Rossi

Vancouver, Canada
March, 2011

Tania

Thirteen days ago, a letter from Chile arrived.

White envelope.

Registered.

Official looking.

Signed by Judge Arturo Leiva.

A bomb concealed in a handful of circuitous sentences.

Judge Leiva writes that he would be extremely thankful if I were to approach the Chilean Consulate in Vancouver to arrange for a sample of my blood to be tested. He explains that a certain Marcelino Romero is on trial for allegedly having performed acts of torture and rape against female political prisoners at the Londres 38 detention centre in Santiago, following the military coup of September 11, 1973. There is evidence to believe, he continues, that one of those women would have been Señora Sol Martínez. There is further evidence to presume that these unspeakable acts might have resulted in Señora Martínez becoming pregnant with Marcelino Romero's child.

Señora Sol Martínez is my mother.

Judge Leiva needs my DNA to determine whether Marcelino Romero is my father.

Until now, Miguel Rivera has been my father.

Miguel—curly fingers, hair shooting up to the sky, face of a naughty boy—principal violinist of Chile's Symphony. Miguel, one of the country's thousands of "disappeared."

I never met Miguel, but he has always been an integral part of my life. My mother and grandmother made sure that I grew to know him as thoroughly as the palms of my hands. My mom would tell me over and over again the story of how they came together when she was twelve and he, fourteen. My grandmother never tired of describing his humble demeanor and the magic of his violin playing.

But my grandma's accounts went much further back in time, to her life as a young woman in Santiago, when all she wanted was to become an elementary school teacher. She insisted on providing detailed explanations of the Chilean cultural and literary scene in those times and, at the drop of a hat, would begin reciting her favourite verses.

She was so passionate about poetry that even her term of endearment for me came from one of her most cherished poems. While my mami had countless names for me—*mi gatita*, "my kitty cat"; *mijita*, "my little daughter"; *chiquitita*, "little one"; *cosa más linda*, "loveliest thing"; "darling"; "lovie"; "precious"; *regalona*, "cuddly one"—for my grandma, I was always "my queen." Morning, afternoon and night, rain or shine, whether I had behaved well or misbehaved, I would be my grandma's queen: "My queen, go and do your homework right now!" "My queen, stop scratching your crotch and sit like a lady." "My queen, come here so that I can braid your hair." "My queen, how can you go out looking like *that?*"

When Queen Elizabeth appeared on television in her ludicrous hats and carting a little purse with who-knows-what inside, I felt completely and utterly cheated. Why on earth would my grandma ever want to call me "my queen"?

One day I mentioned it to her. She burst out laughing and then explained that she didn't call me "my queen" because of Queen Elizabeth, but rather because of a Gabriela Mistral poem called "We Would All Be Queens." In that poem, Mistral talks about her childhood in the Elqui Valley and the friends that she used to play with, imagining that one day they would all have a life of gratification and joy, their dreams and hopes fulfilled forever; that they would all become queens. While brushing my hair, my grandma went on to tell me that when she was a girl she also had wanted to have a prosperous and happy life, but destiny had decided to play havoc with her dreams.

"And as if that hadn't been enough, destiny also decided to mess with my daughter's life!" she added.

"That's my mami," I interjected.

"Yes, my queen, that's your mami," she confirmed as she set the brush down and picked up two colourful hair pins in the shape of butterflies from the top of her dresser. She put one between her teeth—the same way she would hold half a dozen pins when she was doing her sewing—carefully placed the other one on the left side of my head, took the second pin out of her mouth, positioned it on the other side, looked approvingly at me in the mirror and then continued speaking as she rested her hands on my shoulders.

"So, when you were born, I decided to do everything in my power to help you become a queen; to make sure that you can realize your dreams and be a happy, happy person. That's why you're my queen, not because of Queen Elizabeth." She chuckled and then kissed the top of my head. "Now go play!" she commanded, giving me a pat on the butt.

In addition to her recitations and explanations about poetry, my grandmother also offered vivid portraits of the beautiful trees to be found in Santiago's many parks. She also drew and coloured them for me so that I could appreciate the particular shade of lilac of a jacaranda in bloom; the magnificent trunk and red, succulent flowers of a *ceibo*; the vibrant crimsons and golds of *liquidámbars* in autumn. But while I enjoyed her botanical descriptions and her poetry, I was far more interested in hearing about the pleats and cuffs of her chocolate brown school uniform, the cut and length

6

of the home-made percale dresses she wore on Sunday and, most of all, about her engagement and marriage to my grandfather, Andrés—a charming young man who, according to her, looked just like Clark Gable, a famous movie actor.

While my grandmother's memories of her youth intrigued me, the family's stories during the time they lived in a little house on Esmeralda Street in Valdivia enthralled me to the point of delusion. This was the place where my mom had become a rebellious teenager, where my uncle Andresito had fallen in love with his friend Carloncho, where my grandmother had witnessed her son's murder at the hands of the military.

As a child, I was immersed so deeply in those stories that I believed that I had been a witness to them all; that I had lived on Esmeralda Street with my grandma, my mom and the rest of the characters that populated their past.

When I grew old enough to realize that these were nothing but borrowed memories, I felt completely betrayed and for quite a while stubbornly insisted that I had indeed attended the Valdivia Youth Orchestra's concerts; laughed at my grandfather's jokes as the family shared tea and apple *kuchen* at the kitchen table; celebrated Chile's third place in the 1962 World Cup at the town square; travelled to Santiago with my grandmother and met her shrewd and fashionable sister Amparo.

But, by the time I reached my teens, I lost interest in my mother's and grandmother's accounts and even resented not being *Canadian*-Canadian: born here, with a family history that didn't include military coups, concentration camps, resistance movements and relatives who had either been killed or made to disappear.

In those years, my best friends were Karin Russell and Vicki Richards. The three of us lived at Mariposa Housing Co-op, went to Britannia High School and played hockey for the East Vancouver Peewee team. We were like triplets—walked to school together, went to practices and games together, did homework together, hung out on Commercial Drive together, went to the movies together... I never talked about my "Chilean life" with them. They never heard any of my family stories, never learned what had happened to Miguel and my uncle Andresito, my mom's and grandma's ordeal before coming to Canada. Nothing. For them, my family's story was pretty straightforward: my dad had died in an accident, my grandfather of a heart attack, and my mom and grandma had decided to emigrate to Canada.

Karin and Vicki rarely came to my house, as I'd much rather go to theirs. Karin's mom was divorced and worked evening shifts at the telephone company, which meant that Karin could basically do whatever she wanted after school. So, at her place we tried cigarettes and booze for the first time and also watched porno movies that we rented from a fat, sleazy guy who peddled them at Grandview Park.

"Mmmm... I'm sure these beautiful young ladies will want to know what Snow White and the Seven Dwarves were really—and I do mean *really*—doing in that cute little house of theirs in the middle of the forest, eh?" he remarked in a low, enticing tone as he winked and smiled a crooked smile. We were tired and disheartened, having just lost a game to the Westside Thunderbirds, and had stopped to look at the rows and rows of video boxes displayed on a dirty blanket on the grass.

Vicki, who had crouched down to look at the titles and hadn't seen Fatso's gestures, looked up at Karin and me with narrowed eyes and blurted out, genuinely curious, "What the hell does he mean by what Snow White and the Seven Dwarves were really doing?"

"Never mind, let's just go," I urged as I started to walk.

But Fatso wasn't giving up. Now he was waving a video at us and delivering his sales pitch. "Okay, girls. I'll tell you what. Given that obviously you don't know how much fun the fairest one of all and those naughty little men were having in their lovely cottage, I will let you take the video for free. What do you think?" He looked at us inquisitively, waiting for a response.

We shrugged and replied in our usual triplet way, "Sure."

"Okey-dokey then," he continued, sticking his hand into a duffel bag, taking out a few videos, looking at them closely and, finally, offering us the right one. We all reached for it, but he retracted it quickly as he smiled his crooked smile.

"Not so fast, girls, not so fast. Now, you can have this one for free, but you have to promise to bring it back the day after tomorrow and then *rent* another video from me, okay? I only charge four fifty and you can keep it for two days at a time. Isn't that a great deal? I don't really make a profit, girls, I just want to keep young people informed and entertained," he explained with a straight face. "Inform and entertain—that's my motto," he concluded as he now handed us the video.

By the time we got to Karin's place we were *dying* to be informed and entertained. We grabbed a bag of chips and some sodas and made ourselves comfortable on the couch. The first few minutes looked just like a regular movie—an aerial view of a beautiful forest accompanied by romantic orchestral music which then gave way to the sound of deep, masculine voices singing, "Heigh-Ho, Heigh-Ho, It's home from work we go." A line of seven short, muscular men with big beards appeared on a trail in the woods and then we saw the home they were walking towards: a cute little cottage with a red-tiled roof, a rounded wooden door and widows covered with lace curtains. As the men reached the cottage's colourful front garden, the door opened wide and there she was: Snow White herself, a gorgeous white woman with jet black hair and green eyes. She was dressed like Heidi, only she had boobs the size of a football field, and as she walked down the pathway to meet the men she was pursing her crimson lips and rocking her hips just like the hookers we had seen on the Drive.

What Snow White and the seven dwarves did inside their little cottage was very informative and entertaining, indeed. We would've never imagined the many forms that screwing could take between one man and one woman, never mind all the other possible combinations: seven men and one woman, seven men, two men and one woman, two men, etcetera, etcetera. We jumped around the room screaming and giggling, laughed so hard that we wet our pants, replayed some scenes to make sure that we had got it right...

Two days later, we handed the video back to Fatso and rented our next one. He was very interested in our feedback, but we didn't let on that we had actually enjoyed it. We faked a bored expression and declared in a monotone, indifferent voice, "It was okay."

After four or five video sessions, we *did* begin to get bored. They were all variations on the same theme—screwing—except for one that really grossed us out, as it involved a huge, vicious dog, and another one that scared the shit out of us with displays of sadomasochism.

So, when we returned the last movie and Fatso insisted on sticking another one in our hands, we explained that we didn't have time for movies anymore; we had to get ready for final exams, and walked away as fast as we could.

By then we had also lost interest in booze and tobacco. We had finally admitted to each other that drinking and smoking wasn't as fun as it was purported to be; actually, it made us feel like zombies suffering from an acute bout of bronchitis combined with morning sickness, so we began to spend more and more time at Vicki's. She had a stay-at-home mom, a dad who drove a city bus and an older brother in university. I loved their home—it exuded a feeling of "normalcy," completely devoid of any sense of tragedy or loss. There, we would do our homework, listen to music and watch Degrassi Junior High and Street Legal on television, all under the benign supervision of Vicki's mom.

In the summertime, Kits Beach was our favourite place to be. We'd play volleyball, go swimming or just lie lazily on the sand. Once in a while we'd meet boys from the West side and talk and flirt with them, but overall, we just minded our own business.

I often brought my sketch pad along and took down the scene: sailboats like huge birds hovering over the white caps; people of all colours, shapes and sizes enjoying the sun; good-looking, agile guys and gals reaching for the volleyball; cute little kids with their plastic buckets and shovels building sand castles... When I got home, I loved going over my sketches and turning my favourite ones into paintings—airy expanses of blue over which I laid out the whites, golds, greens and reds of the lively figures all about the beach.

When I turned fourteen I took a refereeing course and began to work at the Britannia Ice Rink; I enjoyed reffing the little kids' games, the pay was good and I also welcomed the opportunity to get a few extra hours of skating each week. By then Karin and Vicki had stopped playing hockey and were working at Tim Horton's, so we hardly ever spent time together anymore.

As we drifted apart, I also began to pay attention to the other kids in our school. There were lots of First Nations students who kept pretty much to themselves but turned out to be really friendly when you approached them. That's how I became friends with Dwayne, a fifteen-year-old from Port Hardy who was always carving beautiful sculptures on pieces of red cedar. We would spend hours together at Grandview Park—me, drawing and sketching everything I saw, from the children in the playground to the Vancouver skyline and the North Shore Mountains, and him, working on his latest piece.

He was the first kid from school that I entrusted with my family's stories and it didn't take long for him to start telling me about *his* family and community. That's how I learned about the abuse, and even torture, that Dwayne's grandparents, parents and most of their generation had suffered in residential schools; about the real reasons behind the poverty and epidemics of alcoholism and drug addiction among First Nations people; about the youth's determination to learn about their culture and move forward with their lives.

At Britannia High School, there were also tons of students who had come to Canada as refugees, just like me: Vietnamese who had left their country in squalid boats, Salvadorans and Guatemalans who had literally walked all the way up to Canada, and plenty of Iranians, Ugandans, Ethiopians and Somalians who had also fled from violence.

One of the last times Karin, Vicki and I got together, I told them about Ayanna, a Somalian girl who had disclosed her story to the Current Affairs class I was taking with Ms. Yew. We were having a pizza at Sunrise and the two of them were chattering away about a boy that Vicki really liked, but I just couldn't get into the conversation.

"Hey, Tania, what do you think?" Karin asked me point blank as she pinched my arm.

"Think about what?" I responded absent-mindedly.

"What's the matter with you, woman? Don't you care about your friends' love lives? Get with the program, eh?" she went on in a miffed tone.

"Sure," I answered. "It's just that I can't get this girl's story out of my mind..."

"What girl?" they both wanted to know.

"Ayanna, a girl from Somalia, a refugee. She came here with her mom and her two younger sisters after the father and little brother were killed in their own home," I explained, and then asked, "can you imagine witnessing your own father and brother's murder?"

"Holy shit! That's horrible!" Vicki replied, crunching her face.

"Thank God we were born in Canada and not in some weird, violent country like... Where did you say she was from?" Karin asked as she reached for another slice of pizza.

"Somalia," I repeated.

"Where's *that*?" they both asked.

"East Africa," I responded somberly.

"Mmm... Never heard of it," Karin commented while she chewed on her pizza and screened her mouth with her hand.

"Me neither... But that's really horrible. Poor girl..." Vicki added, letting out a big sigh and shaking her head. "Anyway, where were we?" she continued chirpily, turning her head towards Karin.

I felt like crying. *I* had been born in one of those weird, violent countries and my whole family was from there as well. Not only that, Karin and Vicki didn't even know that Canada was also a violent country, that unspeakable injustices had been committed against the people who had lived here from time immemorial— way before any Europeans had set foot on this land. Somewhere in my heart, I had hoped that Ayanna's story would serve as a bridge so that I could finally disclose *my* family's story to them; that I would finally be able to say, "You know what, you guys? I wasn't born here either. I was only three days old when I came to Canada, which basically means I'm Canadian, but I was born in Chile. My mami, my grandma and I came here as refugees. My dad was killed, my uncle was killed, my mom was in a concentration camp"

But, that evening, I decided that I couldn't tell them any of that, at least not then. Not for a long time; perhaps never.

Eventually I stopped spending time with Karin and Vicki, got closer and closer to Dwayne and became best friends with Ayanna. My mami and grandma were delighted that I was at home most evenings now and welcomed Dwayne and Ayanna with open arms. My grandma expressed her approval of my new friends by preparing her best Chilean specialties to treat them. Dwayne lived with his grandma, mom and siblings just a couple of blocks away in a nice complex that housed urban First Nations families, but Ayanna and her mom and sisters could only afford a small, dark basement apartment near Nanaimo Street. So, my mom encouraged them to apply to Mariposa Housing Co-op and a few months later they moved to the suite upstairs from us.

By now Dwayne, Ayanna and I knew everything there was to know about one another's lives. Hearing their stories, I had come to realize how sheltered and easy my own life had been; I had learned what I knew about suffering through my mom and grandma, but hadn't experienced any real trials and tribulations myself. So I was curious to know where my friends found the strength to keep going in spite of the hardships in their lives. Often, Ayanna got anxiety attacks and I had to hold her until she finally broke down, sobbed for a while on my shoulder and, eventually, calmed down. Dwayne, on the other hand, was the oldest of five kids and had to play the role of father to the family, as his dad was an absent alcoholic. To top it all off, when the man chose to show up at the house, he beat up the grandma, the mom, and the kids, and stole everything in sight before disappearing again. He had been doing that for years, but now that Dwayne was older he had taken it upon himself to fight his father back and keep him off the rest of the family.

According to Ayanna, living with the memory of her dad's and little brother's murders was very hard, but for some mysterious reason she had never considered ending the suffering by choosing death; she wanted to live, to wake up every morning and live. Dwayne would speak of the history of his people, of his desire to contribute to a revival of First Nations' culture.

Humans' love of life had always mystified me. Since I had been able to understand my family's tragedies I had wondered about my mami and grandma's desire to keep on living. Not letting yourself die after your most beloved had been killed was beyond my comprehension.

Whenever I asked my grandma about it, she would hug me effusively and plant kisses on both my cheeks before declaring, "It was all about you, my queen. I wanted to live on so that I could be with you, you, you!"

My mom, on the other hand, would take on a solemn stance when explaining her reasons for choosing life over death. She would stop whatever she was doing, take her glasses off, wipe the lenses with the tail of her shirt, clear her throat and then explain, "First of all, as I have told you many times before, my love, I wanted to raise you and make sure that you grew up to be a good and happy person. When I was in the concentration camp, a few times I did feel like dying; I wanted to die. But when I realized I was pregnant with you, I wanted to keep on living."

"How did you know you were pregnant with *me?*" I would ask for the zillionth time, yearning for the sound of the words I had heard over and over again along the years.

"I just knew it my beautiful kitty cat. I pictured you in my mind exactly the way you are: green eyes, dark hair, long and thick eye lashes, just like Miguel's."

By now my mom's serious face had given way to smiling eyes as she continued, cupping my face in her hands, "But most importantly, I pictured you as the strong, kind and bright girl that you are."

"And that's why you named me Tania, after the heroic guerrilla that fought together with Che Guevara in Bolivia," I would add as I felt a good dose of pride surge up to my face.

"That's right, *mijita*," my mom would confirm. "But you know that there was also another reason why I wanted to live on."

"To fight for a better world," I would offer.

At this point, she would nod approvingly for a few seconds before launching into her usual lesson about social injustices. "Yes, my precious. Because too many people in this world are starving to death."

"Like in Africa," I would add.

"Yes, but in other continents as well."

"In Chile too?" I would ask.

"Yes, my loveliest thing. Many people in Chile go hungry, don't have a house to live in, are sick, don't have a job—"

"So, they don't have any money to buy anything..." I would interject.

"That's right, my darling. And on top of all that, Pinochet and the army are mean to the people," my mom would conclude.

Most certainly, in Canada my mami had the opportunity to continue working for her ideals. She had dedicated long hours to her job as a social worker assisting immigrant women and was also very active in the international movement against the Chilean dictatorship.

But for her that had not been enough. Back in 1986, when I was eleven years old, my mom joined the armed resistance in Chile.

The evening that I heard the truth about her long absence that year was unusually warm for the month of April. The radio was tuned to the six o'clock CBC news. As my mom checked on her chicken casserole and I put the finishing touches on a green salad, we heard Nelson Mandela's voice announcing the formation of the South African Truth and Reconciliation Commission.

"That's great!" my mom commented as she took the clay pot out of the oven and placed it on top of the stove. "I hope theirs is more successful than the Chilean Rettig Comission," she added, opening the lid and breathing in the scent of the food.

"I thought the Rettig Comission had done a good job," I ventured while I tossed the salad.

"Well..." my mother responded, tilting her head to one side, crunching her face into a cluster of wrinkles and gesturing with her right hand from side to side—her very personal way of letting you know that she disagreed and that a thorough explanation of her views would follow shortly.

Here we go, I thought. My mami was so opinionated that sometimes she irritated me to no end. I hastily called my grandma to the table in the hope that dinner would make my mom forget about her critique of the Rettig Commission, but a couple of minutes later, as we sat down to eat, she picked up where she had left off.

"You could say that the Rettig Commission did a fairly good job, but I think it would've been better if they had waited a few more years. 1990 was too soon after the end of the dictatorship; people were still afraid of talking about what had happened to them," she remarked. As she passed the salad bowl to grandma, she continued, "The other problem was that it didn't have any power; they collected quite a bit of information, but nothing came of it, no trials for the torturers and the murderers."

By now my poor mom was getting agitated, her voice had gone up an octave and her cheeks were beginning to colour.

I put my hand on hers in an attempt to calm her down, but she was on a roll, "Besides, many people never presented their cases—people like me, who were in prison after the coup and later took part in the armed resistance movement."

"What do you mean, armed resistance movement?" I shot out, pulling my hand off hers.

My mom went pale when she realized what she had revealed. She held my shocked gaze for a few seconds, her eyes filling with tears. She reached for my hand, but I snatched it away. I couldn't believe what I had heard. After almost dying in prison following the coup, after all they had gone through to escape the country, my mami had gone back to Chile and risked her life? I couldn't fathom my mother, a peace-loving person, taking part in armed operations. And to top it all off, she had left me behind.

My grandma got up, walked around the table and bent over to hug her daughter. By now my mother wasn't looking at me anymore. Her eyes were closed, her hands clutching her head.

"In 1986, your mother went to Chile to be part of the armed resistance movement," my grandma said in a calm, clear voice while she rocked my mom in her arms and looked me in the eye. "Obviously, we couldn't tell you the real reason for her going away. You hadn't even turned twelve yet."

"You could've been killed! You could've been imprisoned all over again!" I cried as I felt my throat begin to tighten.

I was livid. But underneath the anger, I was sad. My mami's political convictions were more important than me.

I found myself standing by the stove, my back to the table. I heard my mom get up from her chair and walk towards me. She rested her hand on my back for a few seconds and then spoke in a low, hoarse voice. "I had to do it, Tania. I had to make a real contribution. I felt that what I was doing here was not enough, so when I was asked to go... I'm sorry that I left you behind, my darling. And you're right—yes, I could've been killed, I could've been imprisoned, but... I don't know how to explain it to you. In my heart, I knew that I would come back in one piece and I did, see?"

I felt my mom's firm grip on my shoulders as she tried to turn me around. I let her do it—my body had gone limp.

My mom's eyes were smiling now as both her hands travelled the length of her body and she repeated, "See? I'm here, *mijita*. Nothing happened to me."

We hugged, then my grandma joined us and the three of us hugged. We cried together. After a while, my grandma suggested that we finish our dinner. For a few minutes, the only voices in the room were those of the radio announcers. I still felt betrayed.

Finally, I heard myself say, "You loved your revolution better than you loved me."

In the silence that followed, I gave up on a response and was getting ready to leave the table when I heard my mother clear her throat—without a doubt, a sign that she was going to offer a lengthy reply. I sat down again.

"I can see how you would come to that conclusion," she said, "but I know what's in my heart and I know that I don't love you any less than I love my ideals. For me, it never worked like that."

She got up and walked to the window. Her breathing was now audible and I could tell that she was fighting back tears. She placed both her hands on the window sill, as if to steady herself, before she continued, "I hate this society that makes us believe that life has to consist of lists—lists that prioritize everything from the most to the least important, even feelings! Well, I'm sorry, but I don't believe in those lists! That's not the way it works for me. Not at all!" she cried out as she turned around.

"Tania, I love you immensely, my darling," she went on after a while, her voice soft and low now as she walked towards me. I started to sob.

My mother knelt next to my chair, put her arms around me and went on speaking. "There are a few things that I need to explain to you—I don't expect you to understand them right away or even ever. I don't expect you to agree with me either, but please listen to what I have to say, okay?" she asked. My grandma handed me a tissue; I blew my nose and then nodded. My mami took my chin in her right hand and looked me in the eye.

"I believe that life must integrate everything, my lovie—it must be like a circle, not like a list. A circle where everything comes together: my ideals, you, grandma, my work, our friends, our dead loved ones, everything and everybody." My mom let go of my chin, sat at the table again and reached for my hand.

"When I was asked to join the armed resistance movement, you were almost twelve and grandma was willing and very capable of taking care of you on her own. At the beginning I hesitated, but finally decided to accept because I wanted to do something significant to help end the dictatorship," she added, her eyes looking for a reaction in mine. But I was still unwilling to yield.

She got up and walked to the sink. She poured herself a glass of water, turned around and then went on, "It's all part of the same love, Tania. It breaks my heart to see people in pain—I want the world to be a better place for everybody, you know that. In 1986, many Chileans were suffering. Pinochet was escalating the violence and there was a strong resistance movement trying to stop him; to get rid of him." She put the glass down on the counter and walked towards me. "I feel honoured to have been part of that movement, *mijita*. Can you at least feel a little bit of pride in your mother?" she asked as she poked me playfully on the ribs.

I had always felt proud of her, but at that moment I wasn't sure whether or not I would ever be able to understand her involvement in the armed resistance in Chile, never mind feel proud of her because of it.

I didn't respond. I blew my nose again and then got up and hugged her. She had left me for almost a year; she *had* chosen her ideals over me. But she was my mother, and I loved her.

We were still in each other's arms when we heard my grandma's voice. "Well... Nobody has asked for my opinion, but I'm going to say what I think anyway, if that's okay with you, m'ladies..."

My mami and I let each other go as we exchanged furtive smiles. "Sure," we said in unison, sitting down in our respective chairs.

"I think that if your mother had joined the resistance movement against Hitler, you would be proud of her, right?" she asked me point blank.

"I guess so..." I responded tentatively.

"And, I'm sure that if your *father*—if those beasts hadn't killed him—if your *father*, and not your mother, had joined the resistance movement, nobody would be talking about whether or not leaving his daughter behind was a good or a bad thing, whether he loved his daughter this much or that much, don't you think?" she went on, still looking me in the eye.

"I guess so..." I repeated.

Grandma stepped closer to me, her voice rising angrily. "Then, for heaven's sake, why can't you take pride in the fact that your mother was part of a movement against a dictator as cruel and ruthless as Hitler, that she went down to Chile to help put an end to the killings and the torturing?"

By now my grandma's face was two inches away from mine and she was yelling. I was taken aback. She hardly ever got angry with me.

"I have to think about it... I don't have a switch to turn my feelings on and off, you know," I responded defensively, getting up and leaving the room.

It took years, and many conversations with my mother about her political views and underground experiences, before I finally came to appreciate why she had gone to Chile in 1986.

When I listened to my mami's stories, I wondered what I would've done if life had dealt me similar circumstances. In all likelihood, I would've joined the exuberant movement striving for justice in the Chile of the sixties and seventies. Maybe I would've taken part in the literacy campaign in the shanty towns of Santiago, the way my mom did. I'm sure I would've offered my art—just like Miguel did—to bring hope to the poor, but I don't know if I would've taken part in the armed resistance to the dictatorship. Even though I grew to admire my mom's courage, I'm glad I haven't had to make those kinds of choices myself.

As for the letter from Judge Arturo Leiva, I've yet to decide whether I'll act on it or not.

The first few days following its delivery, I was both shocked and filled with insatiable curiosity. I carried the letter in my pocket at all times, fingered it, pulled it out, read it, put it back in my pocket once again. I couldn't eat, couldn't sleep. All I could do was think about the message enclosed in those oblique, yet clear words: there was a strong chance that Marcelino Romero, and not Miguel, was my father.

I knew that my mom had been abducted the day of the coup, but I didn't know when she had been taken to Londres 38, the torture centre where Marcelino Romero operated. I spent hours researching calculators for childbirth due dates, but basically they all offered the same information: conception and birth are approximately two hundred and sixty-six days apart. That meant that I would've been conceived on September 23. However, all the calculators also cautioned that many births happen up to two weeks before or after the estimated due date. The answers, then, didn't lie there.

I considered confronting my mother. A few times, I took the letter out of my pocket and practiced in my mind the wording of the bomb I would drop on her. Once, I made it as far as her bed.

But, in the end, I decided that she doesn't deserve this bomb, particularly now that she's so close to the end. She lived a life fraught with hardships and has gained the right to die in peace.

My mami is dying of cancer of the bones, the same ailment that took my grandmother in 1998. It's not surprising, given that they shared so many things in life. Now I wonder if they also shared the knowledge that Marcelino Romero, and not Miguel, may be my biological father.

After the initial shock and curiosity brought on by Judge Leiva's letter, I entered a state of supreme wrath. How could anyone even begin to suggest that a repugnant torturer and rapist might be my father? When I felt as if I was about to explode, I would get in my car and go for long drives on the freeway. There, hidden in the insular protection of my vehicle and tempered by the noise of the traffic, I'd scream and scream until I had no voice left.

Now, I have arrived at a place of exhaustion and exasperating indecision. I don't know what I'll do about Judge Leiva's request. One minute I believe that I will not be able to go on living until I know the truth, but the next I convince myself that Miguel, and only Miguel, is my father. A few days ago, I went as far as picking up the phone and dialing the Chilean Consulate's number, only to hang up before anybody could answer.

Until I muster the courage to make a decision, I will rely on my art to help me pull through these disturbing times.

Yesterday I began working on an exhibition based on my family's history. Every surface of my studio is covered with the sketches, drawings and paintings I have produced along the years. I have also been going through my notebooks and our photo albums, gathering the various objects that my grandma and mom brought with them to Canada: my mother's tapestries, my grandmother's pottery pieces and watercolours.

But as I sit here, surrounded by a disarray of memories, keepsakes, images and words, I wonder if I will ever be able to do justice to the stories that took my family through its many journeys. I don't know if I'll manage to convey the ordinary, yet unique ups and downs of my mami and grandma's daily existence before the Pinochet coup; if I'll have the courage to portray the horror that followed; if I'll dare trace and bring out the underlying forces that shaped my mother and grandmother's lives.

Most daunting of all, though, is the unavoidable challenge of having to delve deep inside myself. If I really want to understand my family's history, I will have to do my best to understand myself as well. After all, a good part of who I am is a result of that history and, conversely, a good part of that history was shaped by my passage through this world.

Art will be my compass, my lens, my tool.

Art as memory.

Art as healing.

Art as creation and beauty.

Art as truth.

Chile

1942–1965

Sol

I met Miguel in March of 1962 at the Valdivia Music Conservatory, where I took piano and musical theory lessons. That year he joined the violin program and, in no time, we became best friends. Until then I had never got close to any of the other students because they were all of German descent, fairly wealthy, quite full of themselves, and went to their own private school: Deutsche Schule. Miguel and I went to public schools; he was studying at Normal School and I had just begun attending Commercial High School.

Shortly after classes began, we were all summoned to the recital room and introduced to Mr. Gronau, a conductor who had come directly from Germany to put together a youth orchestra. He explained that the first presentation was going to consist of two parts: *Concert in D Minor for Piano and Orchestra* by Johann Sebastian Bach, and the *Toy Symphony* by Joseph Haydn. It was to take place in July at the Cervantes Theatre and then we were going to have presentations in several towns close to Valdivia. Ursula Schwazenberg, the most advanced piano student, would play the Bach concert, and the rest of the piano students would have to learn how to play other instruments such as the recorder and the xylophone. The strings students would participate with their own instruments.

Given that Mr. Gronau didn't speak Spanish, he explained everything in German and Mrs. Margot, the director of the conservatory, translated. After the meeting, all the other kids began to talk to him in German, left me and Miguel completely out of the loop. Then I got an idea: I asked Miguel if he had an English class at Normal School and he said yes. So, I suggested that we speak English and he agreed.

"This is a chair."

"That's a table."

"Open the window."

"Shut the door."

We didn't recite it like in school, but said it all as if it were a normal conversation, gesturing with our hands to dramatize a phrase, nodding our heads, shifting out weight from one foot to the other. Sometimes, Miguel would arrange the words in the form of a question: "Is this a table?"

And I would respond with gusto: "Yes, it is!"

We were having great fun and feeling quite pleased with ourselves when Mrs. Margot asked us what language we were speaking.

"English!" we responded at once in an offended tone, as if saying, "You stupid woman, don't you know what English sounds like?"

Mrs. Margot tilted her head and frowned as she examined us with narrowed eyes. Then she turned to Mr. Gronau and, obviously, proceeded to tell him that he could communicate with us in English, because Mr. Gronau began talking to us at the speed of light. Needless to say, Miguel and I didn't understand a word of what he said and were forced to explain, in Spanish, that we really didn't speak any English at all.

When we were walking back along General Lagos Street, I announced to Miguel that I was going to learn to speak English fluently. "You'll see. Mark my words," I declared.

But Miguel didn't respond. I looked at him and noticed that he appeared sad and withdrawn. I asked him what the matter was. All he said was that the orchestra would be going to Loncoche, the town where he was from. As I didn't understand how this could be a reason for sadness and not joy, he confided, "My family's really poor."

I turned to look at him—hands in his pockets, eyes downcast, his cheeks alight with shame. I threaded my arm through his, rested my head on his shoulder and, attempting a cheerful voice, intoned, "Who cares!"

The silence that followed was eloquent. *He* cared, of course, otherwise he wouldn't have entrusted me with his secret.

"It must be hard to be poor..." I finally uttered as I tried to imagine what the word "poor" really meant. Was Miguel's house like those little shacks that proliferated in the outskirts of the city? Had he grown up barefoot, like some of the kids that ran around town begging for a coin or a piece of bread? Did he have zillions of brothers and sisters, faces full of snot, hair a sticky tangle, bodies clothed with a crust of grime?

Miguel shrugged. Then offered, "The hardest of all is living with a drunk."

"Your dad is a drunk?"

"Yeah..."

I had never seen my dad "drunk"; at most, overly talkative and laughing at the drop of a hat as he joked around with friends during a Saturday night dinner at our house. But I *had* seen plenty of drunks on the street, zigzagging their way to nowhere, slurring their swear words or their songs, pausing to vomit as they held on to a lamp post. What would having one of those men inside your house at all times be like?

"Thank goodness you turned out smart," I remarked a bit too enthusiastically as I squeezed Miguel's arm. "Because you have to be smart to have gotten a scholarship to attend Normal School and get free room and board, and the scholarship at the conservatory, no?" I pressed.

"I don't know if I'm smart or not," he responded softly. "What I do know is that I always loved studying... My teacher at the Loncoche School helped me to get the scholarship at the Normal and then my music teacher got me the scholarship at the conservatory. My mom did everything she could to make sure I could keep on studying, even though she can't read or write. But one of these days I will teach her."

"She doesn't know how to read and write?" I heard myself blurt out as I stopped, took my arm from Miguel's and looked at him with an open mouth.

Miguel's face turned beet red. He avoided my eyes and kept on walking ahead of me. I called up to him apologetically, but before I could catch up with his stooped body, he turned and faced me.

"It wasn't her fault. When she was a little girl there was no school in the countryside, and also she had to help her mom bring up her younger brothers and sisters," he explained in a calm, strong voice. He continued, his words now trembling with emotion and determination, "But she's smart, very smart, and one of these days I will teach her how to read and write."

By then we had got to the *Torreón*, so I took Yerbas Buenas Street towards home and Miguel went to catch the bus back to Normal School.

After a few steps, I spun around and yelled, "Miguel!"

He stopped in his tracks and turned towards me, a big smile on his face. "Yes?"

"Come to my house at tea time tomorrow, after our musical theory class!"

"Sure! See you tomorrow! Thanks!"

Walking home I felt light on my feet because I finally had a friend at the conservatory, but my heart was heavy with the feelings and thoughts stemming from my conversation with Miguel. Both my dad and my brother belonged to the Radical Party and were always talking about social injustices and political reforms, but I had never actually met somebody who had grown up poor. I couldn't conceive that Miguel's mom didn't know how to read and write—what was life like when you couldn't read a novel, a poem, a newspaper? What was life like when you couldn't write a letter to your own son?

When I told my mom about the presentations by the Youth Orchestra and about Miguel coming for *onces* the next day, she was very happy to hear about the orchestra, but questioned me no end about Miguel: "And, Señorita, may I ask who this Miguel is? How old is he? Is he from a good family? What school does he go to?"

As I didn't want my mom to veto my invitation to Miguel, I told her that he was from Loncoche, so I didn't know anything about his family, but he was a boarder at the Valdivia Normal School.

Then she stopped the interrogation and smiled. "Mmmm! So, he wants to become a teacher, eh?"

"A teacher and a violinist," I responded.

"That's nice... Very nice," she concluded.

After that first visit, my mom took in Miguel as her protégé and he became a bit of a fixture at our home, just like the boys who played in the Unión Juvenil, the soccer team that my brother Andresito belonged to and that my dad coached.

Back then I had a crush on Tito Ramírez, the team's goalie. Tito was tall and dark, but most importantly to me, he played the guitar and sang beautifully. He and Carloncho were my brother's best friends, so they would come to our house almost every day. Given that Tito was eighteen, I hated the fact that I was only twelve and prayed to God to make time go fast so that I could reach fifteen as soon as possible. For some mysterious reason, I was sure that then Tito would finally fall in love with me and ask me to be his girlfriend.

But, in the end, Tito fell for Silvia and I fell for Miguel.

I became friends with Silvia Wenzel at a track and field practice. We did our warm-up together, and in between jogging and stretching we began to talk. She was fourteen years old and of German descent, tall, slim, pretty, with blonde hair and blue eyes. She lived on Teja Island, right on the river, in a huge white house that her grandmother had inherited from her dad.

The Wenzels were part of the first group of Germans who had arrived at the port of Corral, just west of Valdivia, in 1850. Mr. Wenzel, Silvia's great-grandfather, had brought with him not only his life savings and dreams of a new life, but also his expertise as a master brewer. In no time he had founded the now defunct Wenzel Brewery, still considered the best that Chile ever had.

In 1962, Silvia had just started attending Commercial High School after years at the German school. According to her, she had stopped liking it because the kids were very conceited and she didn't feel comfortable around them. Later I would also learn that the family couldn't afford the exorbitant school fees anymore.

That day at the stadium, we agreed to go to mass together the following Sunday and then for a stroll on the square. As she would take the boat to town, I waited for her at the little dock at the end of Yerbas Buenas Street and from there we walked to the cathedral.

The only Sunday coat I owned back then was a hand-me-down from my Aunt Amparo, which made me look like a huge hairy bear, and not only that, but a huge hairy *purple* bear. My mom would swear that I loved the coat and also tried to foist on me a horrible Russian-style hat that she had made with what was left from the hemming job she had done on the coat, but to no avail. Having to wear the coat was awful enough for me.

On the other hand, Silvia was wearing a beautiful off-white coat that you could tell had been bought new or made to measure for her, just the way she wanted it. When I praised her good taste, she explained that the whole outfit had been a birthday present from a generous cousin in Germany. It was one of those coats that have no buttons and are held closed with a belt made of the same material, looped at the front, just like Marilyn Monroe's famous bathrobe, but longer. She looked like a movie star in her coat, pumps, and matching leather purse, while I felt like a scarecrow beside her in my purple coat, rubber boots, and without a purse because I didn't have one, as my mom had decided that the ones my Aunt Amparo had sent us were too grown up for me.

During mass I prayed to God to help my mom win the lottery which, in my mind, was not impossible because she had been buying the same number combination for about twenty years. All I wanted was for us to be rich because then I could wear the latest fashions and, according to my mom, we would buy a car and a house on Teja Island, plus hire maids to clean and cook, and do the laundry and the ironing.

That Sunday, Silvia caused quite a stir at the square. The boys whistled at her and made all kinds of complimentary remarks, so she kept on blushing, but also seemed to be very proud of herself. All I wanted was to disappear into thin air or for the earth to open up and swallow me because I felt uglier than Cheetah, Tarzan's chimp. But Mario, a boy from our school, came up and asked me if he could walk with me. I almost died from the shock. Then Tito Ramírez came to say hello, and asked me to introduce him to my girlfriend.

Even though Mario was part of the school's track and field team, I had never talked to him, so I was quite nervous and couldn't think of anything to say. But he took initiative, commenting on our performance in the last school competition and congratulating me for having won the fifty metre dash.

As I watched Tito and Silvia walk around the square side by side, talking and giggling as if they were old friends, I realized that I would never have a chance to become Tito's girlfriend. So when Mario asked me to be *his* girlfriend, I accepted in spite of not having the faintest idea of what it would entail. In the end, all it meant was that he would stroll around the *plaza* with me on Sundays and walk me home afterwards.

One of those Sundays, we got to the corner of my house and as I turned to say goodbye, he held my chin in his hand and kissed me. I was completely taken aback, but what really bewildered me was the sensation I got in between my legs: a weird kind of throbbing mixed with an urgent need to pee. That was my first encounter with my own sexuality, something that embarrassed and mystified me for ages.

From as far back as I can remember, my mom would lecture me on the importance of going to school, becoming a professional, not falling for the first boy that crosses your path... One of her favourite times to counsel me was early in the morning as she braided my hair. She would emphasize her points by pulling and twisting, often making me whimper and even shriek with pain. It turned out that she had noticed that Mario was walking me to the corner on Sundays, and that particular day she was at the living room window and saw him kiss me.

When I entered the house I was still walking on clouds and feeling the weird throbbing between my legs, but it all came to an abrupt halt as my mom began to yell, "Sol, listen to me! You're way too young to be thinking about boyfriends! Who is the little twit who kissed you at the corner? Don't you realize that boys only want one thing from girls? Haven't I explained to you a thousand times that you have to dedicate yourself to school and the conservatory? Tell me right now! Who is he? What's his name? Where does he go to school? How old is he? Where does he live? Come here, Sol! Come back here right now and answer me!"

But I didn't. I just kept going up the stairs and locked myself in my room.

Then, that very night, I got my first period. At first I was excited, but then I grew to hate that time of the month, as I had to use homemade sanitary napkins which I had to wash myself, plus wear elastic panties. According to my mom, these girdle-like knickers were supposed to keep the napkin in place, but in my mind, their real function was to squeeze my internal organs and make me the most miserable, uncomfortable girl on earth.

Around that time, I also got my first bra and garter belt, but my excitement about them was also short-lived: I couldn't stand the bra, as it dug into my ribs and made me short of breath, and the garter belt felt like having horse reins hanging from my waist, not to mention the hooks, which jabbed at my thighs. Worst of all, the cups of the bra were too big on me because even though the store carried triple A, my mom insisted on getting double A so that the bra would last.

"Sol, you know that we're not swimming in money, so let's get one that's *crecedorcito*—one that you can grow into?" she half-stated, half-asked, as she exchanged a complicit look with the clerk. Of course, she didn't wait for my response and I knew bet-

ter than to provide one. Now the stupid saleswoman was walking, bra in hand, towards me.

"Darling, let me share a secret with you," she offered in a
hushed, conspiratorial tone, her made-up face a couple of inches
from mine as she bent over to look at me. Her long, red fingernails showed like blood through the lace cups of the bra. "Your
bust will grow very quickly and in no time you will not only fill
this double A brassiere, but will need an A, a B and even a C!"
she added excitedly. Now the woman had straightened up and
her breasts—tightly hugged by a powder-blue banlon top—were
sticking out, right in front of my eyes. Most certainly her bra was
a C or even a D.

"All you have to do in the meantime, my darling, is fill the
ends of the cups with plenty of cotton and you will look very, very
sexy indeed," she added as she walked in her stilettos towards
the counter, ready to ring the cash register and take my mom's
money.

I followed her advice about the cotton and did feel kind of sexy
for a short while at a time, but when I least expected it, the cups
would dent and I'd almost die with embarrassment. Obviously,
the clerk hadn't warned me about this part of the deal. Also, her
prediction about how fast and how much my "bust" would grow
was completely off the mark; it took ages for my breasts to fill the
double A and then the single A bra. Years later I graduated into
a size B, but that's as far as I went—I never have required a C.

Given that none of my friends ever complained about periods

or undergarments, for the longest time I believed that I was not normal. But, as soon as I had the courage to rebel, I stopped wearing bras, girdles and garter belts, and never put one on again in my life.

In 1962, I also became best friends with Gloria, one of my classmates. I loved her wavy, black hair, her loud, husky voice, but above all, her audacity and sense of humour.

One day in March, during recess, Gloria showed me a book that she had taken from her mom's bedside table. It was called *The Positions of Love* and it showed photographs of a man and a woman having sex in unimaginable postures. I thought that it was disgusting, but Gloria insisted that when two people truly love each other, there are no limits to their lovemaking.

In the middle of Math period, Gloria and Doris asked for permission to go to the bathroom and, as they wouldn't stop giggling, the teacher realized that there was something fishy going on, so she followed them. She came back a couple of minutes later with the two of them in tow and gave us a speech about morality while she waved the book about the positions as if it were a flag and repeated, "These girls read por-no-gra-phic literature."

Gloria, on the other hand, repeated at the same time, "That book is not pornographic; it's about love." But to no avail, because they were suspended for several days.

That year our Spanish teacher was Miss Blanca, a beautiful and intelligent young woman who turned out to be a key figure in my life. She understood my feelings of inadequacy, lent me her ear whenever I felt troubled, and guided me through the aches and pains of becoming an adolescent girl in a *machista* society. Not only that, but she also contributed to the awakening of my social and political curiosity.

One day, since I was feeling completely "abnormal," I decided to stay indoors during recess. I was looking out the window at a patch of sky in between the school and the next building when Miss Blanca came back into the classroom.

"Sol, why aren't you going outside for recess? Is something bothering you?"

"I don't know... It's just that I don't think I'm normal... I don't want to be a girl... I hate having periods and wearing a bra. I hate house work... And I don't know if boys want to take advantage of me."

I just blurted it out, without even thinking about it. Only after I finished did I realize what I had done and broke into tears.

But then I felt Miss Blanca's hand on my shoulder and heard her say, "I know how you feel, Sol. Sometimes I also get tired of being a woman. But, actually, I don't think there's anything wrong with you or me. You and I are the normal ones."

I was so happy that I planted a kiss on her cheek and ran out to the schoolyard.

Miss Blanca introduced the class to Pablo Neruda's political writings. She explained that the poet was generally known for his love poems, but that he had a vast body of work dedicated to historical and social issues, among them *General Song*, which had been published clandestinely during the government of President Gabriel González Videla in the late forties and early fifties.

Gloria was the only one who knew about the book—her mom and dad had explained to her that during that period members of the Communist Party were persecuted and killed, and as Neruda was a communist, he had felt forced to leave Chile in order to save his life. He had escaped by crossing the Andes on horseback and eventually had gone to live in Mexico, where he had written General Song. Gloria's mom and dad owned a copy of that first edition of the book and Gloria had already read parts of it.

> Thereupon, from the earth
> made of our bodies, the song was born.
> Song of war, of sun, song of the harvest,
> growing towards the magnitude of the volcanoes.
> We then shared the dripping heart.
> I sank my teeth into that bloody flower
> fulfilling the rite of the earth...

I fell in love with Neruda's poems about *Mapuche* Chief Lautaro; they touched me so deeply that even after all these years I can recite them by heart. I admired Lautaro's bravery and his willingness to sacrifice everything in order to liberate his people. Is that when my revolutionary ideals began to take shape? Did Lautaro show me the way, point me in the direction of justice and a better world? Perhaps. But, when I was twelve years old, I was more preoccupied with being a girl than with being a revolutionary, so much so that for the longest time I fantasized about what would have happened if Lautaro had been a woman.

My secret story went something like this:

> If Lautaro had been a woman, that is to say Lautara, she wouldn't have eaten Pedro de Valdivia's heart in order to absorb his bravery, but instead she would've kissed Pedro de Valdivia in the mouth and their saliva would've come together and become one.
>
> Lautara is gorgeous, so Pedro de Valdivia is mad about her. But as she's extremely intelligent and knows exactly what she's doing—liberating her people—she doesn't fall in love with him but just bamboozles him.
>
> One night, Pedro de Valdivia comes to visit Lautara in her quarters of a Mapuche princess and she invites him in. She's wearing a hand-woven long, black wool dress and all her silver jewelry. A full moon can be seen in between the trees and the song of a lonely owl can be heard in the distance. Lautara has undone her braids and her jet-black hair falls like a waterfall down her shoulders. Her bed is covered with the pelts of wild animals and the aroma of the sweet herbs that Lautara has been burning to call the good spirits swirls up from the coals in the fire.
>
> Pedro de Valdivia comes in, dressed in his conqueror's iron helmet and armour, plus leather boots with spurs, and is carrying his sword in his hand. He has left his horse tied to a tree just outside the door. Lautara is lying down on the bed, resting on one elbow, one of her

legs stretched out and the other one bent. Pedro looks at her with his blue eyes and she holds his gaze with her black eyes. As he begins to take off his helmet, she gets up slowly, like a tigress, and without saying one single word, walks towards him and helps him take off the rest of his iron contraption. When he's finally in his clothes, both of them sit on the bed and she starts caressing him. He closes his eyes and lies on his back as she keeps on caressing him with her left hand while, with her right, she reaches down for the dagger she has hidden under the bed. Then, she kisses him gently in the mouth, but with a little bit of tongue, and as soon as she finishes, she belts out a war cry and thrusts the dagger into his heart. Again Lautara kisses Don Pedro, who has died with the shock. No. Again Lautara kisses Don Pedro, who has died instantly believing that love has killed him. That's how she absorbs the bravery of the conquistador. Then, she runs and runs through the forest until she gets to her Mapuche village.

All the Mapuche are waiting for her, ready for battle, and Lautara leads them on a victorious attack against the Spanish forces, which are completely disorganized and terrorized following the death of their commander in chief. The end.

But as Lautaro was Lautaro and not Lautara, I felt utterly disappointed. Why was it that all the heroes were men? Bernardo O'Higgins, Manuel Rodríguez, the Carrera brothers... The only famous woman was Javiera Carrera, whose great feat had been to sew the first Chilean flag, which probably meant that she also had to sew her brothers' clothes, cook for them, do the laundry and the ironing, *and* clean the whole house; I was certain she also had to embroider tablecloths.

That year, the Needlepoint teacher announced that we had to embroider a tablecloth for a twelve-person table, plus twelve matching napkins. Her name was Señora Esperanza, which means "Hope," but Gloria renamed her Señora Dolores, Señora "Pains," not only because she was a very obnoxious woman, but also for all the pain she wanted to inflict on the students' families on account of the unreasonable and highly expensive tablecloth assignment.

Gloria was quick to point out that, most likely, the great majority of the girls in the class didn't have such big tables at home; she even asked those of us who didn't to put our hands up and only two out of thirty girls kept their hands down. But to no avail, because Señora Dolores didn't budge and insisted that we had to bring the materials to class the following week. Little did she know that the tablecloth assignment would become a battle to the death between her and the school principal, on one side, and Miss Blanca and most of the students and mothers, on the other.

For me, the problem was not the cost or the impractical nature of the assignment; I just couldn't wrap my head around having to spend hours and hours, day after day, month after month, embroidering a tablecloth. And what for? So that you could put it on the table, cover it up with dishes and splash it with grease and food? And the napkins? So much work just to use them to wipe your mouth! In my mind, if I was going to spend so much time and energy making something so beautiful and refined, it belonged on the wall, in a frame, for everybody to admire.

As Miss Blanca was also our homeroom teacher, we discussed the issue of the tablecloth assignment with her. She agreed that it was unreasonable because it would amount to dozens, if not hundreds of hours of work—when would we find the time to study?—while forcing our families to spend an enormous amount of money on something most households can't even use.

"Who on earth needs an embroidered table cloth for a twelve-person table, *plus* matching napkins?" she asked rhetorically while shaking her head and rolling her eyes. She promised to talk to the principal about it and to call a parents' meeting.

That day, when I got home and told my mom about the table-cloth, she was flabbergasted. "Isn't Commercial High School a public school after all? They cannot, and I repeat, *cannot,* force anybody to spend so much money on an assignment like that. And who *is* this Señora Dolores anyway? I bet you she is one of those rich 'ladies' who teaches Needlework so as not to stay home and die of boredom; you know what I mean, one of those made up 'society' women who has never taken an interest in her students, never realized that a good number of them are from working class families, and has no idea what it means to be poor because she's never moved a finger in her whole life. I bet you she pays to have all her housework and cooking done, her clothes cleaned and pressed, and even to have her fingernails and toenails trimmed...

"If it's hard for us to come up with the money for the stupid tablecloth, a household where the father works in a bank and makes a decent salary, can you imagine what it will be like for a poor family, for a housewife that has to make miracles to feed her children? And what about the principal? Does he agree with this absurd imposition? Besides, how can they expect a girl to dedicate herself to her studies if she has to spend her life embroidering?" she asked herself and the walls as she banged cups and plates setting the table for tea time.

Señora Dolores was exactly the way my mom imagined her: a middle aged, upper-middle class woman dressed in fashionable outfits and made up like a magazine model. In fact, she looked like a tropical bird with the amount of green eye shadow she put on her eyelids, plus thick layers of mascara, rouge, and bright red lipstick that matched the colour of her long, pointy finger nails—not to mention her tinted strawberry blonde hair. She wore diamond rings on both hands and tons of gold jewelry.

My mom burst out laughing when I told her that actually the teacher's name was Señora Esperanza, but that Gloria had renamed her Señora Dolores. She said she couldn't agree more with my friend and promised to do everything she could to have the assignment exchanged for something more reasonable.

That's how she became friends with Señora Isabel, Gloria's mom. Together they rallied behind Miss Blanca, organized the rest of the mothers and ended up taking the issue all the way to the Ministry of Education. Finally, instead of embroidering a tablecloth and matching napkins, Señora Dolores was directed to teach us how to sew sheets and simple articles of clothing, and to instruct us on Prenatal Pediatrics.

Obviously, the woman was both incompetent and lazy because all she did was dictate from an ancient book with yellowing pages and brown covers with a fading title: *The Miracle of Life*. One day, as she read about the first trimester of the fetus, Gloria asked her if she could explain to us how a child is conceived. Señora Dolores blushed, took her eyeglasses off, polished them, cleared her throat, and all she managed to say was that Gloria was a very insolent girl.

Another time she dictated about "the bust." It went something like: "When a lady gets pregnant, her bust becomes enlarged because the lacteal glands grow and multiply filling her breasts with ducts through which the milk for her baby comes out. It is necessary to keep the nipples soft and well lubricated so that the baby doesn't have suction problems and also so that the tissue doesn't break. It's advisable then to massage the nipples several times a day with a non-greasy cream, moving your fingers outwards, towards the tip of the nipple."

Gloria put her hand up and asked if a woman had to massage her own nipples or if her husband could do it for her. Señora Dolores' jaw dropped and her mouth opened, but nothing came out for a while. Then she told Gloria that she was the most disrespectful girl she had ever encountered in her seventeen-year career. Gloria thanked her and sat down while the rest of the class burst into giggles.

1962 was also the year that the World Cup was played in Chile. For the whole month of June, the country turned into a gigantic ear as everybody followed the voices of Darío Verdugo and Sergio Silva, the announcers for the games' broadcast on national radio. Our little house on Esmeralda Street was no exception. It became a hub for sports enthusiasts and patriots: the Unión Juvenil boys, Gloria and her family, Silvia, other friends of my parents', and even Miguel, who insisted he had never liked soccer before. Our gatherings often turned into feasts and parties as we ate my mom's delicacies and celebrated Chile's victories with singing and dancing.

The day that Chile beat Yugoslavia and got third place—which for everybody felt like we had won the cup—was momentous not only because of our team's triumph, but also because I witnessed something that I couldn't understand or talk about with anybody. During half-time I helped my mom serve tea and then went in a hurry to the bathroom so as not to miss the beginning of the second period. I opened the door while snapping closed the last hook in my garter belt and walked right into my brother Andresito and his friend Carloncho, entangled in a steamy embrace. As I couldn't believe my eyes I closed them, and when I opened them again the two of them were bounding down the stairs as if nothing had ever happened.

When I got back to the living room, my mom asked, "Why are your cheeks so red, Sol?"

"I don't know... It must be nerves because of the game," I replied.

The rest of the afternoon Andresito and Carloncho acted completely normal, so I decided that what I thought I had seen was just a product of my overactive imagination.

Following the game, the entire country celebrated Chile's victory. In Valdivia, thousands of people gathered at the square and the overflow reached as far up as the Municipal Stadium on Picarte Avenue, a good ten blocks from downtown. The party lasted the whole night, but after an hour or so, my mom and I went back home. My mom invited Silvia to come with us, but she stayed on with Tito, the rest of the boys and my dad. This led my mom to give me a lecture on how Silvia's behaviour was not "ladylike" and to wonder about the kind of upbringing she was receiving from her family. So, a few days later, when my friend asked me to her house for *onces*, I had to beg my mom to let me go. Finally she gave in after I promised I would conduct myself like an angel and would tell her all about the visit when I got back. I think that my mom's curiosity got the better of her; nobody knew anything about Silvia's family, other than the fact that they lived in a big house by the river and had owned a famous brewery.

That Sunday, I left our house at about four and took the boat at the end of Yerbas Buenas Street. It was a beautiful day and you could see Villarrica Volcano in the distance. The water was bluer than ever and huge, cottony clouds sailed across the sky.

Silvia was waiting for me on the other side of the river and seemed happy to see me, but as we were walking towards her house, I realized that she was extremely nervous.

Just as we started to climb the steps towards the front door, she stopped and faced me. "Sol, I have something to tell you. My house is not the way you imagine it. On the outside, it looks big and beautiful and it used to be very beautiful, but now we only use a few rooms in the front."

I just shrugged as if to say that I didn't care about that, but she continued, "Also, my mom is ill... Well... She's mentally ill, the same as her brother Willy, my uncle... Besides, my uncle is also in a wheelchair."

"And who takes care of them?" I asked.

"My *oma*. My grandma."

I told her not to worry, but the truth is that I got the jitters because I'd never been in the company of a mentally ill person before.

Silvia must've read my mind because she added, "My mom and my uncle are not violent, Sol. Besides, we won't have *onces* with them. We'll go up to my room and listen to the radio and talk." Then she put her hand on my shoulder and continued, "This is the first time I have ever invited a friend to my house."

What would life be like if you felt you couldn't invite your friends to your house, introduce them to your nearest and dearest? I thought of Miguel and our conversation about his growing up in poverty, his sadness and shame over his situation, his feelings of inadequacy... And here I was, just about to enter Silvia's home, my friend's private and secret world—her first peer ever to do that. I felt sorry for her, but also proud of myself—obviously, in the few months we had been friends, she had come to trust me. I turned and gave her a tight hug.

Silvia's grandma, mom and uncle were sitting at a round table, having tea and bread. The mom and the uncle just looked at us with vacant eyes, but the grandma got up to greet us, gave us both a kiss, and said that Silvia had told her many wonderful things about my family. I fell in love with the old lady right away: tiny, silver hair tied in a bun high up on her head and huge blue eyes that sparkled with what I then interpreted as inquisitiveness, but later on in life came to understand as pain, deep pain, the kind that makes you wonder, "Why me? Why did life deal me this set of circumstances?"

Silvia's room was on the second floor and had tall windows overlooking the river. Compared to my own room, it was gigantic, and it also had a full ensuite bathroom, for her exclusive use. I walked around admiring her desk, book case, chest of drawers, vanity table, double bed and wardrobe with mirror doors... Silvia was not only beautiful, but she also had things that I could only dream about. Besides, she had all the freedom in the world and most likely, she would become Tito's official girlfriend as soon as he made up his mind and declared his love for her.

While we sipped our tea and munched on McKay cookies, we listened to Ricardo García's "Discomanía" and talked about the World Cup and our aspirations as track and field athletes. We both had a crush on Alberto Fouilloux, a forward on the national soccer team, so we decided to send him a letter. Silvia took some writing paper from a drawer in her desk and we sat together to compose the letter.

> Dear Alberto:
>
> Our names are Sol and Silvia and we're best friends.
>
> We're writing to congratulate you on your excellent performance as a member of the national team. We are athletes as well (we do track and field), so we understand perfectly well how proud you must feel to represent our country. Our golden dream is to participate in the Olympics, but we'll have to wait a bit because we're only twelve and fourteen years old.
>
> Also, we would like to congratulate you for being a university student as well as a soccer player. We're both very good students at the Commercial High School and when we graduate we will go to university for sure.
>
> As you can see, we're not stupid little girls, but interesting people. So we hope that you will want to write to us so that we can get to know one another a little better.

We pondered endlessly about the closing.

"With our love," I suggested.

"No! That's too daring," Silvia responded as she chewed on the end of the pen.

"Sincerely," I offered then.

"No! That's too businesslike," Silvia replied this time.

After a few more moments of chewing, she proposed, "With admiration and affection."

"Yes! Perfect!" I agreed.

We signed our full names, folded the blue paper and put it inside the envelope Silvia had taken from a wooden box on top of a shelf. As Silvia's handwriting was prettier than mine, we had decided that she should pen the letter. So, I wrote Alberto's name and address on the envelope, which I did with great care and pride.

We were so excited about our letter that we decided to go to the post office and mail it right away.

We walked back to town crossing the Pedro de Valdivia Bridge and stopped for a while to look at the regattas training on the river. Silvia told me that her dad had been the captain of the Phoenix Club team; that she remembered him as being very handsome and fun to be with, but he hadn't been able to withstand her mom's illness and had died of a heart attack.

"And you didn't have any brothers or sisters?" I asked.

"I had a younger brother, but he drowned in the river when he was two years old. That's why my mom began to go crazy," she responded.

I hugged her again and whispered in her ear, "Silvia, I'm really happy that you invited me to your house."

I could feel the emotion in Silvia's voice as she hugged me

back. "Thanks, Sol. I love *your* house. The truth is that I feel a lot more comfortable with your family than with my own."

What an irony, I thought. *I'm jealous of her life and she's jealous of mine.*

After we mailed the letter, Silvia invited me to the new Café Palace, which had just opened at the Prales building. When we got there all the tables were taken, so we sat at the bar. I didn't know what to have, so in the end Silvia ordered two *completos,* hot dogs with everything: mayo, sauerkraut, tomato and avocado. We were eating and talking quite happily when, all of a sudden, the wiener in my sandwich shot out of the bread and landed inside the pant leg cuff of the gentleman sitting next to me, reading the newspaper.

I whispered in Silvia's ear what had happened, then we both looked down surreptitiously and saw the wiener sitting on end in the gentleman's cuff.

As he hadn't noticed anything, Silvia leaned over me and said, "Sir, excuse me... You see... My friend dropped her wiener..."

The gentleman looked at her as if she were crazy and Silvia repeated, "My friend dropped her wiener and now it's sitting inside your pant leg cuff."

The gentleman looked at her, looked at me and then looked down and saw the wiener. His face went red with anger as he jumped up yelled, "This is unbelievable! Look at these girls! Aren't there any good manners left in today's youth? Look at the mess they've made of my pants... You can't even sit to read the newspaper in peace anymore... Now I'll have to send my suit to the cleaners and it's quite likely that the grease stains won't even come out!"

He went on and on while he grabbed a paper napkin, plucked the wiener out of his pants' cuff and put it on my plate. I felt like telling him that I could take his pants home with me because my mom knew how to take stains out of clothes without having to pay an arm and a leg at the cleaners, but I got such a case of the giggles imagining the gentleman taking his pants off at the Palace that I took off for the bathroom instead. When I came out, Silvia was waiting for me at the door and the gentleman had left.

As expected, when I got home my mom wanted to know everything about Silvia's family and about her house. I told her that the house was huge and quite nice but looked abandoned; that the little brother had drowned in the river and the mom had gone crazy; that the uncle was mentally ill as well, and not only that, was in a wheelchair; that the grandmother looked after her two children; and Silvia's dad had died of a heart attack. My mom listened with her mouth open and then started to cry and couldn't stop. Then I told her that Silvia had invited me to the new Café Palace, and everything that had happened with the hotdog and the gentleman with the newspaper. She stopped crying and couldn't stop laughing. When my dad and brother came home we told them the story about the Palace and they couldn't stop laughing either.

Back in March, shortly after our first meeting with Mr. Gronau, the Valdivia Youth Orchestra was formed and, amazingly enough, Mr. Gronau appointed Miguel as first violin and I was assigned the xylophone. Our first public performance took place at the Cervantes Theatre on July 21, 1962. The concert was a huge success, the theatre was full to the brim and the public applauded so much that we had to come out three times to bow. Everybody was there: my parents and their friends, my brother and the Unión Juvenil boys, Gloria with her mom and dad, Miss Blanca, Silvia, Mario and other kids from our school.

That afternoon my mom took me to Yolanda's to get my hair done for the first time in my life. Now when I look at pictures of that day I cannot help but laugh at my hairdo, but back then it was the latest fashion—it was called "nest" because it looked like a bird's nest—and it added a good two to three inches to your height. My mom had also bought me a new pair of shoes with a bit of a heel and had made me a new dress: sky blue, tailored down to the waist, no collar, three-quarter sleeves, and a skirt that came out at the hips and went back in at the knees—a style that made me look as if I actually had hips! All in all, I felt like a movie star as I stood on the Cervantes' stage behind my xylophone.

Miguel had been quite worried because, according to him, he had nothing decent to wear, but my mom convinced him that his black suit and white shirt were perfectly appropriate. She offered to clean and iron them, Andresito lent him a tie and Miguel ended up looking very elegant indeed. But Mr. Gronau looked the most elegant of all in his tuxedo, white shirt and red velvet bow tie. This came as a surprise to all, as we had never seen him dressed up before. In fact, he was always clad in a pair of jeans and an old sweater. Besides, he was extremely goofy and unpretentious; during rehearsals he made us laugh with his singing and dancing as he conducted the orchestra. Looking back, I realize that he was an outstanding educator who made us feel at ease while tapping into our best musical abilities.

The three Sundays following the Cervantes performance, we travelled to nearby towns in what was presented as a program for the dissemination of culture. Austral University put both its yellow buses—"The Big Ducky" and "The Little Ducky"—at our disposal and off we went, instruments and all, to a handful of communities that had never hosted a concert of classical European music before.

The bus trips were lively and fun; we would talk and eat the snacks our mothers had prepared for us, but above all, we would sing. Miguel and I taught Mr. Gronau some Chilean songs and he taught us "Am Brunner von dem Tore," a piece about a beautiful tree that German people remember when they leave their country. When I asked Mr. Gronau why he had left Germany, he replied that he had always wanted to travel around the world and Austral University had offered him the opportunity to do something he loved: work with young music lovers for a couple of years. He added that he did miss his country, but that he also loved living in Chile. I remember thinking that it must be ter-

63

rible to be so far away from your own land, from the place where you were born and grew up, from your friends and family, from your own language... I told myself that I would never be able to do something like that.

On the last of those three Sundays we visited Loncoche, Miguel's hometown. From behind the curtain, Miguel pointed out his mom and brothers and sisters to me. They were sitting in the front row, wide-eyed and perfectly still, their feet and knees sealed together, their clasped hands resting on their laps. They were wearing what looked like their Sunday outfits: freshly starched and ironed, but painfully old-fashioned and threadbare. And not only that, the kids were wearing their school shoes, obviously the only ones they owned. Miguel must've seen them through my eyes because when I turned to look at him, his face was beet red, he couldn't look me in the eye and his forehead was pearled with perspiration. I took my handkerchief out of my pocket, wiped his forehead and gave him a peck on the cheek. Then Mr. Gronau called us to take our places on the stage.

I had seen Miguel play many times before, but that day, when I looked at him as he put the violin on his shoulder and started to play, full of inspiration, the way he always played, I got a strange sensation in my stomach—a mixture of sadness and joy. Never before had I noticed his beautiful hands, his long, curly fingers, his grey-green eyes and his never-ending, thick eyelashes. I longed to touch him, to extend my hand across the stage and cradle his small ears; I even envied the smooth surface of the violin where his chin rested.

The day before, Miguel had told me his sister had written to say that we were both invited for lunch, so we took off as soon as the concert was over. Miguel's house turned out to be much more destitute than I could've ever imagined: a small construction of uneven planks with a rusty tin roof.

When we went in, it took me a while to get used to the darkness, but I could hear somebody snoring loudly in the back corner of the room. It was Miguel's dad. The brothers and sisters were sitting at the table and the mom, bent over an open hearth. When she saw us standing by the door, she came to greet us. She made excuses for her husband—"He's very tired after a long week of work and he woke up with a headache today," she explained—and then proceeded to apologize for her humble home.

I didn't know what to say or where to set my eyes, as the entire scene spoke of grinding poverty and the family's shame saturated the air.

While we ate the thick semolina soup that Miguel's mom served for lunch, she and I talked about the concert, Valdivia, school. Miguel didn't say a word and the brothers and sisters just listened and watched with big eyes.

That evening, on our way back to Valdivia, as the bus rode through rain and darkness and everybody else slept, Miguel and I felt each other's skin and explored the inside of each other's mouths with the ardent curiosity of novices. I can still taste the coffee and milk flavour of Miguel's mouth, smell the scent of LeSancy soap on his neck, feel the weight of his arm on my shoulder, the warmth of his thigh against mine.

The next day we met at the *Torreón* on our way to the conservatory and for a few eternal moments we stared at each other in plain daylight without knowing what to say. Then, Miguel took my hand in his and kissed it; I kissed his hand in return and proceeded to tell him that I liked his curly fingers. He assured me that he liked everything about me: my fingers, my hands, my eyes, everything. I replied that I also liked his ears, his eyes and his eyelashes. He caressed my hair, bent over and whispered in my ear, "Sol, I love you."

"I love you too and when I grow up I want to marry you," I responded.

"Me too," he said.

We walked hand in hand to the conservatory and after class we sat for a while on the dock at the end of Yerbas Buenas Street and kissed. We also talked about what to do, whether to tell my mom or not, and decided to wait because at the time she was very busy getting ready to travel to Santiago, given that she had won a prize in the Imperial Baking Powder contest. As Miguel put it, in the meantime, we would have a "clandestine" love, like Pablo Neruda and Matilde Urrutia's in the early fifties.

While my mom was in Santiago, I caught my brother and Carloncho hugging and kissing several times: on the couch, in the kitchen, going up the stairs... Now I knew that I wasn't just "seeing things" and I also knew that *they* knew I had seen them. I didn't know what to do. Then, one day as I was lighting the fire to prepare *onces,* both of them came into the kitchen and after much shuffling and fidgeting, Andresito announced that they wanted to talk to me.

I busied myself with the stove, my back to them, as I attempted to come to terms with what I knew they would tell me: that they were perverts, degenerates, faggots, *maricones,* the worst kind of men that could ever exist. How could my brother be like that? What was wrong with him? How could the person that I had looked up to all my life be a *maricón?* He was handsome, virile and charming. Plenty of girls would have been happy to have him as a boyfriend, but he had never been known to have fallen for a girl; this made my mom happy, as she insisted that there was plenty of time for love after finishing school and becoming a professional. But now I knew the real reason behind my brother's apparent level-headedness and I hated him for it.

I could feel myself boiling inside as I picked up the cast iron pan from the top of the stove, turned around and shouted at the top of my lungs, *"Maricones de mierda!* Fucking faggots, get out of here before I break your skull!" Without thinking twice about it, I hurled the pan in the direction of Andresito and Carloncho.

Next thing I knew, my brother was rocking me in his arms and whispering, "It's not the way you think, Sol. We're not perverts—Carloncho and I are in love. We know it's not normal, it's weird, but we can't help it. We really love each other..."

When I heard Carloncho's steps leaving the room, I pulled away from my brother and looked at him. Tears were streaming down his cheeks. I had never seen my brother cry and the sight moved me to the core. He claimed that he and Carloncho were truly in love. How could that be?

"Miguel and I are in love with each other too," I confessed to him.

Andresito smiled as he wiped his face with the back of his hand.

"But we don't know if Mom will let us be boyfriend and girl-friend. You know how she's always lecturing me about boys. So, for now, we're having a 'clandestine' relationship, just like you and Carloncho," I pressed on.

Andresito hugged me tighter as he responded, "She loves Miguel and knows that he's a great guy. She'll understand." Then he wondered out loud, "Maybe she will also understand if we tell her that Carloncho and I are in love."

The image of our mom fainting, or crying hysterically, soap opera style, came to my mind. "I doubt it, but you could try," I responded.

What I was really thinking was that seeing her in absolute shock would put some sense into my brother's head. Perhaps, after recovering from the bombshell, our mom would be able to convince him that he was just being stupid. She could make him stop being a faggot.

A couple of weeks later, I changed my tune into a self-serving rationale, and in a moment of anger, I betrayed my brother by planting an insidious seed of curiosity in our mom's head. In my twelve-year old mind I fancied that, after all, she just *might* understand his dilemma, and if she did, why wouldn't she approve of Miguel's and my relationship?

Soledad

Destiny is a powerful force. It doesn't matter how many plans you make, how much you want this, that, or the other, because inevitably destiny ends up imposing its own will. When I was young, I did my best to welcome my lot with resignation and joy, but after the military coup and everything that those beasts did to our family, I lost my desire to live and all I longed for was death. Needless to say, as much as I wanted to, I didn't die and life took its own course once again.

My daughter, Sol, doesn't believe in destiny. She gave me a lecture once about the importance of being "an actor" in your own life, which confused me no end—it sounded to me like she was talking about life as if it were a Hollywood movie.

"Mom!" she shot back when I commented about it. "That's not what I mean! I'm using the word 'actor' as it relates to *being active,* making choices, deciding for yourself what you're going to do with your life," she went on in her usual know-it-all way while she rolled her eyes.

"Yeah... Like when you decided to be tortured and raped," I

responded nonchalantly.

I knew I was being cruel, but I also knew that she would have to admit that there are certain things in life, important things, that have nothing to do with your own choices.

She was taken aback and I could see the hurt in her eyes. I was about to say, "Sorry," when she responded, "That's got to do with the forces of history—with the dialectical relationship between society and the individual, with alienation and exploitation—"

"—When you decide to come off your high horse and stop speaking in Greek, let me know. Bye, bye," I cut in as I walked out of the room, waving my hand Queen Elizabeth-style.

I knew that she had read plenty of books and was always discussing her ideas about capitalism and the revolution with her friends, but I never became interested in any of that. I don't think you need big words to know what's right and what's wrong; to know that the choices you make in life are tiny compared to what destiny has in store for you.

But I have to admit that sometimes those choices do make a big difference—like my decision not to wear a girdle the day that Andrés turned twenty years old.

I met Andrés on Sunday, March 1, 1942, when he and his family moved to the house right across the way, on Allende Padín Street in Santiago.

It was sweltering hot, so our mom sent me and my sister Amparo to the corner store to get four ice-cold bottles of pop. We were walking briskly back along Club Hípico Avenue so that the pop wouldn't get warm, when we saw a *golondrina*—a horse-drawn moving cart—filled to the brim with furniture turn the corner of our street. In between beds, tables and chairs, I could make out an older man and a dark, handsome boy with a moustache á la Clark Gable.

While we were waiting for my dad to open the front gate, the boy came up to say hello. He shook my hand and Amparo's, asked us our names and introduced himself as Andrés Martínez. He was nineteen years old, had just finished his accounting studies at the Advanced Commercial High School and was about to start working at the National Savings Bank.

I was sixteen and had two more years at Santa Teresa Normal School before graduating as an elementary school teacher. For as long as I could remember I had wanted to become a teacher, and I applied myself to my studies with utmost dedication. I spent most evenings doing my homework, got up at six o'clock in the morning, reviewed my schoolwork while having breakfast and then took the long walk to Santa Teresa, on the corner of Bascuñán and Tucapel Streets.

It turned out that Andrés had been watching me, because one day he came out of his house just as I was leaving and asked if he could accompany me. I could feel myself blush as I uttered a quick "Sure" in a high-pitched, overly enthusiastic voice. My heart was racing and my knees felt like wool because I had liked the boy from day one, but never thought that he could be interested in me. Besides, I didn't know what my mom would say if she found out that the neighbour from across the street had walked me to school. For a moment I considered going back inside and asking for permission, but what if she said no?

By now Andrés had offered to carry my school bag and we were already near the corner, so I just kept on walking beside him. I felt shy and self-conscious in my brown school uniform, knee-high socks and lumpy shoes, but it didn't take long for my nervousness to give way to a feeling of ease as Andrés began to tell me about his soccer team, his work at the bank and his involvement in the Radical Youth. He was a great admirer of Presidents Pedro Aguirre Cerda and Juan Antonio Ríos and asked me if I wanted to hear about the party's principles.

"I know you'll understand them because you're a well-educated person," he stated enthusiastically.

I just shrugged, as if to say, "I don't know," but felt good inside because obviously he considered me to be smart.

"Soledad, the Radical Party is a humanist organization. We believe in reason, ethics and justice, those are our three basic principles," he explained as he took a cigarette out of the left inside pocket of his jacket.

At school, we had studied humanist philosophies, so I was proud to be able to respond firmly, "Yes, but I know that humanists don't believe in God and religion and I don't agree with that."

"You don't need religion to be a good person or to build a just society, Soledad," he replied, holding the cigarette between

73

his lips and searching for a box of matches in his coat's outside pockets. When he found it, he took a match out, struck it against the side of the box, stopped walking for a few seconds and lit the cigarette. Then he continued, "What you need is education. E-du-ca-tion. We believe that to govern is to educate. There must be a system of public, free education for all. For all," he repeated as he stressed each syllable with a vigorous thrust at the air with his right hand. "You're studying to be a school teacher, so you have to agree with that, eh?" he pressed on as he stopped and turned to look at me, a big grin on his face and a twinkle in the eye, as if to say, "See? I got you with this one."

Obviously, I did agree with the principle of free education for all and told him so. But in that moment, I was more charmed by his passionate demeanour than by his philosophical and political positions. He was not only good looking, friendly and polite, but also intelligent and articulate, and he didn't hesitate to show his enthusiasm for his ideas.

"What about you, Soledad? What are *your* interests?" he asked all of a sudden, interrupting my reveries.

"Me?" I shot out, panicked.

"Yes, you m'lady," he replied with a chuckle, pointing at me with his right index finger.

I cleared my throat while I tried to decide which, of all my interests, would impress him the most. Cooking, baking, sewing and embroidering were out of the question. Botany? No. "Poetry," I finally responded. "I love poetry," I added with conviction.

"Poetry, eh? That's nice... And who are your favourite poets?" he wanted to know.

This time I didn't have to think twice about it. "Gabriela Mistral, Juana de Ibarburú, Alfonsina Storni, Gustavo Adolfo Béquer and Rubén Darío," I responded. "Yes, those are my very favourite ones."

"Do you just like to read their poetry or do you also recite it?" he asked now.

"Both. I love reading it over and over again, because the meaning of a poem changes depending on what's happening in your own life. And then there are a few that I like to recite," I offered.

He asked me to recite a poem for him, but by then we had already got to the corner of my school—I had to go to class and he had to go catch the streetcar for work.

We stood in silence for a few moments. Then he placed the strap of my school bag across my shoulders and held my hand. "Soledad, can I walk you to school every day?" he whispered very close to my ear.

"I don't know... I'll have to ask my mom for permission," I responded.

"But would you like it if we did this walk together every morning?" he insisted.

"Yes," I replied.

"Then I'm sure you will be able to convince your mom that

it's good for both of us. That we enjoy our conversations..." he asserted while moving a strand of hair from the side of my face to behind my ear.

Feeling his hands filled my body with a lovely tingling sensation. I wanted to stay in that very position with him for a long, long time. But then the school bell rang and I had to rush before the front gate got locked.

"I'll ask my mom as soon as I get home," I yelled as I ran sideways towards the gate.

He was standing in the same spot, hands in his pockets, big smile in his face, watching me. As I was about to fly through the open gate, I waved and he waved back.

That afternoon, I asked my mom for permission to walk to school with Andrés. "He walked me this morning and we had a great time—he told me lots of things about the Radical Party, about how banks operate... And I told him about poetry..." I explained, praying that she would say yes.

I was standing at the kitchen door and she, in front of the counter, chopping vegetables for that evening's *carbonada* soup. I could only see her back and the repetitive movement of her right arm as I heard the quick tapping of the knife against the wooden board. She paused for a moment and then resumed her work.

"Soledad, don't forget that you have been studying hard to become a school teacher," she began, pausing again and walking towards the sink to wash her hands. She picked up the tea towel, took a step towards me and continued, "Andrés is a very nice young man, my daughter, but why don't you wait until you finish school to start your friendship with him?" she suggested, looking at me with pleading eyes.

I was crushed. Wait two years before being able to talk to Andrés? I felt my throat tighten. "Please, mom, it's only a morning walk, that's all... And I will continue studying hard and you'll see—I will graduate as a school teacher, I promise." By now my eyes were filling with tears.

My mom put her arms around me and rocked me back and forth as she whispered in my ear, "Okay, Soledad, it's okay, it's okay. He can walk you to school in the mornings." Then she returned to her task, her gaze towards the sky as she repeated, "Please, God, help her to keep her promise, help her to keep her promise..."

The morning walks became a daily occurrence and a few weeks later Andrés declared his love for me.

That Monday, I left the house at the usual time, but Andrés was not at his front door. I busied myself with the padlock as I waited for him to come out, but to no avail. Finally, I began to walk as slowly as I could, casting discreet glances at his house. By the time I got to Club Hípico Street I had given up and was feeling upset and confused, but when I turned the corner, Andrés was standing there, waiting for me, a huge smile on his face.

"Andrés!" I cried out.

"Soledad!" he responded excitedly while he grabbed my school bag and slung it across his shoulder. "I must've left my house earlier than usual because I waited and waited for you and when you didn't come out, I walked to the corner to find you," he explained as he took my hand in his. "I didn't know what to think—I thought you might've decided not to walk to school with me anymore," he continued as he kissed my fingers.

"I thought the same about you," I responded, feeling my heart gallop inside my chest.

"No, that would never happen," he said in a serious tone, and then continued as he cupped my face in his hands. "I'm crazy about you, Soledad. All I do is think of you. Let's be boyfriend and girlfriend," he added, his voice hoarse with emotion.

My heart was about to race out of my mouth, so much so that I had a hard time breathing, never mind speaking. "I don't know if my mom will let me have a boyfriend," I said tentatively, "I'll have to ask her for permission." I felt a pang of anxiety as I considered my mom's most likely response.

"Oh, I'm sure she'll approve," Andrés asserted confidently. "I know she doesn't know me very well, but I think she likes me!" he added with a chuckle.

"Yes, she does like you, but she doesn't think I should have a boyfriend while I'm going to school," I clarified.

By now we were walking along Mirador Street. Andrés had taken my hand in his once again and was looking at it attentively.

"You have beautiful hands, Soledad... Actually, you're beautiful all over, my chocolate muffin," he declared, alluding to my brown uniform.

We stopped just short of the corner of Bascuñán Street to avoid being seen by my teachers and fellow students. He embraced me tenderly and planted a gentle kiss on my mouth.

That afternoon, I managed to convince my mom to give me permission to go steady with Andrés and for the longest time life became a big cottony cloud.

A few evenings a week, he would come by and together we would listen to a lovely radio program called "Thirty Minutes with Eglantina," which combined poetry and music. Other days, my mom would give me permission to go wait for him outside the bank, near Plaza Italia, and then we would walk down Alameda Boulevard or have a stroll on Ahumada Street and around the Plaza de Armas. Time continued to elapse, until the afternoon of January 10, 1943, the day Andrés turned twenty, when our life changed forever.

That day, we celebrated his birthday with a luncheon at his house. For a present, I had made him a handkerchief with a drawn-thread border all around and his monogram embroidered in gothic letters, in shadow stitch, all in white. My mom had given me the money for the materials a few weeks before and I had gone with Amparo to Gath & Chávez to find the fabric and the embroidery floss. Amparo had helped me with the design and then it had taken me hours and hours of hard work to finish it on time. It turned out beautiful.

In the afternoon, I was allowed to go downtown with Andrés. We took the streetcar to the *Alameda* and then walked to Café Paula for some delicious *lúcuma* ice cream. Afterwards, we went for a stroll around Plaza de Armas and then Andrés suggested that we go to Cousiño Park because the heat downtown was unbearable; besides, that way we would be closer to home and wouldn't have to rush to get back.

I was nervous because my mom had given me permission to go downtown, not to Cousiño Park, but Andrés was so excited and besides, as it was his birthday, I couldn't say no. We went to catch the streetcar, Andrés happily playing with his new handkerchief, putting it in his pocket, taking it out of his pocket, feeling it on his cheek... He would sniff it and then hug me and kiss me. I was floating in the air...

I could hardly feel the heat with so much greenery and Andrés suggested that we cross the park diagonally so as to end up at the corner of Beaucheff and Rondizzoni Avenues, near our street. We walked holding hands, and halfway through we came across an area that looked denser, like a mini forest with weeping willows, chestnut and linden trees, and various shrubs and vines. Andrés wanted us to sit down in the shade for a little while because it was still early and I didn't have to be home until seven. I said that I didn't want to get my dress dirty, but he put his jacket on the grass and pulled me down by the hand.

Then he started to kiss me, hug me and touch me all over. Next thing I knew, one of his hands was travelling up my thighs. I thought about my girdle sitting inside my dresser's top drawer—if I had been wearing it, that's as far as Andrés would've been able to go, but now his hand had made it inside my underpants.

My mom would always say that no matter how hot it is, ladies must always wear a girdle so as not to go around displaying all that loose flesh. She would insist that this is what distinguishes ladies from non-ladies, but at that age you think you know everything and that your mother is a dunce, so Amparo and I used to laugh at her and as soon as the good weather started, off went the girdle.

Andrés tried to take off my underwear, but I resisted. Then he unbuttoned his fly and drew aside the crotch piece of my panties with his hand. After that, I don't really know what happened until I felt a piercing pain. I screamed, but he covered my mouth with his. Following the pain, I didn't feel much other than him on top of me, moving as if he were riding a horse until, all of a sudden, he exploded. After a while I started to suffocate and also felt something sticky run down my thigh, so I pushed him gently aside. Then he took his new handkerchief out of his pocket and put it in between my legs. My lovely birthday present, made with such love and dedication, turned into a complete mess, filthy with blood and semen.

After a couple of months of not getting my period, feeling nauseous and not knowing what to do or who to turn to, my mom caught me crying on my bed and I had no choice but to tell her that I was pregnant. Even though she was obviously disappointed, she comforted me and made me promise that I would tell Andrés the very next day.

That afternoon, Andrés came to get me and we went to Santa Lucía Hill. We walked up slowly and finally stopped at one of the terraces to look at the city down below. I was quite silent and when Andrés tried to hug me, I felt like he was smothering me, so I wouldn't let him. He started to get impatient and finally said, "My little princess, what's wrong? Why don't you want me to hug you?"

I whispered in his ear, "I'm pregnant."

Andrés took a cigarette out of his coat's inside pocket, lit it and stood there, looking down on Alameda Boulevard as if I hadn't said anything. Back then, Andrés used to smoke a brand of cigarettes called Embajadores Especiales, which doesn't exist anymore. They were really strong, and as my stomach was so sensitive, I started to get nauseous. But I just stood there, waiting for him to respond while I listened to an organ grinder play on and on somewhere nearby.

Time kept on ticking and Andrés wouldn't speak. I began to feel panic stricken and, without thinking twice about it, turned around and ran towards the steps that would take me down to the street and the bus stop. The only thing I wanted was to go home. Then I felt him grab me by the arm and heard his voice asking me not to go, saying that he hadn't responded right away because he was reflecting on the situation.

We walked down together and sat on a park bench. There were some lovely blue morning glory in between the shrubs and the sweet aroma of the eucalyptus trees made me feel better. Andrés hugged me and said, "Bonbon, forgive me for what I did to you at Cousiño Park. I never thought that you would get pregnant... I had planned to propose to you after you graduated from Normal School, but I will propose to you now." Then he took my hand in his, looked at me in the eye and said, "Soledad, will you marry me?"

I nodded and broke down with relief.

He hugged me, kissed my wet cheeks and then suggested that we go for a walk on Alameda Boulevard. By then Andrés was back to being his talkative old self and started to speak about this, that and the other: "I bet you our son will be the best soccer player in Chile. I will get a loan from the bank to get all our furniture. We're going to have a big wedding. This has to be celebrated properly."

I felt like my soul had come back into my body and told him that at Gath & Chávez I had seen some beautiful dining room sets, with a corner curio and a pretty, small side board, not like the huge, unwieldy piece of furniture we had in my house.

"Yes, bonbon. We're going to buy whatever you want because you will be the *dueña de casa*—the owner of the home, the house-wife—and at home, you will be the only boss," he assured me. He asked me when I wanted to get married.

"As soon as possible, but I have to consult with my mom," I

replied. Then he promised to come by that very evening to ask my dad for my hand.

My dad came back from the tracks at about eight, and five minutes later Andrés rang the bell. My mom went to open the door while Amparo and I went up to our room. My dad was sitting in the living room, listening to the radio, and at that moment he had started singing because they were playing one of his favourite tangos, "Don't Rush White Face." As we made our way towards the stairs, he said, "Bah, I wonder who it is at this time in the evening..."

Amparo and I just played the fool and kept on walking. When Andrés came in, my dad greeted him with great effusiveness, "How are you, Mr. Martínez? How is the National Savings Bank doing? Do Chileans actually save their money?" Then he shouted, "Soledad, it's Andrés!"

We had sat down at the top of the stairs, so we heard Andrés tell him that he had come to talk to him, not me." What an honour, man! What an honour! And what is the purpose of your visit?" my dad asked.

There was a tense moment of silence as my mom started going up the stairs. She signaled to us with her hand to go to our room. The three of us sat on my bed while we heard my dad's and Andrés' muffled voices in the living room. I tip-toed to the bedroom door just as my dad was saying, "Soledad has to finish school before getting married. She only has one year left, so we can plan the wedding for next January or February."

"But I want to marry her now, don Federico, and Soledad agrees," responded Andrés.

Obviously, my dad was dumbfounded. "Did that girl go crazy? What's going on with her? She wasn't happy until she was admitted to Normal School and has always said that all she wants is to become a school teacher!" Then he shouted, "Soledad, come here!"

By the time I made it downstairs I was crying, so my dad figured out the situation in a flash and charged against Andrés, "You fucking asshole, who do you think you are! You have stained my family's and my daughter's honour! Get out of my house before I beat the shit out of you and don't let me see you ever again!"

He opened the door, but Andrés didn't move. By now my mom had joined us and she asked my dad to calm down because he was going to alert the neighbours. So, he slammed the door, sank in an armchair, took his head in both his hands and repeated several times: "No, no, no, no..."

Then Andrés spoke. "Don Federico, I ask for your forgiveness for what I did to Soledad, but I didn't do it to take advantage of her. I love her and that's why I want to marry her, not because she's pregnant."

My dad looked at me for a long while and, with eyes full of contempt, said to me, "How could you do this, Soledad? How? I always trusted you."

A long silence followed. My mom and I sat on the couch;

Andrés sat beside me and put his arm around my shoulders. Finally, my mom suggested that we decide on the wedding date as soon as possible. While my mom hugged me, my dad nodded in agreement, got up and hugged his future son-in-law. We called Amparo to come down and Andrés crossed the street to get his family. They looked confused, as if they didn't know whether to be happy or sad, but then my dad offered a toast in our honour, Andrés' dad toasted in honour of the union of the two families and everybody hugged.

In those days, it was not unusual for young couples to marry "in a hurry" due to an unexpected pregnancy. That had been the case with a girl from our street the year before—the poor thing had married when her belly was already showing, causing the neighbours to gossip and giggle every time she left her house. Apparently, her boyfriend had tried to "escape," but had finally given in when the girl's brothers had threatened to beat him up. Andrés hadn't hesitated to ask me to marry him when he learned that I was pregnant, but all the same, I had never thought that I would "have to" get married. I was certain that I would finish Normal School, get a job, and then get married and have children. But here I was, marrying in a hurry and giving up my dreams of becoming a teacher. Furthermore, I would become the object of the neighbours' gossip: a loose girl, a whore, a "man catcher," a source of shame for my family and a bad example for the other girls on the street. "Look at Soledad, there she goes, who would've ever imagined that she was that kind of girl? She seemed to be decent, but you never know with these girls... Thank God the boy turned out to be good and has agreed to marry her."

I wondered why my mom hadn't explained anything to me, why she hadn't told me about the facts of life, love and desire, the menstrual cycle and ovulation. I also hated myself for not having been strong enough to say "No" to Andrés at Cousiño Park, and I resented the fact that he hadn't waited to make love to me after we got married, as God commanded.

But those questions didn't have any relevance now, as I was already pregnant and I would get married in less than two weeks.

Back then, country people would bring flocks of turkeys to Santiago and exchange birds for used clothing. Even though my mom had never cooked a turkey in her life, after going through her *María Cenicienta Cookbook*, she got it into her head that we had to have a roasted turkey for the wedding banquet. Every day she would send us out to check if there were any men with turkeys around the neighbourhood. About a week before the date, Amparo and I had gone to Señora Ada's store to get some bread, when we saw a man with a flock of turkeys on the other side of Rondizzoni Avenue. We ran across the street and told him to come to our house. My mom had already put together some old pants and shoes of my dad's because country people always preferred men's to women's clothing and most of the time they asked for shoes. The man must've had about a dozen turkeys with him, all tied to a cane. We ran back home, giggling the whole way, the man with his turkey racket behind us. My mom came to open the gate right away and, after negotiating for a while, we had a huge turkey in the backyard.

Amparo and I named the turkey Pepo, even though my mom

warned us that if we gave the bird a name we would grow fond of it. Of course, we didn't listen and had to pay the consequences the day before the wedding, when we had to kill poor Pepo.

At first my mom thought that she could kill it the same way as a hen, but it was impossible. When she finally got a hold of the turkey and tried to twist its neck, nothing happened, the animal scurried out of her hands and kept on running around the backyard. Then she decided that we had to cut his neck. Amparo and I held Pepo tight on top of a rock, his neck completely stretched, and my mom slashed it with her kitchen machete. The head jumped up and away as if it still had a will of its own and the poor animal sprang up, headless, and started to run in circles, leaving a trail of blood all over the backyard while horrible noises escaped from its severed neck.

Amparo and I were paralyzed, screaming in a panic while my mom ran after Pepo with her machete in hand. Finally, the turkey stopped in its tracks and fell over. It took us hours and a lot of scrubbing to clean all the blood off the backyard and our clothes, but in the end there was not a trace. My mom made us promise that we wouldn't tell anybody about it and the next day all the guests loved the roasted turkey, except us. Actually, we didn't even try it.

I often think about Pepo now, of my first encounter with a violent killing: the hideous sounds coming out of the turkey's gaping neck, the blood, Amparo's and my own screaming, and then the secrecy surrounding the whole event. Perhaps this was an omen of what was to come in our lives.

Up until Andresito was born, we lived at *Pension* La Serena, on the corner of Catedral and Maturana Streets. Señora Mafalda, the owner, welcomed us as if we had been her own children and treated me like a queen. When she heard that I was pregnant, she started making me soft boiled eggs for breakfast and chicken broth for lunch, and wouldn't let me go to bed before serving me a good size bowl of warm donkey milk and an *hayuya* roll with butter and jam.

Early in the morning, a man would come by selling bread, which he carried in wooden boxes hanging on the sides of a horse. I would wake up when he blew his whistle, throw my robe on and go down to buy a few buns because the pregnancy made me hungry at all hours. Also, a country man would come by with a she-donkey, milk her right there on the street and sell the milk. While I was pregnant I never got sick and I'm sure it was because of my nightly bowl of donkey milk.

The rest of the people that lived at the *pension* were men on their own and they treated me with great respect and consideration. Señora Mafalda made sure everybody was content, prepared good food and at lunch time turned on the radio so we could listen to La Pichanga, a comedy about life in a *pension*, which made us laugh no end. After the men went back to work, the two of us stayed in the dining room listening to "The Right to Live" while I did some knitting or embroidering. Then I had my daily nap and Mrs. Mafalda woke me up for *onces*. We tuned into Radio Minería and listened to "Discomanía" with Raúl Matas, who was the best announcer the country ever had.

Back then, Sonia and Miriam had just started their singing career and Ester Soré was Negra Linda, a national treasure. Los Panchos were causing a stir, Leo Marini was hardly twenty years old and Libertad Lamarque not only sang beautiful tangos, but was also a famous movie star. But my favourite was Malú Gatica, especially when she sang:

Serene and clear night
blue sky, night of magic
wrapped in the mist of love
listen to the whisper of the breeze
the breath of the trees.
The one I long for will hear my song in the shadows
tremble with emotion and call my name...

Even though I was sad because I hadn't been able to continue going to school, I was in love with Andrés, I was expecting my first child and I was happy.

One afternoon in April, I went to visit my mom. It was a typical autumn day, fresh and full of sun. I got off the streetcar at the other side of Cousiño Park and crossed it diagonally. After a while, I realized that I was following the same route Andrés and I had taken on his birthday. I sat on a bench wondering what my classmates at Normal School might be doing at that time—perhaps discussing a Gabriela Mistral poem or doing a scientific experiment. I ached to be there with them, but I couldn't be. I was going to have a child. Then, I promised myself that if it was a girl, I would educate her about the facts of life sooner rather than later; I would teach her how to take care of herself, how to say "No" so that nobody could take advantage of her. If it was a boy, I would make sure that he respected girls and didn't let lust steer his actions.

The Andes looked so close that it seemed like I could touch them with my hand, the trees were dressed in different hues of yellow, red, brown and orange, and the leaves crackled under my steps. I went into the wooded area and found the place where Andrés and I had conceived our child. I put my sweater on the ground and sat down to think about how that moment had changed my life forever. I was about to leave when I remembered that we had buried the handkerchief underneath an enormous weeping willow.

I started digging until I found it. I wrapped it in my own handkerchief and put it in my purse. When I got to my mom's, I went straight to the bathroom with the excuse of having to urinate every five minutes and scrubbed my fingernails. I didn't say anything to Andrés about the handkerchief because I wanted to surprise him. I washed it and left it in bleach overnight; all the stains came off and it looked like new again. I ironed it and put it in the drawer with the other handkerchiefs, right on top, so that Andrés could see it, but days went by and he didn't say anything, nor did he use it. After about a week, I decided to put it away as a memento.

That was my first disappointment in Andrés, but not my last. A short while before Andresito was born, my husband didn't come home until five in the morning. Unable to sleep, I was lying in bed wondering where he was, what he was doing, who he was with, when he opened the door and stumbled into our room. He smelled of liquor and cheap perfume, was missing a sock and his shirt collar was stained with lipstick. How could Andrés kiss, hug and make love to another woman? What had happened to his promises of eternal love? He never explained, and during our twenty-one years together there were many other occasions when he came home in the wee hours of the night, half-drunk and showing signs of having slept with somebody else.

My son Andresito was born at two twenty in the morning on September 23, 1943, at the maternity ward of the Salvador Hospital in Santiago.

It was around six o'clock in the evening and I was walking up Catedral Street towards Plaza Brasil when I felt my belly go hard. At first I didn't pay much attention to it, as it had happened many times in the previous month, but when it went hard again, just a few minutes later, I knew that the time for my child to be born had finally arrived.

I went into a corner store, asked the lady to use the phone and called Andrés at the bank. I walked back home, and just as I was coming out of the house with my suitcase, Andrés pulled up in a taxi and off we went to the hospital.

To get to the maternity ward, we had to go through a beautiful interior courtyard full of orange trees in bloom, and then down a covered gallery with a tiled floor in a white and red zig-zag design. Andrés was directed to sit in a small waiting room and I was ushered into the midwife's office. She listened to the child's heartbeat with one of those wooden horns they used back then and examined my insides. She determined that everything was in order and that my baby would be born some time during the course of the night.

A bit before two in the morning, I was taken into the delivery room. During those last moments of labour I kept thinking that it wasn't possible to feel such enormous pain and still be alive. In the distance, I could hear the midwife asking me all kinds of questions: "What's your name? Where do you live? What does your husband do for a living?" I wanted to answer her, but all I could do was scream. Then, I was overcome by an unstoppable desire to push, even though I was certain that if I did, I would break into pieces.

I felt myself open at the very roots and heard the midwife say that the child was coming. I pushed for the last time and my entire being escaped from in between my legs.

"It's a little man, Soledad," the midwife announced as I lifted my head and saw her holding a bloodied baby by the feet. "A beautiful boy with all his parts," she added as she gave him a gentle slap on the buttocks. My son let out his first cry and I rested my head and closed my eyes.

After Andresito was born, we went to live in a little house on Herrera Street, near Quinta Normal. By then Andrés had been able to secure a loan from the bank, so we got all our furniture at Gath & Chávez and I was finally able to fulfill my desire to become a full-fledged *dueña de casa*, a housewife.

I loved taking care of my baby and my home. The house had quite a large garden in the back with beautiful trees, and an assortment of flowers: camellias, fuchsias, hydrangea, roses... I could spend hours looking after my garden while Andresito slept under the purple jacarandas and the perfumed acacias.

I would do my grocery shopping up the street at Plaza Brasil, and when my son got older, we would stop at the playground for a few minutes so that he could go on the swings or climb on the slide. But what he liked the best was to play tag with the neighbourhood kids, going around and around a gigantic *ceibo* tree that sat like a sentinel right in the middle of the square.

Andrés adored our son and loved spending time with him when he came home from work. At the beginning, he was afraid that he wouldn't know how to hold the newborn, that he would drop him, but he learned, and would spend long whiles walking him around the house and talking to him in baby language. When Andresito got older, they would play ball in the backyard and Andrés would also take him to his soccer games at Quinta Normal on Saturday afternoons.

Then, one hot summer day at the end of January, 1949, Andrés announced that he had been transferred to the city of Valdivia where he would be in charge of organizing the savings department of the bank. "We're leaving for Valdivia," he announced when he got home that evening. He didn't even say "Hi."

I froze and didn't know what to do or say, and as our son

Andresito stared at us both with his mouth open, Andrés picked him up with one arm, hugged me with his other arm and repeated: "We're leaving for Valdivia."

"Valdivia," I muttered, while remembering the postcard that my friend Rina had sent me when she had gone there on holidays with her family the previous summer: the ample and blue Calle-Calle River, cotton clouds in the sky, and the bridge with its grand white pillars and its half-moon arches opening over the river.

"What do you mean, 'We're leaving for Valdivia?'" I finally asked him.

In between jokes, he explained, "Let me introduce you to the Registered Accountant, the exemplary Mr. Andrés Martínez," (big bow followed by cha-cha steps with me), "Head of the Savings Department of the State Bank of the beautiful city of Valdivia" (tickles on Andresito's tummy), "awarded a fifteen percent raise over and above his already generous salary" (raising his voice while putting his arms out and extending his hands in the style of a Radical Party politician), "Who will shortly leave for the 'Pearl of the South' in the company of his beautiful and charming wife, Mrs. Soledad de Martínez" (waltzing around with me), "And his precocious five-and-a-half-year-old heir, Andrés Martínez Jr." (whirling Andresito in the air), "All expenses paid, yes ladies and gentlemen, boys and girls, all travel expenses paid by the honourable treasury of our beloved country, Chile" (voice and gestures in the style of Caluga Clown).

We used his two weeks of annual holidays to pack our things and at the beginning of March we left for "The Pearl of the South" in the regular train that departed Santiago's Central Station at six o'clock in the evening.

The compartment we were assigned was quite pretty: it had facing red velvet seats that at night came together and became a bed, and a wooden box above the window, which when lowered turned into a bunk bed. I had cried quite a bit after saying good-bye to my family, but by the time we got to Rancagua, I was feeling much better. The vineyards were heavy with grapes, you could see some beautiful clay ovens in the countryside and the Andes looked lovely, dressed in the pinks and oranges of the setting sun. Andresito had fallen asleep and Andrés and I were looking out the window in silence. He had his arm around me and before I knew it we were kissing and ended up making love on the train seat. All I managed to do before half our clothes were off was pull down the blind. I knew that I wasn't quite at the end of my dangerous days, but I didn't worry about it and told myself, "It will be God's will."

By the next morning the landscape had changed completely; we were going through forests and more forests, thick with enormous ferns and varieties of trees I had never seen before. Other than the common pine-trees, I only recognized the *araucarias* from pictures I had seen in my geography schoolbooks. There seemed to be water everywhere and we crossed one river after another. Most beautiful of all were the volcanoes with their snow-capped peaks and their craters, like open mouths wanting to take a bite off a wandering cloud.

The fields also looked different from those in the central region: instead of vineyards, the main crops were wheat, potatoes and alfalfa. I had always thought that what gave the Chilean countryside its special character were the small adobe houses with their clay ovens in the front yard and the *huasos*—cowboys with wide-brimmed hats and short, colourful ponchos; but during that trip, I realized that in Santiago we knew very little about the rest of the country. The houses of the *campesinos* that I could see from the train were made of wood, there were no clay ovens and the men were wearing short-brimmed hats and long, heavy ponchos made of raw, un-dyed wool.

At about eleven o'clock we got to Antilhue, where we had to move to the first-class car because the sleeping car continued south towards Osorno and Puerto Montt. A steam engine was placed at the head of our section of the train and we set off along the river for Valdivia. I had never seen such a beautiful, wide, blue river in my life. The train made two more stops, in Pishuinco and Huellelhue, and we finally arrived in Valdivia at about one o'clock in the afternoon.

At the station we took a taxi to a *pension* on Carampangue Street, which had been recommended to Andrés by the bank manager. I was fascinated by the wooden houses and their chimneys, the humid air and the sweet aroma of burning wood. Everything was so different from Santiago: the shape and size of the buildings, the lush vegetation, an expansive feeling of openness and freshness...

After a couple of weeks at the *pension*, we found a house on Esmeralda Street and life began to take its course. I sorely missed my family, but also welcomed the opportunity to have a fresh start in life in a completely new place. Oddly enough, what I missed the most was the sight of the Andes, which were omnipresent in Santiago. Every time I left the house I would look for the mountains before remembering that they're not visible from Valdivia. Then I would walk to the river and rest my eyes in its blue waters for a while. If it was a clear day, you could see Villarrica Volcano in the distance and that also helped to ease my homesickness for Santiago and the *cordillera*.

What I had the most trouble getting used to was the stormy weather. I never knew it could rain so much; it was like a constant deluge. There were nights when the wind was so strong that I was certain the roof would fly away, or Andresito would wake up with the thunder and lightning and get in my bed, crying. After a while we all got used to it and slept through the night.

Sol was born on December 1 of that year. By that time it's already summer in the central region, but in Valdivia, other than the occasional nice day, it's still raining. My mom had come from Santiago to help out, and the night I had to go to the clinic there was a huge storm. She was so scared that it was hard to tell whether she would be looking after Andresito or the other way around.

The storm didn't stop all night, and in the morning the thunder and lightning were still going strong. The clinic was housed in a huge, old, yellow house and the delivery room was on the second floor. It had big windows looking on to the street so, as I pushed and pushed, I could see the rain washing down and hear its pitter-patter against the glass. Then, at the same moment Sol came out of my womb, a huge bolt of lightning lit up the room and the electric lights flickered off for a few seconds. My girl's first cry coincided with a clap of thunder that made everything shake. It was eight o'clock in the morning.

On July 16, 1962, I got a telegram signed by Mrs. Elena Vergara de la Cruz, Director of the Nestlé Institute of Domestic Economy in Santiago, informing me that I had won third prize in the Imperial Baking Powder contest. I had submitted my apple *kuchen* recipe a few months before, and then concluded that most likely I didn't stand a chance, given that thousands of housewives from all over Chile would be sending in their own creations as well. But, against all odds, I had won! I was so happy that I skipped and whooped around the house like a madwoman until I decided to go to the bank and break the news to Andrés.

He seemed surprised and even annoyed to see me show up unexpectedly at his work, but when I told him about the award he almost burst with pride and danced his way around his colleagues' desks as he read the telegram out loud and with great enthusiasm for everyone to hear.

His good mood was short-lived, though. That evening, when I informed him that I would be travelling to Santiago in September, all expenses paid, to receive my prize and cook my recipe in front of the TV cameras, his face fell and he didn't hesitate to shout that I shouldn't go, as it would be utterly irresponsible on my part to abandon the family, even if it was for just one week. But, I was determined to go no matter what. I talked it over with my new friend Isabel who was the mother of Sol's classmate, Gloria, and also with my old friends Laura, Paulina and Maruja; they all encouraged me to go and offered to take charge of my housework. So, even though Andrés' opposition put a damper on my happiness, I didn't allow it to stop me from taking the train to Santiago.

My mom and Amparo were waiting for me at Central Station and I was surprised to see how elegant my sister looked in her fashionable two-piece tailored suit, patent leather high heels and matching purse, and short-brimmed raffia hat. The house on Allende Padín had also changed dramatically because of the expensive furniture Amparo had bought the year before, following our dad's death. Even though the new decor was very nice indeed, I felt that my old home had lost its warmth and taken on the looks of a display shop window. But, I praised my sister and the house anyway and proceeded to thoroughly enjoy my mom's Sunday cooking.

The next evening I went to pick up Amparo at Los Gobelinos, the department store where she worked. When she saw me she became quite nervous, and instead of walking towards the bus stop she suggested that we sit for a few moments at the square. There she told me that she was going to introduce me to the man she loved. I was astounded, but managed to hug her and say that

I had no idea she had a boyfriend. I asked her why she hadn't told me.

Her chin was quivering when she whispered, "Héctor is a married man..."

Next thing I knew, I was shouting, "Amparo! Don't you realize that you're destroying a family? Haven't you stopped to think of this man's wife and children?"

Now tears were streaming down Amparo's cheeks as she responded, "Héctor doesn't love his wife anymore, Soledad... He doesn't even sleep with her. He wants to divorce her." She blew her nose, wiped the tears off her face, took my hand and added, "He's not the way you imagine him. He's not a womanizer. He's truly in love with me, but also has the responsibility of his family and cannot leave them. I have come to accept that reality and have decided not to demand anything from him. The only thing I want is his love."

"You deserve much better than that, Amparo. You deserve somebody who's free to love you, who can marry you and start a family, the way it should be," I replied.

My sister assured me that she didn't feel like having children anymore, that she was too old for that. All she wanted, she said, was for Héctor to love her.

I felt sorry for her; obviously my sister felt lonely. We were very close to each other when we were young, but we had grown apart after my move to Valdivia. Back then, only the wealthy could afford to have a telephone, so we just used regular mail. As I didn't have time to write lengthy personal letters, I would usually just send one page a week to both my mom and Amparo, and my mom would reply in the same way. But that evening I made a mental note to write to Amparo separately and encourage her to confide in me once again.

We walked slowly toward Paula Café. Héctor was waiting at the entrance: regular height, thin, dark skin, brown eyes, black hair and a pencil moustache—nothing special at all. He certainly was very affectionate with Amparo and did his best to be charming and thoughtful; he told me that he felt like he had known me for years because my sister was always talking about me. As we sipped our tea, he repeated several times that Amparo was the love of his life. I felt like telling him that he probably said the same thing to his wife, but of course I didn't.

Amparo had met Héctor a couple of years earlier—he worked for a company that imported leather goods from Argentina and stocked several downtown stores, including Los Gobelinos. After a while they had started to travel together and, as he knew the customs agents at the border, she was able to bring into the country a variety of merchandise, free of duty. Then, with the utmost discretion, she sold these articles directly to her most loyal customers—at discounted prices, but still with a substantial profit margin. That was how she put together the money to start her own business. Back then, nobody but Amparo herself could've imagined that in a few years she would become a very wealthy and powerful woman.

Towards the end of that week in Santiago, following my public presentation and the awards ceremony, my mom, Amparo and I made ourselves some tea, sat on the couch, wrapped ourselves in a blanket and tuned into "The Great Stage of Love" with Mireya Latorre and Emilio Gaete. For a while I felt like we were re-living old times of closeness and intimacy, moments from before my marriage. We listened in silence to the familiar voices of Chile's "romantic couple," exchanging glances of complicity and squeezing each other's hands when the words pulled at our emotions. At some point, Mireya said, "I don't want to hear about your infinite love for me anymore. I want you to show it to me. I want you to be faithful to me. I'm tired of this invisible love."

It was as if somebody had pushed a button on the three of us, because we started to cry in unison. Then Amparo and I got the giggles, but stopped in our tracks when we heard our mom's voice: "Mireya Latorre is right. What's the sense in being called 'my love, my sweetheart, my baby, my life, my honey,' if at the same time they're two-timing you? It doesn't make any sense." For the first time in our lives, our mom was talking to us about her emotions, her pain.

After a few moments of silence I asked, "Were you and our dad in love when you got married?"

"Of course! Very much in love. But a few years later he began to have lovers and everything got spoiled," she answered. Then she asked, "Has Andrés been faithful to you?"

At first I didn't know what to say. All I could hear was my heart thumping.

I offered, "The truth is that I don't know. I think that sometimes he goes to see ladies of the night... But in spite of everything, I know that deep down he loves me and I'm happy," I answered tentatively.

"Happy... Happy... That word has the ring of a bad joke," I heard Amparo say. She shot my mother a look of bitterness. "What does it mean to be happy? I would've been happy with Yoshi, but that turned into nothing. Happiness is a ridiculous illusion." Our mom tried to hug her, but Amparo pushed her away. "I will never forgive you for rejecting Yoshi Okano! He was the love of my life, but you didn't care about my happiness! All you cared about was people's gossip!"

My mom turned pale at the sudden outburst. It had been years since Amparo had lost Yoshi and yet, looking at her in this moment, you would think it had been barely a week. Mom could only repeat what she had said many times before: "Amparo, that relationship couldn't last, not just because he was Japanese. Don't forget that he was also very rich and his family would've never accepted that he marry a poor Chilean girl."

In between sobs and tears, and with her voice full of sarcasm, Amparo muttered several times under her breath, "A poor Chilean girl, a poor Chilean girl, a poor Chilean girl..."

I remember perfectly well the first time that Amparo met Yoshi, the love of her youth. She had just graduated from high school and was looking for a job, so when she saw an advertisement for a nice-looking young lady to work as a salesperson for Okano Toys, she decided to apply. I went downtown with her and waited at the Plaza de Armas with Andresito while she went to the store to find out more details about the job. It took her almost an hour and when she came back, she told me that she had been hired. It turned out that Yoshi Okano had interviewed her and offered her the position on the spot. He was only twenty years old then, but as the owner's son he had the authority to hire and fire. It didn't take long for the two of them to start dating, and a few weeks later Amparo confided that she and Yoshi were in love.

"I was wondering what was going on—you have looked so happy lately," I commented as I hugged her and planted a peck on her cheek.

"Oh, he's so sweet, Soledad," she responded, kissing me back. "I love him, love him, love him!" she sang, opera style, as she took me by the hands and we spun around the way we had as kids.

It had been a while since we had had a moment of closeness, as now I was a married woman living with her husband and child in her own separate home. Until my wedding, Amparo and I had shared a bedroom, which made it hard to keep secrets from each other. When I got pregnant with Andresito, for example, she was the first one to know and had gone out of her way to be kind and supportive. "Everything will be okay, sister, you'll see, you'll see," she would assure me, sitting on my bed and stroking my hair as I sobbed, my face buried in my pillow.

We were still spinning around when it occurred to me that if our mom hadn't explained the facts of life to me, she hadn't explained them to Amparo either.

"Amparo!" I cried out as I pulled on her hands and we came to a stop.

"What's the matter?" she demanded, a look of confusion on her face.

"Nothing—sorry—nothing is the matter... I just want to explain a few things to you." We sat down at the dining room table and I told her everything I had learned about love and desire, ovulation, conception and all the rest. I had learned the hard way, but I wasn't going to let my little sister make the same mistakes.

She listened carefully, thanked me for the lesson and assured me that she would not allow Yoshi to go overboard with his affection. "I'll keep him in line," she joked.

I suggested that she tell our mom about Yoshi, but Amparo said that she wanted to wait for a while as she was afraid that our mom wouldn't approve of her Japanese boyfriend; the war had just ended and there was a lot of anti-Japanese and anti-German sentiment going around. After about three months, I concluded that there was nothing wrong with Yoshi; on the contrary, he was a very nice person. I had met him a couple of times and had been impressed by how well mannered he was—he treated me as if I were the Queen of England and was always sending little toys for Andresito—so I decided to invite our mom and Amparo over on a Saturday afternoon while Andrés played soccer and my dad was at the horse track.

After I poured the tea, I told our mom that Amparo had something to tell her. She looked at Amparo with wide open eyes, probably thinking that now her other daughter had become pregnant out of wedlock, but I assured her that Amparo had good news.

My sister's voice was hardly audible. "I have a boyfriend," she said.

"Oh, that's nice, Amparo, and who's the lucky boy?" our mom asked as she reached for the sugar.

Amparo looked at me. I nodded, but she couldn't say any more, so I added, "It's Yoshi Okano, the son of the owners of Okano Toys."

Our mom's hand stopped mid-air. Her face fell. For a few seconds, she didn't move or say a word. I looked at Amparo; her eyes had filled with tears. Finally, our mom poured the sugar into her tea, stirred it and rested the spoon on her saucer with a loud clink. Then, turning her head towards my sister, but eluding Amparo's gaze, her voice loaded with contempt, she said, "A Japanese boy? Why, Amparo, when there are so many Chilean boys available?

Tears were running down Amparo's face now, but it only took a second for her sadness to turn into anger. "I don't care one bit about how many Chilean boys are available because I'm in love with Yoshi Okano and he's in love with me!" she shouted as she got up from the table.

I told our mom that Yoshi was a thoughtful, well mannered boy; explained that at Normal School we had learned that Japanese people are very well-educated and intelligent. I also showed her the toys that Yoshi had sent along for Andresito, but to no avail. Our mom didn't say a word for the rest of the afternoon and, in the end, she never accepted Yoshi because—according to her—"the yellow race" was a threat to humanity.

That was my first encounter with that kind of prejudice. I was used to hearing people's derogatory remarks on account of a person's dark skin, poverty or lack of education, but to witness my own mother's ignorance and intolerance saddened and angered me to no end. Over the following weeks I asked her many times to give Yoshi a chance, to at least meet him once and then judge him for who he was as a human being, but she wouldn't hear of it.

As it turned out, the Okanos didn't approve of their son's Chilean girlfriend either and a couple of months later the relationship came to an abrupt ending. Yoshi assured Amparo that he was still in love with her, but also made it clear that he wouldn't go against his parents' wishes. My sister stopped working at the toy store and got a job at Los Gobelinos, where she was employed for many years to come. A few months later, on the social pages of *El Mercurio*, we read that Yoshi Okano had married a Japanese girl.

For a long time Amparo was angry at me for having "forced"

her to tell our mom about Yoshi. "I always knew that she wouldn't approve! I told you so!" she would yell in an accusatory tone.

After we learned about Yoshi's wedding, Amparo took a week off work and stayed in bed, claiming to have a bad cold. I went to visit her a few times and tried to make her see that having a secret love affair with Yoshi wouldn't have worked anyway, that she had to get on with her life.

"Yeah, it's easy for you to tell me to get on with my life... You married the man you love," she would respond, full of resentment.

Eventually, she seemed to have recovered and went back to being her cheerful old self. A couple of years later she decided to start saving to open her own store, and now she was well on her way to doing so. But obviously she had never really gotten over Yoshi.

"A poor Chilean girl, a poor Chilean girl, a poor Chilean girl..." she was repeating now, her voice charged with bitterness and self-loathing. "You two wait and see," she added, looking at my mom and me with frigid eyes as she nodded and smirked.

By now my mom was crying. I was in shock: at the drop of a hat, my sister had turned into a cold, mean stranger. A few days earlier she had introduced me to her lover and I had promised myself to correspond with her more intimately and more often. Now I wasn't sure—I didn't know what I would say to this new persona.

I wonder if that was the moment when her soul began to turn

black; her resentment and greed so strong that when she felt threatened, she didn't hesitate to cause immense hardship and pain to her own family.

Upon my homecoming, I was given a beautiful reception by my family and friends. Everybody was waiting for me at the railway station and as I walked off the train the kids sang a rendition of "The World Cup Rock'n Roll," with words they had adapted to suit the story of my award:

> The 1962 baking contest
> Is a national festivity
> Of flour, eggs and milk
> And Imperial baking powder
> Celebrating our triumphs
> We will dance the rock'n roll
>
> Take it, whip it, bake it
> Goooooooooooal by Soledad
> With her delicious apple *kuchen*
> She has won her big award

I didn't know whether to laugh or to cry.

Most moving of all was to see Andrés. He was all smiles and, as he handed me a bouquet of red roses, he whispered sweet things into my ear. Obviously, he had had a change of heart after hearing my dedication of the *bolero* "Sabor a Mí" to him when I was interviewed on national radio.

At lunch time he got a little tipsy and every two minutes he would want to make a toast in my honour: "To the best looking and smartest housewife in Chile!" "To Mrs. Soledad de Martínez, wife of Andrés Martínez, Director of the Savings Department of the Valdivia State Bank!" "To my wife, whose good looks beat Brigitte Bardot's by a country mile!"

That week, he got in my bed every night and we made love as if we had been on our honeymoon. I was ecstatic.

A few days after my return, Miss Blanca, Sol's Spanish and home teacher, suggested that I apply for a position at the Girls' Technical School. The principal, Mrs. Zoraida Fahual, was a good friend of hers and had mentioned that she needed a pastry-making teacher to work as a substitute and as an evening instructor. According to Miss Blanca, I had better qualifications than many of the ladies that worked there already because I had studied at Normal School and now I had also gotten an award in the Imperial Baking Powder contest. I was in heaven: Andrés and I were in love again, I had a wonderful family and loyal friends, and now I would also fulfill my dream of becoming a teacher. But the fears I had harboured inside me since my youth took a hold of me and marred what could've been the happiest two weeks of my life.

I had noticed that Sol was acting rather strangely, so a couple of days before Andresito's nineteenth birthday I pressed her to tell me what the matter was.

She blushed, her eyes wide, and blurted out, "The thing is that I'm in love with Miguel and he's in love with me. We want to go steady, but we don't know if you'll approve."

I couldn't believe my ears. My daughter was only twelve years old and she wanted to have a boyfriend! What about school, the conservatory, university? What if she got pregnant out of wedlock, the way I had?

"I can't believe it! I thought that Miguel was an honourable boy and never imagined that he'd take advantage of you while I was in Santiago!" I heard myself shout.

"Don't be ridiculous, that's not what happened! Miguel and I have been in love for quite a while now!" Sol shouted back.

I didn't know what to think or say. I had always liked Miguel; actually, I had come to love the boy—he was not only thoughtful and sensitive, but was also studying to become a teacher and played the violin beautifully. But I couldn't allow my daughter to have a boyfriend at such an early age, so I said, "Absolutely not." I insisted that they were acting irresponsibly and even banned Miguel from coming to our house ever again.

At first my daughter just looked at me in disbelief. Then, choking back tears, she yelled, "When it's convenient for you, then you find me responsible, like when you abandoned your family and I had to become the housewife! You should have your eye on your son instead of me because he is the one who has been doing weird stuff, not me!"

I begged her to tell me what she meant, but she refused: "Question him, not me."

That afternoon, when Andresito came home, I asked him to go to Sol's room with me—she had been hiding there since our argument. He looked puzzled, but didn't hesitate to follow me up the stairs.

Sol, puffy-eyed and her nose bright red from crying, was lying in bed. Andresito sat beside her, patted her head and asked her what the matter was. Sol sat up, hugged him and whispered something in his ear. Andresito looked at her, then looked at me, and stood up while Sol declared that she had lied to me, that she hadn't seen her brother do anything weird. She assured me that she had only said those words in anger.

Andresito asked me to sit on the bed, sat beside me and took my hand. His head was buried in his chest. My heart was pounding—I was sure he was going to tell me that he had to get married because some girl was pregnant with his child. Then I heard him say, "Carloncho and I are in love with each other. We truly love each other."

It took me a while to understand the words. *Carloncho and I are in love with each other. We truly love each other.* Then I put two and two together: Sol had caught Andresito and Carloncho "in the act" while I was in Santiago. My son and his best friend were *maricones*, perverts.

It was my fault. Somehow, my son knew that I hadn't wanted to have him, that I had always resented getting pregnant with him before finishing school, that because of him I had gotten married "in a hurry." I had also been a bad mother: I hadn't taught him the difference between right and wrong and he had turned out to be a pervert. Yes. It was my fault.

I slapped my son across the face and ran out of the room.

I have a vague recollection of the following days: Andresito's birthday party, the fact that Carloncho was reportedly "sick" and couldn't come, my own lying about having a cold so as to justify my constant sniffling. Finally, I decided to open up to my friend Isabel. After all, she was a health-care professional and seemed to be a very "modern" woman, judging from her daughter Gloria's behaviour at school and her own firm stance against Mrs. Dolores, the Needlepoint teacher.

I showed up at the end of her shift at the regional hospital and explained that I needed her help. We went for a cup of tea at a nearby café and I poured my heart out to her.

She listened attentively and then, with great compassion in her voice, proceeded to say that she understood me completely, but that she didn't think there was anything wrong with my son and Carloncho. "You know what, Soledad? I also used to think that homosexuals are abnormal, but not anymore," she confessed.

I was puzzled. "How come? What made you change your mind?" I asked.

"I don't know if you remember this or if you actually know this—the government made sure to keep it under tabs—but in the late forties and early fifties communists were persecuted and killed," she explained as she looked at me inquisitively.

Now I was even more puzzled. "Yes?" I responded tentatively.

"Well, they didn't only kill communists, Soledad. They also killed homosexuals. I learned this from a colleague, a male nurse. He had had an affair with his best friend's wife and the wronged husband had taken revenge by accusing him of being a faggot and turning him in to the police. He was sent up north, to Pisagua concentration camp, with hundreds of real homosexuals and communists. Fortunately, his family pulled some strings and he was freed instead of—"

I was getting impatient, so I cut her off. "But what's that got to do with changing your mind about faggots?" I asked.

"Sorry, Soledad. Okay, to cut a long story short, what happened to Juan—that was my colleague's name—got me thinking: to the government of the time, communists and homosexuals were one and the same, monsters, freaks that needed to be eliminated. Well, as a communist myself, I knew that I wasn't a freak. And if we communists weren't freaks, maybe homosexuals weren't either... See what I mean?" she continued.

I nodded. I could see the way she was going, but I wanted to hear a definitive answer right away.

Isabel went on, "So, I began to do research. I got my hands on every book and article about homosexuality I could find. By then I was already married to Carlos, also a communist, so I got him thinking and researching as well. Finally, we both came to realize that homosexuals have no choice, the same way that you or I are attracted to the opposite sex, they're drawn to people of the same sex. They can't help it. There have been homosexuals in every society at all times in history, and in many cultures they have not been shunned, but accepted for who they are. But in this country—as in many others—we've been taught to hate them, to believe that they're perverts. Even many of my communist comrades, people who supposedly have a critical mind, despise homosexuals and consider them to be freaks, but they're human beings, Soledad, just like the rest of us. They fall in love, have professions, have values and beliefs—they're definitely not freaks. Anybody with an open mind will understand that," Isabel concluded keenly.

I had never heard anybody explain homosexuality this way before. It made sense to me and I wanted to believe Isabel's views, particularly after she informed me that great artists such as Leonardo da Vinci, Oscar Wilde and Cole Porter were believed to have been homosexual. But still, I couldn't bring myself to accept my son the way he was. I wanted to see him walk around the square holding hands with a girl; I wanted him married to a girl; I wanted grandchildren from him. I didn't want him to live a life of secrecy as a *mariposón*, a pansy. I asked Isabel if this could just be "bad habits," something that he would outgrow.

She smiled and then responded, shaking her head, "Perhaps, Soledad, perhaps... but I don't think so. He's already nineteen years old. If he were twelve or thirteen, maybe we could say that he's just experimenting with his sexuality, but at nineteen..."

All the same, I held on to the hope that my son would turn into a "normal" man. All he needs, I told myself, is to find the right girl.

Regarding Sol, after talking to Isabel about it, I decided to allow her and Miguel to be girlfriend and boyfriend. I asked Andrés to have a good talk with the boy and I explained the facts of life to Sol. My daughter was elated. She gave me a big hug and then ran out to the conservatory to break the news to Miguel.

In terms of Andresito, I didn't talk to him about his "problem" again and made Sol and Isabel promise that they would never mention it to anybody. As far as Andrés was concerned, I decided to act as if nothing had ever happened. *He will die if he ever hears about it,* I thought.

It was a beautiful Saturday afternoon and Andrés and Andresito had gone to the Municipal Stadium to have their weekly Union Juvenil practice. Sol was helping me make a Primavera cake for *onces* when we heard loud knocking on the front door. It was Tito Ramírez, who had run all the way from the stadium to tell us that Andrés had collapsed on the field and an ambulance had taken him to the emergency room of the Regional Hospital.

When we got there, Andresito was waiting for us at the entrance. His head was buried in his chest and his whole body was trembling. Andrés was dead. I looked at my son and, for the first time in my life, saw his naked face. It was as if he had shed a veil to reveal a pale, almost transparent shell. The pain had also opened a door deep into his eyes—a tunnel the colour of honey. Sol's face, on the other hand, was contorted, transformed by anguish, tied into a knot. I was numb.

For the longest time I didn't experience any emotions over my husband's death other than feeling like a traitor because I couldn't cry, couldn't bring myself to be sad. My memories of that time are blotchy: people coming and going, Andrés' sisters, my mom and Amparo staying at our place, Carloncho showing up after several days of not coming to our house, Andrés' funeral—a horse-drawn black hearse followed by the family and dozens of friends marching slowly up Picarte Avenue, all the way to the cemetery.

Right before the funeral, a few black outfits showed up on my bed, complete with shoes, stockings and even underwear. I never found out for sure, but I suspect that Amparo brought them from Santiago, together with mourning garments for the kids.

My friends organized the wake and we stayed up all night, talking, eating, playing music, singing and even dancing. Tito Ramírez brought his guitar along and as Miguel always carried his violin with him everywhere he went, they played impromptu renditions of Andrés' favourite songs and provided background music for my poetry recitations. My husband's sisters related stories about him as a child—he had always been outgoing and witty—and his colleagues from the bank repeated some of the jokes and riddles he had told them over the years.

Then Tito started to play the "World Cup Rock'n Roll" and I began dancing with Sol, Gloria and Silvia without even knowing. Everybody joined in, until all of a sudden I felt an uncontrollable urge to weep and wail. It was as if a switch had been turned on inside me. From then on, anything and everything would make me cry: a melody on the radio, the aroma of my own cooking, the memory of Andrés' hand on my waist... But then I would think that everything had just been a bad dream; that I would wake up and Andrés would be right there, next to me, his body molded to mine.

At times, I would get angry and shout and scream. This was the utmost case of disloyalty and infidelity, worse than an affair, far worse than going to the ladies of the night: Andrés had left me just like that. The days prior to his death had been filled with so much joy and love! Why leave then, when we had a whole life ahead us! I wondered if he had felt ill and never said anything. I couldn't comprehend how a person could just drop dead.

But as days and weeks passed, I had no choice but to accept my new reality. Besides, now I was the head of the family and needed to earn our keep.

My first day of classes at the Girls' Technical School was nerve-racking. That morning, when I went into Mrs. Zoraida's office to say hello, my voice was quivering and my knees shaking. She got up from her chair, walked around her desk and greeted me with a long, tight hug. She said that she was very happy to have me as part of her teaching staff and that she was certain that I would distinguish myself as an excellent educator.

At first my students acted a bit strange, as if they weren't sure of what to do or say, probably because they had heard of my husband's recent passing. But, little by little, I relaxed, they relaxed, and, in the end, the day turned out to be very rewarding, albeit exhausting. With the passing of time, as I gained knowledge and experience, my job became less taxing and I looked forward to spending my days at the Technical School.

At home, the kids behaved like angels and took it upon themselves to help with the house chores. A few months later, after Andresito graduated and got a job, I decided to hire a girl to do the ironing—Isabel's maid's cousin. She was a lanky fifteen-year-old who had just come from the countryside to live in the city with her aunt at the Corvi housing project. The poor thing was called Bovine, but there was nothing bovine about her. Actually, she was very smart and an excellent worker—it didn't take her any time to learn to do the starching and to use the electric iron.

At the beginning, even though I kept scolding Sol and Andresito, they wouldn't stop laughing when I talked about Bovine or when Bovine was in the house. So, one day, I said to her, "Look, Bovine, I know that your mom must've had a very good reason to give you your name, but tell me in all honesty: do you like it?"

She turned beet red and told me that no, she hated her name. Then I asked her if there was another name that she would rather go by.

Without thinking twice about it, she blurted out, "Marilyn,

for Marilyn Monroe."

This time, I had to stop myself from laughing because Bovine had a very dark complexion and was as skinny as a rake, but I managed to say to her with a straight face, "Okay then, from now on, what about being called Marilyn instead of Bovine while you're in this house?"

She blushed again and gave me a big hug and a kiss on the cheek for an answer.

Of course, when I told the kids that Bovine would now be called Marilyn, they laughed even harder, but eventually they got used to it.

Mondays and Tuesdays after work I would do the laundry in my newly acquired Hoovermatic and Marilyn would come on Thursday afternoon to do the ironing, once all the clothes had had a chance to dry. She had lunch with us, and as soon as we finished the dishes, she'd settle at the kitchen table with her ironing and I'd leave for work. I always managed to make an extra *kuchen* to bring home, and on my way back I'd get *hayuyas* at the bakery and some ham and cheese at the Nilo delicatessen shop. When I got home, Marilyn would've finished the ironing, set the table and boiled the water, and we would sit down to eat and talk. After *onces*, I would send her home with a good care package of leftover bread and *kuchen*.

I grew very fond of that girl and the following year I managed to get her accepted as a student at the Technical School, where she trained to be a seamstress. That Christmas I gave her a secondhand sewing machine that I bought from Tito Ramírez' mom, and that way she was able to start making a bit of money doing alterations until she learned her trade well and got herself a good clientele. For years she kept on coming to do the ironing, even though I knew she could make better money with her sewing. I think she had also grown fond of us and enjoyed spending Thursday afternoons at our house.

A couple of years after Andrés died, I fell for Helmut Meyer, the owner of the Cervantes Theatre. In the end, he turned out to be not only a shameless Don Juan, but also a soulless Nazi. He had come to Chile after the war posing as a businessman in search of a better life, but he was actually a run-away Nazi who never gave up his ideology of hatred and contempt for people he considered his "inferiors." Later on, I also learned that Miss Blanca, Sol's Spanish teacher, had been another one of his many lovers and he made sure the military imprisoned and then executed her because she was a communist.

Helmut Meyer conquered my heart by giving me a beautiful piano for my daughter, Sol. He showed up one day in his blue Opel pick-up truck, carrying the piano in the back together with two men who took it down and put it in our living room. Everything happened so quickly that I didn't even have time to react.

For quite a while he had been courting me—calling to offer me free tickets for the Cervantes, sitting beside me when the lights went off, walking up to greet me when he saw me on the street.

The man was undoubtedly good looking: tall, elegant, dark hair, and with a pair of velvety hazel eyes that made my heart gallop. Besides, he was thoughtful and quite the gentleman, so much so that every time he saw me he would bow and kiss my hand.

Several times at the theatre he tried to put his arm around my shoulders, but I squirmed out of his embrace promptly even though the weight of his arm made me perspire with emotion. He was persistent and continued to shower me with attention until he showed up with the piano. When I understood his plot and wanted to return it, Sol had already fallen in love with the piano and would spend the whole afternoon playing. Of course I never told the truth to her and Andresito—instead I said that I had bought it from Mr. Meyer on monthly installments. In fact, I bought it from him on weekly installments—not of money, but sex.

A few days after the piano delivery, Helmut phoned to invite me to the theatre once again, this time to the opening of *The Sound of Music*. He sat beside me and that was it. We didn't even see the movie. We got up in silence; he took hold of my elbow and guided me to a back door that opened into a garage where his pick-up truck was parked. There we made love for the first time. Then we began to go once a week to a little hotel at the end of General Lagos Street. The last time we went there was two days before the coup.

After all that happened, I never became interested in a man again and I would never have exchanged my peace of mind for ten pianos or a complete orchestra.

Chile

March 1, 1967 – September 10, 1973

Sol

In March of 1967, I began to study Social Work at the University of Chile. Miguel had moved to Santiago two years earlier, as he had been awarded a full scholarship to pursue his violin studies. We were euphoric. After an eternity of communicating by mail and seeing each other only during the holidays, we would be living in the same town again, this time in the capital city of the country.

On my first day of classes, we had agreed to meet for lunch. I was running late, so I bolted into the cafétería trying to figure out how I would find Miguel in the midst of the hustle and bustle of that hub of student activity. Instead, I was met by absolute silence and stillness. Everybody had turned into statues—dozens of spoons were suspended halfway between bowls and mouth, while all eyes were fixed on one single point: a tall, long-haired boy wearing John Lennon glasses. It was Raúl, President of the Student Federation, standing on top of a table.

I was drawn immediately to his convincing and calm words, the clear ring of his voice—not at all strident, but still full of emotion. Much of what he said that day I had already heard from Miguel, Miss Blanca, Gloria, my brother, my father: we lived in an unjust world where the rich exploited the poor, where many people starved to death while others indulged in luxury; we were part of a society in dire need of change. Also, the images of Miguel's home and family were still imprinted in my mind. Certainly, these were issues I knew about, but Raúl's speech brought them into focus for me. He was a natural leader: clear, humble, patient, disciplined, and with a vocabulary that could persuade even tables and chairs.

After he finished his speech and jumped off the table, Raúl was surrounded by students wanting to talk to him. I waited patiently and finally made my way to the front of the small crowd.

"I want to do something," I said. "What can I do?"

He smiled and invited me to go talk to him at the Student Union's office that afternoon. That's how, encouraged by Raúl, I got to La Esperanza, a shanty town in the south end of Santiago.

I had never seen such poverty in my whole life: shacks made of tin and cardboard where an entire family spent the night huddled together on the dirt floor covered with a few sheets of newspaper; thirty-year-old women as wrinkled as raisins and with no teeth in their mouths; men made of skin and bones, their eyes popping with the anger and shame they carried inside for not being able to provide for their families; a dirty pot filled with dirty water on top of a feeble bonfire, going by the name of "soup"; children with bellies like barrels and legs like pins; children splashing around in the stench of an open sewer; children dying, the way the children of the poor die, with no fuss, no melodrama, simply dying in their mothers' arms.

There I met Señora Guillermina. Her youngest baby, "Blondie," the blue-eyed one, the one that looked so much like her aunt Filomena and had won her daddy's heart—Manuelita was her actual name—had died just a little while ago. She had also been her older brothers' pride: they had loved to take her around the neighbourhood inside a wooden box that the gentleman from La Tranquera grocery store had given them and to which they had added a set of wheels they had found in the dump. But the baby girl had decided to become an angel just before turning seven months and, most likely, she was now flying around, who knows where, dressed as a butterfly or disguised as a cicada while she sang songs to the sun.

Señora Guillermina, her old man, Don Arnulfo, and their five children had come to Santiago from Potrero Chico Grande, inland from Curicó. They had come to the capital city looking for a better life—they had been migrant countryside workers and had grown tired of the constant comings and goings and the instability. Besides, some friends had told them that in Santiago Don Arnulfo would definitely find a job in construction and Señora Guillermina could work as a laundry woman. Also, the kids could finally start going to school. But it was already three months since they had arrived and nothing had turned up. If it hadn't been for the neighbours who had helped them to set up the shack, the children who panhandled on the main street and came back with a few coins, plus the good-hearted ladies who shared their tea and bread with them, Señora Guillermina wouldn't have known what to do. Even her own milk had dried up, and now that she thought about it, perhaps her baby had died because the only thing she had been giving her in the last few weeks was warm tea—quite weak, but with a little bit of burned sugar to take away the bitter taste.

Señora Guillermina's grief streamed down her face when she talked about her baby, or when she whispered in my ear that her children went to bed hungry every night and her old man had walked all day but hadn't been able to get one bit of work. Her cheeks would be flooded with tears, but she didn't make any noise at all. It was as if at that moment her voice had left her body and joined the world of the dead.

For the longest time I didn't know what to do other than contribute to the situation with the noisy evidence of my own anxiety. Whatever I was learning in the Department of Social Work, if anything at all, I'd forget completely when I went to La Esperanza, and all I could think of was to show up with a dozen *hayuyas,* a piece of *chanco* cheese, a few slices of ham, a bag of pinto beans, some potatoes, a couple of onions. At the beginning I would spend the bit of money my mom sent me for the bus and other minor expenses; a few weeks later I began to dig into my food allowance until finally, I had to stop because by May 15 I had nearly exhausted my monthly stipend.

That evening I decided to go to the caféteria before taking the bus back home to my grandma and aunt Amparo's place. I was looking for Miguel, but above all, I was looking for an answer to my dilemma; I felt completely powerless in the face of what I witnessed during my visits to La Esperanza and I couldn't get Señora Guillermina and her family off my mind. Everything seemed completely absurd compared to that crude reality. What was the sense in enjoying one of Bach's fugues, understanding the psycho-social experiments of Wilhelm Reich, Karl Marx's analysis of the capitalist system or Simon de Beauvoir's feminist proposals if at the same time there were so many people starving to death?

Raúl and Miguel were having a coffee, and right away they knew that something was wrong. Miguel comforted me with hugs and kisses while Raúl guided me with his words.

"Sol, it doesn't make sense to go hungry yourself so that you can play tricks with the stomachs of Señora Guillermina's children once in a while," he said while taking my hand. "First, you have to take care of yourself, okay? Your own health is important. Second, you're not solving anything. That situation is the result of years and years of injustices."

"But what can I do, then?" I cried out in desperation.

"Why don't you become involved in the literacy campaign—that would be a good contribution, something that could lead to many other changes," he offered.

"Yeah... But I wouldn't know where to start, what to do," I responded hesitantly.

"Sol, you won't be doing it alone—the Federation is already holding workshops in many shanty towns around Santiago. I'll let the people in charge know that you are interested and they'll help you set the program up in La Esperanza," he concluded as he got up and put his coat on.

"Okay, sure," I replied, wondering how it would all work, questioning in my mind the importance of learning how to read and write when you didn't have enough food to eat, a place to live, a job... But I decided to give it a shot.

Pastor, an arts and literature student, was in charge of the literacy campaign in the South end of Santiago. The following week, he took me on the back of his motorcycle to La Esperanza. This time, I was empty-handed and, on our way there, I explained my discomfort to Pastor. In response, when we arrived at Señora Guillermina's shack, my new friend took paper and pencil crayons out of his bag and produced a series of pictures for the kids: toothless cows with a daisy behind their ears, traveling ants wearing wide-brimmed hats while they carried leather suitcases in their tiny hands, zigzagging polka-dotted caterpillars with lumpy shoes on their feet. The children couldn't stop laughing and then had great fun drawing their own creations with Pastor's materials.

Señora Guillermina and Don Arnulfo told us that neither had ever gone to school, but along the way she had learned to read a few things here and there and Don Arnulfo was good with numbers, though not at all with letters. When we explained about the literacy campaign promoted by the Student Federation in shanty towns around Santiago, they took an immediate interest. The kids were sent out to pass the word around, and a while later we were a group of more than twenty people sitting on pieces of cardboard and newspaper around a bonfire.

At the beginning, you could only hear the crackling of the fire and the children's giggles. Then Señora Guillermina began to tell the odyssey of the family's journey to Santiago, their hope for a better life, the tragedy of their baby Manuelita, the desperation of not having work, food, or a decent house to live in. Everybody nodded, their hands extended towards the fire, their mouths closed tight, their eyes downcast. But, little by little, other stories, other preoccupations began to emerge and rise over the filigree of smoke, first in whispers, then like a chorus of common understandings and coincidences. From that circle of voices, we got the first word that would serve as a starting point for our educational work: *casa*, "house."

On Saturday mornings, Pastor and I would arrive in La Esperanza at around ten o'clock. We met in Señora Guillermina's place during the winter months, but as soon as the weather improved, we held our learning circles outdoors. The kids would help us to pitch a few poles and we'd build an improvised awning with a couple of old sheets I brought from home. There we would settle and start to read and talk with whoever wanted to take part.

Pastor made a compilation of Latin American and Spanish poetry and one afternoon, at the Federation of Students' office, I spent a few hours cutting the stencils and mimeographing fifteen copies of the booklet we named "Word Masons." That's how, for the first time in their lives, the dwellers of La Esperanza had the opportunity to read or hear the words of Gabriela Mistral, Pablo Neruda, Alfonsina Storni, Federico García Lorca, Antonio Machado and Juana de Ibarburú.

A few weeks later, some of the participants began to bring their own poems. With downcast eyes they'd hand us a shaky sheet of paper and ask us to read it to the group. The words buzzed between the columns of dust while everybody widened their eyes and half-opened their mouths as if yearning to be nourished by those words, caravans of bandy-legged little spiders, carriers of so many emotions. Several years later, when the Allende government created the Quimantú Publishing House, some of those poems made it into an anthology of popular poetry with an introduction by Pablo Neruda.

Miguel and I didn't make love until I started school in Santiago. In Valdivia we had staged practices and drills in between shrubs and bushes by the river, leaning against a tree at the Saval Park, on the couch while my mom was at work, or hidden behind a piano at the conservatory. In Santiago we finally discovered the possibilities of pleasure afforded by the comfort of a bed and the privacy of a room.

Miguel's room on the third floor of the men's dormitories became our "study room" and a witness to our juicy trespasses. Lunch hour, twenty minutes between classes, any moment was propitious for a trip to the dorms. One of the two just had to ask,

"Do you want to go study for a little while?" in a tone of extreme indifference, but with eyes full of laughter and complicity, and we'd abandon professors, friends, books and bowls of soup.

It was absolutely forbidden for women to go into the men's rooms—and vice versa—under threat of expulsion from the university. So, at the beginning of the year, fear kept us in line: not one step past the common room on the ground floor of the building. But it only took a few days for our apprehension to evaporate and our excitement to grow, as we realized that we *could* make it to the third floor undiscovered; we just had to be cautious. Finally, right after lunch on a Wednesday afternoon, Miguel walked up and down the stairs a few times making sure that there wasn't anybody in sight, let out a conspiratorial whistle and I took the run of my life. In a matter of seconds, I was inside his room.

Our "study sessions" became a daily practice and there were days when we made the trip up the stairs more than once. We'd giggle our way under the sheets while the Andes, blushing with embarrassment, leaned in through the window and watched us.

The following summer, we told my mom that we wanted to live together. She wouldn't hear of it. Andresito tried to talk her into it, but she didn't budge, so Miguel and I ended up getting married in a simple ceremony attended by my mom, my brother, Tito and Silvia, Gloria and her parents. My mom cooked a beautiful luncheon and we celebrated with music and dancing for the rest of the day.

Back in Santiago, we went to live in a rooming house in the Parque Bustamante neighbourhood.

The ad in the paper specified clearly that this particular room had a private bathroom. After inspecting dozens of filthy shared bathrooms, we had decided that no matter what, we'd rent a room with a private bathroom. And—voilà!—here was exactly what we wanted! Furthermore, the rent wasn't one cent higher than what was charged for a room with a shared bathroom. Obviously, we were facing a miracle.

No such thing. What the ad didn't specify was that this was the "service room," a dark and poky little space, and that the "private bathroom"—a thimble with a shower head that hung from the middle of the ceiling and caused a flood every time you switched on the tap—was on the other side of the backyard. Hot water? Of course not! Servants didn't deserve hot water. The ad also didn't mention that the landlady, Señora Clarita, was a widow with an aristocratic past whose current situation had relegated her to the kitchen and living room, while she managed to survive by renting the rest of the rooms, including the maid's quarters.

We were so sick and tired of looking unsuccessfully for a room with a private bathroom that we decided to make Señora Clarita's arrangement work the best we could, and to confront our cramped circumstances and the cold with creativity and good humour. We got ourselves an electric hotplate and an enameled pot, and every morning we'd take turns sitting on the toilet, shivering with cold, while the other poured a waterfall of warm water on his or her shoulders and scrubbed him or her with a soapy sponge. These were called "sitting baths."

The bedroom was so small that we could only fit a single bed and a small dresser. There was no closet or wardrobe to hang our clothes in; instead, the upper part of one of the walls was crossed by a row of nails. It only took one night of chills and tooth chattering to bring the clothes off the nails and on top of the bed as an extra blanket. This became known as our "nordic quilt." "The library" was a collection of apple crates with books, tucked under the bed, and "the pantry," a shoe box with a tin of Nescafé, a bowl of sugar and a package of Hucke cookies. The sweetened condensed milk was kept in "the refrigerator"—an empty tin of Nido powder milk outside the door that opened onto the backyard. "The banquet" took place every Saturday at lunch time, right after the weekly parcel from my mom was delivered: a roasted chicken, homemade bread, *chanco* cheese, the homemade doughnuts we called *calzones rotos* and fruit.

The door to our room was off Señora Clarita's kitchen, so every time we went in or out we had to exchange niceties with her. "I'm so glaaaaaaaaaaaad!" she would exclaim in the morning as a conclusion to our daily "goodmorninghowareyouthismornin-gwellthankyouandyou?" She'd be wearing her usual pink velvet house coat, pink fuzzy slippers, rollers on her head and a thick layer of white cream on her face.

"I'm so glaaaaaaaaaaaad!" she'd exclaim again at the end of the day, her three-storey coiffure, false eyelashes and half a pound of compact powder and blush in perfect place, when we went through her kitchen again, but in the opposite direction, this time as a conclusion to our exchange of "didyouhaveagoodayyes-thankyouandyou?"

Was I happy in that room? Yes, except for one night, when I cried my eyes out while Miguel snored away and the alarm clock, its implacable tic-tac and green numbers floating in the darkness, drove me into a bout of existentialist anxiety. I was crying because Miguel had refused to kiss my toes.

We had just come back from seeing *My Beloved John*, a Swedish production that revolutionized Chile with its combination of sensuality and boldness. The movie showed scenes never witnessed on the big screen before, but there was one that fascinated me more than any other: without taking his gaze away from her eyes, John removed the sheet that covered his blonde, slim and naked lover, and proceeded to kiss her toes, one by one, slowly and diligently. For the rest of the movie, I couldn't stop dreaming of the moment we'd go back to our room where I'd lie down on the bed like a Swedish beauty and enjoy the boundless pleasure of having Miguel kiss my toes. But when we finally made our way through the kitchen, managed to get rid of Señora Clarita and entered our private quarters, Miguel said that he was too tired and we'd have to leave the toe kissing for another time.

In the summer of 1968, right after our wedding, Miguel and I went to the Villarrica region for our honeymoon. We borrowed Gloria's rickety *Citroneta*; Silvia lent us a huge green canvas tent that her grandfather had brought back from Germany after the First World War; my mom attended to filling bags and baskets with bedspreads and blankets, beef jerky and sausages, bread and fruit; and we left on a clear February morning, the tiny car overflowing with joy. We were on our way to the mysterious volcano that crowned the Calle-Calle river.

In our comings and goings we met Nicolasa Meliquén, a *Mapuche* spinner, weaver, embroiderer and silversmith. She lived by herself in a little wooden house by a river in the foothills of the Andes, a few kilometres from a reserve. There, she raised chickens, goats and sheep, tended a huge vegetable garden and worked at her art.

She invited us to pitch the tent by the river and for a whole week shared her food and stories with us. Evenings were particularly special, as the three of us would sit by a bonfire to drink *mate*, eat roasted hazelnuts, talk, and listen to Miguel's violin while the moon and the volcano played hide-and-go-seek with the clouds.

One of those nights, I asked Miguel to play my favourite piece: "Memory of a Beloved Place," by Tchaikovsky.

"Look!" I cried out excitedly. It was as if the stars had ears and, moved by the nostalgic beauty of the music, had decided to start rolling down the sky, like tears of light.

Miguel turned his gaze upwards. "Wow!" he exclaimed, amazed by the spectacle.

Nicolasa, however, didn't take her eyes off the fire. "You have to be careful—you don't make the sky cry in vain," she pronounced solemnly.

A few years later, as Pinochet and the army began their violent takeover, I would remember her prophetic words. But, back in 1968, we couldn't have imagined those future events.

In our conversations with Nicolasa, we learned about the German, British, French, Italian and Yugoslavian settlers that had taken possession of what was left of the *Mapuche* territory in the first decades of the twentieth century. We also heard of the 1934 massacre at Alto Bío-Bío and the 1961 killings on the coast of Arauco.

"The genocide didn't stop with the Spaniards or the campaign of extermination led by the Chilean government in the nineteenth century," Nicolasa said.

Prior to meeting Nicolasa I'd had a romantic view of the *Mapuche*. I knew that they had resisted the conquest fiercely, that the Spaniards had never been able to subdue them fully, but I didn't know that the Chilean state had conspired to steal their land and even used armed force to repress them. Our school history books didn't provide that information.

When I mentioned that to her, she smiled.

"The official history is written by the victors, the conquerors, the oppressors," she said. "We don't have the means or the power to write our side of events, so we carry our history in our hearts and in our tongues, we pass it down from generation to generation and the spirits of our dead make sure that we don't forget."

At that point in my life I wasn't too interested in the world of the spirits, I just wanted to know more about *this* world. Why was there so much inequality and injustice? Why were the facts of history hidden from us? Above all, I wanted to know what could be done to change things, to ensure that the poor were not poor anymore, that they didn't starve to death, that they had access to education, health care, all the rights that people like me took for granted. I knew that the literacy campaign was contributing to improve the situation at La Esperanza, but it felt like a drop in a bucket. Wasn't there a more widespread, quicker way?

When I was younger, my dad and my brother had explained the principles of the Radical Party to me, the formation of the Popular Front back in the forties and fifties, the social reforms that had benefitted the country as the result of those governments. But later on, Miguel and Gloria had been quick to point out that Gabriel González Videla—a Radical president—had outlawed the Communist Party, even though the communists had helped to elect him; thousands of communists had been killed and many others had gone into exile, including Pablo Neruda. Salvador Allende had been a candidate for the country's presidency several times since then, representing a number of coalitions of leftist parties, however, he had never been successful. Would he win the 1970 elections? Would his government propel the necessary changes to turn Chile into a truly just society?

1969 and 1970 were intense years at La Esperanza as we continued our literacy work and also prepared for the upcoming presidential elections. By then a great majority of the residents had learned quite a bit about letters and words, blackboards and notebooks, but even more about their rights.

Several times, the Christian Democratic government of Eduardo Frei sent the police to evict the inhabitants of La Esperanza from the empty lot where they had become squatters; every time, they would return and erect their pieces of tin and cardboard once again. Several times, they made it to downtown Santiago to demand solutions to their situation; every time, they were welcomed by police batons and water cannons. Driven by stubbornness and hope, they continued to struggle. I was right in the thick of most of those battles and, as time went on, I became more and more convinced that change could only be brought about by the direct actions of the oppressed. I was sure that mainstream politics and politicians with their rhetoric and empty promises would never benefit people like Señora Guillermina.

Miguel, Raúl, Pastor and Gloria disagreed. They believed that traditional politics could work; that if Salvador Allende was elected president, radical changes would take place because the program of his Popular Unity Coalition included key reforms—the nationalization of the copper mines, the banks and other important industries, plus a far-reaching agrarian reform.

In spite of my reservations, on Sunday, September 4, 1970, I voted for Salvador Allende. I wanted to believe that his "Peaceful Road to Socialism" would work. Besides, the enthusiasm for his candidacy was contagious and, both at the university and at La Esperanza, my friends were united in their resolution to make him our next president.

That evening, hundreds of thousands poured into the streets of every village and city in a gigantic celebration of Allende's victory. They chanted: "*Se siente, se siente, Allende presidente*," "You can feel it, you can feel it, Allende is the president."

Workers, shanty town dwellers, students and large numbers of professionals and intellectuals filled the night air with their shouts of joy, while the upper classes and many Chileans of the middle sectors double-locked their doors, overtaken by fear and disgust.

Allende spoke to the crowd from the Santiago headquarters of the Chilean Federation of Students, right on Alameda Boulevard. He vowed to take the country out of underdevelopment: "This is the first government in Chile's history that is truly democratic, national, popular and revolutionary," he concluded.

Then he asked his supporters to go home quietly. Our opponents needed to realize that he hadn't been elected by an unruly mob; that communists and socialists didn't eat babies, rape women, loot and rob, as the campaign of the right had asserted.

Miguel and I were there that evening, at the Federation of Students' headquarters. Our dear friend Raúl—the Federation's President—had the honour of introducing Allende, and after our new new president finished his speech, Raúl took us by the hand and invited us to go onto the balcony and join Allende while he waved at the crowd.

The next day, we got a call from my brother: the television cameras had broadcasted our image to the entire country and in Valdivia he had seen us on a gigantic screen while celebrating at the Plaza de Armas with Tito, Silvia and thousands of others. Our mom, on the other hand, had taken refuge at home and bolted her door, fearing that "the Marxist hordes" would take over the city and turn the country into a violent and totalitarian state.

Soledad

The late sixties and early seventies were bitter-sweet for me: I had a lover, but I didn't have love and I still missed Andrés immensely; I had finally fulfilled the dearest dream of my youth: to become a teacher; I had failed miserably as a mother: my son was a pervert and even though he had told me he wasn't friends with Carloncho anymore and assured me that he would start dating girls, he never had; my daughter married Miguel in an uneventful ceremony and shattered my illusions of a big, beautiful wedding—the best I could do was to sew a red pantsuit for her, since she wouldn't hear of a white dress, and prepare a nice luncheon, including a lovely wedding cake; and, on top of everything, it turned out that both my children were communists. It was as if destiny had decided to test me every step of the way.

I took solace in painting watercolours and making pottery and spent all my spare time in solitude, pretending that I was at peace with myself.

When the 1970 presidential elections came around, Helmut Meyer and my sister Amparo convinced me to vote for Jorge

Alessandri, the right-wing candidate. Though the standard of living had improved considerably during the Eduardo Frei government—inflation was under control, staples were fairly inexpensive and now everybody could afford to have a television set and a phone—Helmut and Amparo made me see that electing Alessandri was the only way to stop Salvador Allende and his communist cohorts, and that voting for the Christian Democrats would only help Allende.

Sol, Andresito, Tito and Silvia, my friend Isabel, Mrs. Zoraida—the Technical School's principal—and Miss Blanca, on the other hand, tried to talk me into voting for Allende, but I wouldn't hear of it; I didn't want Chile to become another Russia or Cuba. So, when Allende won the election, I was devastated.

That evening, alone in my house, I watched the results on national television and witnessed the gigantic rally that celebrated the Popular Unity's victory in Santiago. The final blow came when I saw Sol and Miguel on the balcony of the Federation of Students' building, standing right next to Allende. First, I thought that my eyes were betraying me; I couldn't understand what they would be doing there. But then, as I got closer to the screen, there was no doubt in my mind. It was them. I turned the television off in disgust.

Then, the phone rang. It was my sister Amparo: she had just seen her niece on national television and wanted to know what I thought about it and, furthermore, what I was going to do about it. But all I could do was cry. Cry because I didn't know what to think, what to say, or what to do.

"Don't you realize that your daughter is staining the whole family's reputation?" my sister shouted in my ear. "Soledad, you have to do something about it. You are her mother. You have to stop her from shaming us in this way."

In the end, I promised her that I would talk to Sol, but I never did; she wouldn't listen to me anyway. She had been living in Santiago for years, was a married woman and was also about to graduate as a social worker. She had become a know-it-all and didn't give a hoot about what I thought.

That night, when I went to bed, I made sure that the door was double-locked and then decided to jam a chair against it; what if the celebrating mob got out of hand and went on a looting rampage? If Andresito came home that night, which I doubted, he would have to ring the bell.

As I lay in bed, I could hear the Valdivia crowd cheering and singing happily in the distance, but all I felt was bitterness and fear. In the last few years I had gotten used to the bitterness, but this kind of fear was new to me—fear of something big and nebulous at the same time, of outside forces that would steer my life into the unknown.

The first year of the Allende government was fairly uneventful, but then chaos set in: there was such a shortage of food that you had to line up for hours to buy a chicken or a pound of meat; half the buses were off the road due to the lack of spare parts, so it was virtually impossible to use public transit; the truck owners went on strike and blockaded the roads which resulted in the whole country coming to a halt; doctors went on strike.

I started joining the anti-government demonstrations because the situation had become truly unbearable. Marilyn, the girl who did the ironing, was the only one who agreed to join me, as the rest of my friends were all Allende supporters. We would bang our pots and pans and shout until we had no voice left.

One day, Isabel came to talk to me. I hadn't seen her for months. She explained that she understood my frustration with the state of affairs in the country, "But maybe you don't know that an embargo has been declared by the United States, Soledad— that's why there are no spare parts, no fuel. Also, the distribution companies and the wealthy are hoarding staples, and the truck owners are being paid by the CIA to stage their strike."

I wouldn't have any of it. I told her that, in my view, the chaos was the result of the incompetence of the Allende government.

"In part you're right," she agreed, "there is incompetence and inexperience, but the main forces behind the confusion are the wealthy and the U.S. government."

I didn't believe her, just as I didn't want to believe my children and the rest of my friends. In the end, I stopped seeing all of them and didn't talk to them until after the military coup. As far as Andresito was concerned, we became virtual strangers living under the same roof.

Sol

In November of 1971, shanty town La Esperanza became *Campamento* Che Guevara: a community made up of one hundred and six small brick houses, a central square, a school, a clinic, a soccer field and paved streets lined with young plane trees. Six months earlier, after much paperwork and many comings and goings, the Allende government had finally given the squatters the title to the land and the materials to build new houses.

Helping my friends with the construction filled me with pleasure, even though each day I ended up with a sore back, and scratches and bruises all over my body. I had never imagined that a brick could have so many dimensions: its weight, its texture, its colour—but, above all, the profound significance of putting one brick on top of another, the magic of erecting a wall, the miracle of building a house. "Brick," a word that generated joy and dignity and that was followed by many others: work, food, nutrition, water, bathroom, sewage, electricity, gas, school, clinic, library, garden, music, theatre, photography, cinema.

The day of the inauguration, we celebrated with pots of pork beans steaming over a collective fire and a show that included the theatre group interpreting a play based on the dewellers' experiences, followed by the folk ensemble with their ponchos and guitars singing music by Víctor Jara, Violeta Parra, Inti Illimani and Quilapayún.

At *Campamento* Che Guevara, I learned to use a weapon. In the event of an imminent military coup, the communal assembly decided we would defend the *campamento* with our lives.

In February of 1973, seven months before the coup, I went back to Valdivia for a few days after spending several weeks with Nicolasa and her people on their reserve in the Villarrica region.

By then it was virtually impossible to hold a rational conversation with my mother; she was nothing more than a poor public employee, owner of a few appliances acquired on monthly installments, but acted and talked as if she were Rockefeller's wife. She would go red in the face while parroting what *El Mercurio* printed with CIA money, repeating the complaints of the landowners, industrialists and truck owners, and defending the rights of the money merchants. She accused Andresito and me of having abandoned our principles and values, all the while regurgitating what her sister Amparo and Helmut Meyer had put in her head: Allende was a pervert and the Marxist hordes had driven the country into chaos.

We weren't able to set our differences aside. The day before

I left, she begged me to listen to reason, to abandon my "communist" activities.

"Daughter, you can't trust those down-and-outs in the shanty towns; they'll mug you, they'll stab you in the back," she said.

"There's nothing to worry about, mom; I have known these people for years and they're completely trustworthy. They're my friends. They love me, respect me, and I love them and respect them," I replied.

She didn't understand. She got angry. She accused me of being a terrible daughter. She even burst into tears and, turning her eyes to the sky, asked God why he had punished her so severely, why he had allowed the communists to brainwash me.

I got angry. I yelled at her, "Stop your stupid nonsense, mother! For your information, I'm a thinking human being—in case you hadn't noticed. Your brains have been washed—not mine. Actually, I don't think you even have any brains left underneath that ridiculous hairdo of yours. I'm sick and tired of your crap!"

"Yes, of course, please forgive me, m'lady... I forgot that you're the biggest expert in everything there's to know on planet earth and its surroundings," she responded, putting on a fake, subservient tone and bowing. Then, she yelled back as she fingered her hair and tilted her head, a frown on her forehead, "And what's wrong with my hairdo, anyway!"

My mom's shoulder-length hair was permed now and she wore it parted in the middle. I didn't respond. *If she wants to go around looking like a brunette British judge, that's her business,* I thought as I left the room.

I was angry at her, but above all I was sad: I couldn't believe that my mom, an intelligent, resourceful woman, had fallen for the right-wing propaganda. How could I make her open her eyes and use her head, realize that she was just being used by the powers that be? Finally, my brother talked me into letting it go; every family in the country seemed to be divided, as things had become more and more polarized.

"Give it time. She'll come around. You'll see," he concluded.

The following afternoon, Andresito and I crossed the Pedro de Valdivia Bridge and went to visit Silvia and Tito in the big white house across the river. They had been married for several years now and had two beautiful children. Silvia's mom and uncle looked as if they hadn't aged, but her grandmother, now over seventy, resembled a porcelain miniature fissured by time. She moved more slowly than the last time I had seen her, but her bright blue eyes were still as alive as when she was younger. She offered to look after the kids for a while and the four of us went to the Raussmann to enjoy some *crudos*—tartar steaks—and catch up on the latest news.

As usual, the café oozed aromas and voices, joy and friendship. We sat in our favourite spot, right in the thick of things, and Don Willie had just put a plate of *crudos* and mugs of beer on the table when the place was overtaken by an eerie silence. In front of the counter, a group of young men had materialized, all dressed in black, truncheons in their hands and white swastikas printed on the fronts of their shirts. The leader, a tall, blonde and blue-eyed man, knocked on the counter several times before jumping towards the door to intercept a couple attempting to leave the café unnoticed. The other members of the group proceeded to take on combat positions and demonstrate their skill with the truncheons, scattering nearby customers who had to hop out of the way so as not to get an unexpected blow.

At the end of the demonstration, the leader read a declaration against the Allende government and international communism, and in praise of the fatherland and freedom. He assured us that the organization they belonged to was large and well-armed, and that all its members were ready and willing to die in defense of the established order. He let out a war-cry and the group left with a spraying of pistol and machine gun fire against the ceiling. The whole operation hadn't lasted for more than three minutes.

When I was able to catch my breath, I realized that I was under the table, holding on to my brother's hands; the four mugs of beer and the plate of *crudos*, now shattered to pieces, lay in a puddle on the tile floor. I couldn't stop shivering and Silvia was crying in astonishment—the leader, son of landowners south of Valdivia, had been her boyfriend when she was attending German School.

Five of the six members of the group were obviously of German descent, but the sixth one was Juan Paillal, a morose and sullen *Mapuche* boy who, a few weeks before, had participated in the literacy classes in Villarrica. Juan had come to believe what the landowners had told him all along: that the *Mapuche* were an inferior race. His self-hatred ran so deep that he had joined a Nazi organization.

By June of 1973, the defense strategy for *Campamento* Che Guevara was in place. I had my position in the rearguard, in charge of logistical support, together with the rest of the women and children. At the general assembly where the plan was finalized, I complained up and down because it seemed to me that it was *machista* to decide that the women could not be in the vanguard, together with the men. But Señora Guillermina popped my feminist bubble when she whispered in my ear, "Don't be silly, *mijita*, just go along with it. You don't have to pretend to be so brave."

The evening of September 10, Miguel came home exhausted. For months he had been working sixteen hours a day, seven days a week. I was exhausted as well: in addition to my paid work, I was dedicating long hours to *Campamento* Che Guevara. It felt like we hardly saw each other anymore and when we did, we argued about politics.

Our positions had begun to differ a while back. For him, the government's attempts to reach a compromise with the opposition and the military were worth supporting. For me, that was downright stupid and ignorant, and I told him so—it basically meant giving in to their demands and betraying our principles and the Señoras Guillerminas of Chile. I wanted to see Allende's peaceful road to socialism turn into a real revolution and I knew that my friends at the *campamento* were more than ready to go the extra yard to get there. Miguel couldn't come around to seeing it that way, he couldn't get his head wrapped around the fact that the rich and their subservient army were not "peace lovers" and would do anything to hold on to their privileges. So, given that every time the topic came up we ended up having an argument, we had agreed not to talk about it again.

But that evening I was in a bad mood; I couldn't keep on ignoring the bitter thorn of truth that kept jabbing at me: we weren't prepared for a coup d'état. At the *campamento*, a few old guns wouldn't be enough to resist the onslaught of a whole army, and besides, Miguel and those who thought like him were in as much or even more denial than us, claiming that the military wouldn't attack an unarmed people. However, we did agree that each day was taking us closer and closer to an unclear ending.

That's why I busied myself with housework instead of striking up a conversation with Miguel. And that's why, when he told me that the next morning the Symphony would be offering yet another concert for "national harmony and peace," this time at the University of Chile, I yelled, exasperated, "How much longer are you going to continue with your idiocy? Don't you realize that the political right and the military don't give a damn about the Symphony and its concerts for 'national harmony and peace'? Has your brain gone soft? Why is it that you don't realize that, at this point in time, your stupid violin is good for nothing?"

Chile

September 11, 1973 – June 17, 1974

Sol

The morning of September 11, 1973, we woke up to the roar of helicopters hovering over downtown Santiago. We turned on the radio just as Allende was beginning to address the country. It wasn't easy to hear him—there was a lot of static and interference, plus the whole building was shaking and tinkling to the rhythm of tanks crawling down the street. By then Miguel had become the National Symphony's first violinist, I had a job at the Women's Centre in the Central Station neighbourhood and we were living in a nice apartment at the San Nicolás Towers on Providencia Avenue.

"—My words do not carry bitterness, but deception. Let them serve as punishment for those who have betrayed their own patriotic oaths—" Allende was saying.

Then he mentioned the names of a couple of generals. Obviously, this was the military coup d'état we had anticipated but hoped would never take place. What was going to happen now? Was Allende resigning?

"—At this historical crossroads, I can only say the following to the workers: I will not resign! I will offer my life in exchange for the loyalty that the people have afforded me—" he was stating now in a firm, unwavering voice.

Miguel and I looked at each other in disbelief. We knew that Allende was a principled, brave man, but never imagined that he would sacrifice his life for his beliefs. We held on to each other's hands as we continued to listen.

"—I am certain that the seeds we have sown in the conscience of thousands and thousands of Chileans will not be destroyed. The military do have the force to overpower us, but neither sheer force nor crime will ever put a stop to social processes. History belongs to us and is made by the people—"

The deafening sound of low-flying bomber jets buried Allende's words. I got up and looked out the window: the long, cloud-like wake of two planes crisscrossed the bright, blue sky. The line of tanks continued to crawl towards downtown. I looked at Miguel. He was still sitting on the bed, his hands clutching his head.

"I have to go to *Campamento* Che Guevara, we have to get ready to resist," I said.

He looked up, a frown in his forehead. "Are you sure? What if—" he started.

"Miguel, I have to go. And you should be going to the university. Aren't you supposed to be there this morning?" I butted in.

He nodded.

"We can't just stay home and do nothing," I went on.

"You're right," he agreed somberly.

We got dressed in a flash. Miguel picked up his violin, I grabbed my bag and we hurried down the stairs. At the door to the street we gave each other a quick hug and a peck on the cheek. Why didn't I turn to look at him? Why didn't I tell him that in spite of our political disagreements, I was still in love with him? Why did I urge him to go to the university?

The streets were half empty of civilians. Hundreds of soldiers were getting off military trucks and buses and congregating everywhere. It was a weird scene, completely different from anything I had ever experienced. I felt a pang of fear, but ignored it and kept on walking. The grocer across the street was rolling down the metal curtain on his shop. I got our daily veggies and fruit from him.

"Where are you going, Señora Sol?" he asked, but didn't wait for an answer. "You shouldn't be outdoors. Go home," he urged.

I just smiled and kept going. All the shops were closing now. There were scatterings of people here and there. Everybody was in a hurry to get somewhere. No one was talking. No one was laughing. No one was honking their horns or screeching their tires. There were no street vendors, no music in the air. The noisy, bustling Santiago that I knew had been replaced by a hushed, muted place.

At the corner of San Diego Street and Diez de Julio Avenue,

there was a group of people that needed to get to the south end of the city. A young woman with a small wicker suitcase in her hand whispered to me that she worked as a live-in maid for a family on Bulnes Avenue, right across from the presidential palace, and that her boss had sent her back home because most likely something huge was going to happen. Together we climbed on the back of a truck that offered to take us.

When we got to stop number 36 of the Gran Avenida, the *Campamento* Che Guevara had already been cordoned off. I made up a stupid story about my little daughter being sick, in an effort to persuade some of the young soldiers to let me cross the barriers, but to no avail. They didn't let me through.

Sitting on the curb, I cried in frustration until a pick-up truck agreed to give me a ride. I ran along empty streets towards my home. On the way, I realized that if I actually was the disciplined activist I purported to be, I should be thinking of how to get to my emergency meeting point with Raúl instead of my house. Then I remembered that I had hidden my notebook—the one where I jotted down shopping lists, the words to songs I liked, bits of information related to my job and the *Campamento* Che Guevara work, plus reminders of meetings and deadlines—inside the double bottom of our desk. First I would burn it, then go to meet Raúl.

It was too late. From a block away, I saw that the Torres San Nicolás were surrounded by military vehicles and soldiers were taking people out of the buildings and throwing them inside their trucks as if they were sacks of potatoes. They pushed and kicked them towards the vehicles, their eyes blindfolded, their hands tied behind their backs.

I walked towards Costanera Avenue not knowing what to do, completely devoid of ideas and feeling empty, like a dress hanging on the line. While I looked at the chocolate water of the Mapocho river skipping along the rocks, aunt Amparo came to my mind, now living in her new house on Pedro de Valdivia Norte, just a few blocks from where I was.

It had been months since I'd seen my aunt Amparo, or "aunt Amparito" as I used to call her when I was a kid. Back then, I was my aunt's special girl, and the truth is that for years she was my hero as well. Beautiful, charming, elegant, independent—she was the utmost example of an emancipated and intelligent woman. As a teenager, I aspired to be like her: liberated from domestic chores, dedicated to her work, successful in a world dominated by men, and with enough money and the necessary freedom to do whatever she pleased. However, our mutual admiration came tumbling down after I started university and became involved in political activism.

The last time I had seen my aunt was a few days before Christmas when I had gone by one of her stores to say hello and wish her a happy holiday season. She had welcomed me with her usual combination of mistrust and arrogance. As always, she was impeccably dressed and made up, and the first thing she did was to poke fun at my clean face, my jeans, my clogs, my woven bag and embroidered shirt. I didn't fall into her trap. I praised her good taste and commended her for her beautiful merchandise. But she continued to provoke me. She asked me if I had been invited to one of President Allende's orgies—after all, I was a "close" friend of his, wasn't I? She told me that given the total ineptitude of the Armed Forces, which allowed the country to continue sinking into the totalitarianism and chaos of international communism, she had had no other option but to acquire her own arsenal in case the Marxist hordes tried to take away what she had earned with so much work and sacrifice. I didn't say a thing. I felt angry, then I wanted to laugh at her absurd remarks. Then I felt sad: for her, for me, for my family, for the country.

Nine months later, I was ringing her doorbell while Santiago shook under the whizz and thunder of the Hawker Hunters on their way downtown.

One of the maids opened the door, accompanied by a huge bulldog with impressive teeth. My aunt followed, holding a small lapdog covered with ribbons and bows, as the city burst with the explosion of bombs.

Instinctively, I threw myself on the ground, but without losing her composure, Aunt Amparo yelled, "*Ay*, you stupid little girl, get up and come in. Can't you see that nothing will happen here? Only your president will turn into a bloody rag, just as he deserves."

I would've left, but at that point I knew that there was no possible meeting with Raúl or anybody else; all I could do was try to make contact with Miguel. So, in desperation, I went in.

Aunt Amparo made me sit down in the living room in a springy maroon velvet armchair. She left the room followed by the small mutt and when she came back, a cigarette in one hand and a whiskey on the rocks in the other, she turned the television on at full blast. By now the mutt had jumped onto my lap and wouldn't stop licking my hand. My aunt made herself comfortable on the couch and proceeded to watch the screen with a grin on her face while I had to swallow my disgust at every communiqué, invective and harangue by the four generals of the military junta that had taken over the country: "—Due to, number one, the extreme moral and social crisis that the country is going through; number two, the inability of the Allende government to control this chaotic situation; number three, the proliferation of paramilitary groups supported and trained by the Popular Unity political parties, a situation that will inevitably lead to a civil war—"

There were four men in uniform sitting behind a desk, but one was clearly in charge: Augusto Pinochet, the general that Allende had appointed Commander in Chief of the Chilean Armed Forces just a few weeks before. He stood out not only because he was reading the communiqué, but also because he exuded more arrogance and contempt than the other three put together. A few minutes later, each one of them took the mic and pledged their unconditional support to Pinochet and to "the new order in our fatherland."

When the generals stopped talking, my aunt started. "My heart bleeds just thinking that my only niece turned out to be a communist. I can't believe that you had all the opportunities I never had in my life: music classes, sports, university, everything.

And what did you do with your life? Nothing. Absolutely nothing. You married a poor fool whose only skill is to know how to play the violin and, on top of everything else, you dress like a hippie, dedicate yourself to 'helping' the thugs in the shanty towns of Santiago, and for sure you also take drugs. Who knows what my sister Soledad did to deserve abnormal children, heaven forbid." She leaned forward and touched on wood three times on the coffee table imported from France. "If you had turned out normal—like so many girls that are part of my clientele—you could've learned to manage my businesses and shared my wealth, including this beautiful house, everybody's envy, my utmost pride. But, instead, you became an insolent, stupid, disheveled girl, and a communist to boot."

Sitting in my aunt Amparo's velvet armchair, all I could do was think of Miguel; I tried to imagine where he could be and where we would meet now that it was impossible to go back to our apartment. I wanted to warn him that our building was cordoned off. What if he tried to go back and was arrested? I thought about going to the University of Chile, but by then the military had already imposed an indefinite curfew.

When my aunt paused to light another cigarette, I asked if I could use her phone and consult the phone book. For a few seconds she looked at me with suspicion while exhaling rings of smoke.

Then she said, "Look, Sol, from this house you're not going to call any of your guerrilla friends, do you hear me?"

I explained that I just wanted to find Miguel at the University of Chile, where the Symphony was scheduled to offer a concert that morning.

My aunt got the giggles. "A concert by the Symphony? The only concert this morning was the one you heard at my gate; the one that put an end to this Marxist regime that kept us in chains for years," she proclaimed, while pointing at the telephone on a small table in the hallway and getting one of the maids to bring the phonebook to me.

For more than fifteen minutes, I called all the numbers listed for the university, but all I got was a busy signal. I dialed our own home number and then my mom's and brother's in Valdivia; the lines were either busy or kept on ringing. I had no alternative but to wait until the curfew was called off. Then I would go looking for Miguel.

The afternoon crawled on: heavy, viscous, suffocating. What were my friends at the *Campamento* Che Guevara doing at that time? Had they piled the old tires we had been collecting for months and built a burning barricade at the entrance? Had they taken their combat positions? Were they wondering why I wasn't there? Did they think that I had betrayed them and backed out of my commitment to defend the *campamento* alongside them?

At one point my aunt asked me if I wanted something to eat. I declined, but nevertheless she urged me to get up and follow her—she wanted to show me her pantry, a huge room off the kitchen.

"As you can see, my dear niece, I never had to line up and deprive myself of my favourite dishes," she said proudly as she opened freezers overflowing with meats and seafood and unlocked cupboards filled with groceries. "My friends made sure to keep me well-supplied during the periods of shortages. And, if you had turned out to be just a bit smarter and more respectful of your aunt, you could have also enjoyed this beautiful food," she added.

Back in the living room, she opened her heart to me as she sipped on yet another whiskey on the rocks. She even cried as she told me about Yoshi, the love of her life.

"I would've wanted to have children, but in the end I never got married... I decided to dedicate my life to my businesses, to give it all to my work, and it did pay off, as you can see," she added as her left hand made an arc encompassing the furniture, the Asian carpets, the artwork on the walls. "Sol, I loved you as if you were my own daughter," she confessed, choking back the tears. "Why did you do this to me? Why?"

I told her that I hadn't done anything to her, that I was just living my life on the basis of my own beliefs, my own principles.

She got angry. "Arrogant little girl! Do you think that because you went to university you're the only one to have principles? For your information, I have my principles, too, and I didn't learn them from a book, but from years and years of hard work, sacrifice and loneliness... And do you want to know what my principles are called?"

By now my aunt was slurring her words and I had started to feel sorry for her, but then I heard her say, "Fatherland and liberty."

Of course! Of course she would have joined the fascist group. Still, I shuddered at the thought that my own aunt could be in sympathy with them. In the last few months they had gone from staging flash actions like the one I had witnessed at the café in Valdivia to blowing up bridges and assassinating union and political leaders.

Our conversation was interrupted by the screeching tires of a vehicle turning the corner at full speed and braking in front of the house. My aunt got up with a certain difficulty, but managed to zigzag her way to open the door. She let in three military men, accompanied by two hooded individuals dressed in black, with swastikas printed on the front of their shirts. Without uttering a word, they pulled me off the armchair, blindfolded me, tied my hands behind my back and pushed me out of the house. When I woke up, I was lying on the cement floor of a dark place, together with dozens of other bodies, soaked in my own urine.

Soledad

The morning of September 11 was sunny and bright. As usual, I got up early, took a shower, put the kettle on and turned on the radio to listen to the seven o'clock news while I prepared breakfast.

Instead of the usual newsreel, however, the announcer repeated the same communiqué over and over again: "Sectors of the Armed Forces have revolted and are advancing towards La Moneda, the presidential palace. Sectors of the Armed Forces have revolted and are advancing towards La Moneda—"

I felt a huge sense of relief; finally the country would go back to normal. Andresito had spent the night at home, so I woke him up and gave him the news with a big grin on my face.

He got dressed in a hurry and left without even having a cup of coffee. On his way out, he yelled, "Stop celebrating because the coup will not be successful."

Then I heard Salvador Allende's voice stating that he wasn't going to resign, that they would have to take him dead out of

La Moneda. That was his last speech, the one about the great avenues, which became famous worldwide. A little while later, they started to broadcast one military communiqué after another. I felt a pang of fear for my children, but then I thought that in no time the military would call on the Christian Democrats and the political right to govern the country, so I decided to hoist the Chilean flag on the pole in our garden.

That morning I tried calling Sol in Santiago, but all the lines seemed to be jammed or disconnected and I couldn't get through. Finally, three days later, I was able to get a hold of my sister, but she assured me that she didn't know anything about my daughter's whereabouts.

When I begged her to go to Sol and Miguel's apartment, she replied, "Are you crazy? Why would I want to risk my life for Sol? She cooked her own goose, so let her eat it."

Finally, my friend Rina agreed to go and check on my daughter and son-in-law, but the next day she called back to say that unfortunately she hadn't been able to get near Torres San Nicolás because the military had surrounded the area and wouldn't let anybody in.

Isabel and Carlos were also desperate because they hadn't been able to locate Gloria in Santiago, either. I hadn't seen them in months, but they didn't hesitate to give me a hug when I showed up at their door and explained my dilemma. We decided that in the next couple of days they would continue to phone Gloria's place, Isabel's sister in Santiago and José Joaquín Aguirre Hospital, where Gloria was doing her internship as a medical student. I committed to keep trying Sol and Miguel's number, the Municipal Theatre—headquarters for the National Symphony—and the Women's Centre where Sol worked.

We were unsuccessful. All the numbers either rang endlessly or had a busy signal, except for the hospital's switchboard where the receptionist insisted that Gloria hadn't been to work since the day of the "military pronouncement."

Then, in the early morning of September 18, tragedy struck.

I was lying in bed unable to sleep, thinking about Sol and Miguel, wondering about where they would be, when I heard a vehicle turning the corner of Carampangue Street. I ran into Andresito's bedroom. He was already sitting up on his bed, getting dressed. He hugged me and prompted me to go put my robe and slippers on.

In the street, a shouting voice broke the silence, followed by four car doors slamming shut. "Private Peláez, Private Mansilla, cover the back—over there! Private Vega, Private Soto, both sides of the house! Private Gaete, the front door!"

I went into the hallway and found Andresito standing there, in the dark. I kissed his hands, his cheeks...

He put his arm on my shoulders and whispered in my ear, "Stay calm. We have no reason to be afraid. I already burned all the Popular Unity documents I had at home. They won't find anything that will compromise us."

172

There was more shouting and the sound of running footsteps, and then the front door burst open.

"Peláez, to the living room! Mansilla, the dining room! Soto, the kitchen! Vega and Gaete, the bedrooms and bathroom!"

One by one, the lights were switched on. Finally, the upstairs hallway ceiling lamp lit up.

There were neither invitations nor orders to go downstairs. Instead, two soldiers pushed and shoved us to the bottom of the staircase. Then, the sergeant in charge forced Andresito against the wall and jabbed his crotch with his machine gun. My son screamed in pain, and the next thing I knew, I was kicking the sergeant on the calves and punching him on the back. He bashed my face with the butt of his gun as he turned, twisted my left arm behind my back and forced me to sit on one of the dining room chairs. From that privileged position, I witnessed what unfolded next.

In the living room, Private Peláez slashed the sofa and the armchairs with his bayonet. When he was finished, he stuck his hand into each tear and took out wool and straw. Then, he turned his attention to the teak cupboard with our RCA television set on top and the Blaukpunt radio and Dual record player inside. He concluded that none of the artifacts had bombs inside and that the cupboard didn't seem to have a double bottom. The piano was next. He swept the figurines and doilies off the top with his right arm and then tried to force it open, but to no avail. Frustrated, he charged against it with the butt of his gun.

In the dining room, Private Mansilla proceeded to gut the chair seats. He even asked me to get up so that he could take care of the chair I was sitting on. Then, he made me sit again, this time on top of a pile of rags, straw and wool. He turned to the sideboard and the curio. The Sunday dishes and glasses fell with a deafening shatter as he made sure that neither piece of furniture had double walls or bottoms.

In the kitchen, I could hear Private Soto taking my Mademsa stove and fridge apart, and disemboweling the cupboards where I kept the groceries, plates, pots and pans. In the meantime, from upstairs came the sound of Privates Vega and Gaete engaging in vigorous combat with our wool mattresses, the ones that Marilyn had helped me wash and remake the summer before. A crash announced the slamming of the water tank lid against the tile floor in the bathroom, followed by another scandal of breakage, most likely my beautiful little Hoovermatic washing machine.

"There are no arms, Sergeant Molina," the privates announced, one after the other.

"Privates Peláez and Mansilla, get spades from the vehicle and tackle the garden. Privates Soto and Vega, get crowbars and take care of the floor. Gaete, help as needed."

As I witnessed the floorboards being pulled up one by one, I thought of my beautiful rose bushes and my rhododendrons, of the fact that Spring was around the corner and soon my garden would be in bloom...

"There's nothing, my Sergeant—we haven't found anything," the soldiers announced after a while.

"The books—take all the books out, make a pile on the sidewalk and set them on fire," commanded Sergeant Molina at the top of his lungs, stressing his order with several knocks with the barrel of his gun on Andresito's back. "These communists learn all their tricks from books," he added with the satisfaction of somebody who believes he has just stated an irrefutable truth.

Until then, I had been frozen in terror and disbelief, but when I heard the command about burning the books, I heard myself shout, "No! Not the books!"

Sergeant Molina's blow to the back of my head slammed my face against the table top. Pieces of my shattered glasses dug into my eyelids and cheeks and I felt myself fall into a blue world.

My daughter Sol and my son Andresito were babies. Even though in real life they were six years apart, in this blue world they were both babies, about nine months old. They were sitting, naked, inside the wicker crib that we had bought at Gath & Chávez when Andresito was about to be born. The crib had an organdy white ruffle all around and a tulle net over top, which made it look like a sailboat. The crib was floating in this blue world while my babies gurgled, laughed, sucked their toes and examined their belly buttons. I contemplated my children with the conviction that they were the most beautiful beings in the whole universe. I closed my eyes for a few moments so as to get my fill of this sublime love, to delight in the lightness of my own body which was now floating over the sailboat-crib. I wanted to engrave in my memory the wide-open smile of my Sol, the honey eyes of my Andresito, the rolls on my babies' legs, the dimples on their miniature elbows. I opened my eyes so as to continue enjoying the delicious image of my children, but the crib was empty.

My own scream brought me back to reality. At first all I could see was shadows sprinkled with tiny colour lights, while the throbbing on my cheekbone hardly allowed me to hear. My sense of smell hadn't betrayed me, though. From the bathroom, the aroma of *Lavanda Atkinson* reached me in waves, and from the half-open door to the kitchen came the sweetish smell of meat and sour milk, gas and coffee. I forced myself to sit up again and saw that my son was still standing against the wall, arms and legs spread apart.

Once in a while, Sergeant Molina shouted, "Watch it, you fucking communist! Stay still, don't make me turn you into minced meat right here! Watch it, because the temptation is too much!"

Then I heard a thump. My son had not been able to stay upright anymore and was now a bundle on the floor.

Sergeant Molina went berserk. "What are you doing, you fucking asshole? Get up before it's too late, you fucking communist! So you and your communist cohorts had a plan to kill us all, eh? What did you know about *Plan Z*? Tell me! Were you in charge of killing me? Here, take this! Let's see who's going to kill who, eh?"

I sprang off the chair and charged at the sergeant, but before I could get to him, I tripped and fell on my face. The last thing I remember before closing my eyes is a black boot, a dark smudge sprinkled with stars.

When I woke up, the house was silent and morning light was streaming in through the windows. I got up with great difficulty. Even though one of my eyes was half closed by the swelling on my cheek, I was able to take note of the deplorable state in which the military had left our house. Andresito was nowhere to be seen. I found some undergarments, a skirt, a sweater and a pair of shoes in my bedroom, and went to the bathroom to wash myself the best I could. Then I gathered up strength and left for the square to find a taxi.

The cab driver was shocked when he saw me, and even though I asked him to take me straight to the military barracks, he said that first we would have to make a stop at the hospital. He walked me to the emergency room himself, where the doctor on duty treated me. She didn't even ask me what had happened—in just a few days people had learned not to talk, not to ask. My cheekbone was cracked, several molars were loose, my face showed multiple lacerations and my body was bruised all over. Fortunately, my eyes were intact. She plucked the pieces of glass off my face, disinfected the wounds, made me rinse my mouth with an antiseptic solution, and ordered that I take plenty of fluids and refrain from speaking for at least a week—she explained that it was important to keep my face as still as possible. She gave me a prescription for painkillers, but I didn't want to fill it because I knew that the drugs would knock me out and I had to find my son.

The taxi driver took me to Caupolicán Regiment, where I asked to speak to Captain Riquelme. He had been a client of Andrés' at the bank and had helped the Unión Juvenil by providing the team with a bus whenever they had an out-of-town tournament. They made me wait at the entrance and a little while later a soldier came out to tell me that if I was looking for my son, Captain Riquelme wanted me to know that he was not at the barracks. He suggested that I go to the public prison on Teja Island.

There was great commotion on the Pedro de Valdivia Bridge; the traffic was stalled and small groups of people were looking over the railing. I rolled down my window and called out to a young woman to ask what was happening.

She walked up to the cab and whispered, "Corpses. There are dozens of corpses in the river."

She was as white as a ghost.

I paid the driver, thanked him for all his help and got out of the cab. What if my son's body was down there? But by then the military had figured out what was happening and were dispersing the small groups.

"Move on, move on," they repeated as they used their semi-automatic machine guns to push people away from the railing.

I walked towards the prison as fast as I could. When I arrived, there was a long line waiting for visiting hours to begin. Then

I saw Silvia, who had gone to visit Tito, and Mrs. Zoraida, my boss, who had gone to visit Miss Blanca. They couldn't believe their eyes when they saw the state I was in. Through hand signs and trying to speak with my mouth half closed, I explained to them what had happened. I felt sad and ashamed because I had stopped talking to them for political reasons, but obviously they hadn't forgotten our friendship. They hugged me and promised to help in whatever way they could. I felt like crying, but decided that I couldn't crumble; I had to stay strong. I had to find my son.

As the gates opened, word got around that twelve prisoners had been executed. Everybody went silent as the queue began to move.

When we got to the front and Silvia gave the officer in charge Tito's full name, he scanned the papers he was holding in his hand and then shouted, "Executed for subversive activities against the fatherland."

Before we had time to react, he gestured her aside and waited impatiently until Mrs. Zoraida gave him Miss Blanca's name. He scanned his lists again and shouted, "Executed for subversive activities against the fatherland."

I gave him Andresito's name and after a few eternal seconds, he shouted, "He's not in these premises."

By then two soldiers were pushing Silvia and Mrs. Zoraida out and telling them to go to the morgue to claim the bodies. Silvia had a sort of a nervous fit and began to swear and kick and punch one of the soldiers. I was frozen. The only thought on my mind was that now I didn't know where I would find Andresito. Finally, Mrs. Zoraida was able to calm Silvia down before the military arrested *her*, and we all left for the morgue.

I found Andresito in the basement of the building, at the entrance to a room full of corpses, on the floor, together with many others, as if instead of human beings they had been soulless animals. My son was on his back, his clothes torn to pieces and soaked in dried-up blood, barefoot, his right leg bent backwards and his arms, limp. His honey eyes were looking at the ceiling and the grimace in his mouth could've very well been taken for a smile.

I closed his eyes, covered his face with kisses, and for a moment I wanted to believe that he was sleeping. But all of a sudden, the paleness in his face brought me back to reality and then I knew with certainty that Andresito was dead. He had been murdered. I felt a stab in the chest. All I wanted was to kill his murderer with my own hands. I wanted to find Sergeant Molina and stab him with my butcher knife until he was dead. I don't know what happened next because when I came to, somebody was kneeling beside me. It was a young soldier, praying an Our Father. He helped me to sit up and offered to call an ambulance that could take Andresito's body home.

I don't know for how long I sat on the floor beside my son, his head on my lap. I asked him to forgive me for not understanding him, for not accepting him the way he was. Sitting there, on the tiled floor of the Valdivia morgue, I realized that I had spent a good part of my life preoccupied with trivialities; I had never really appreciated the gift of being alive. Following Andrés' death, I had grown to feel bitter about life instead of appreciating the fact that we had spent more than twenty years together. Furthermore, I had felt sorry for myself for having a "perverted" son and an "odd" daughter. I had grown to dislike my own children, to loathe their political ideals.

Finally, two male nurses arrived to lift Andresito onto a stretcher and we left for our house. I cleared the kitchen floor the best I could, put a sheet down and asked the men to place Andresito on top. Then I called Isabel.

As I could hardly open my mouth, it took her a while to figure out who was phoning, but as soon as she realized it was me she hung up, and in moments she showed up at my door with Carlos. Together we washed my son's wounds, cleaned him, combed his hair and dressed him in his Sunday suit. I promised him that his murderers would be punished; that one day justice would be done. Only then was I able to cry.

We kept a vigil during that whole afternoon and evening, and the next morning we buried him at the Valdivia General Cemetery, beside his father.

Sol

I don't know how long I was lying on the floor, in the dark. Then, a pair of hands plucked me from amongst my *compañeros* and dragged me to a different room. There, they hurled me onto a bed of bare springs—the torture instrument that became known as "the grill."

My body plunged again and again into a dark and turbulent zone inhabited by underwater beings. Some were small and slimy, incisive invaders of orifices; others reached gigantic proportions and were armed with powerful tentacles capable of suffocating me, crushing me to a pulp.

A couple of words would have been enough to put an end to the suffering, but for some inexplicable reason, during those encounters with my torturers, I managed to forget everything: the people I loved and who loved me, my name and my surname, even my pain. I abandoned my poor body to its own fate and the only thing I wished for was death, but to no avail. Every time, I was hurled back alive into the room full of people.

As children, my brother Andresito and I would play "blind

hen" with the neighbourhood kids. Eeny-meeny-mainy-mo—the "winner" was blindfolded, turned around several times and left standing in the middle of nowhere, looking at the inside of his or her own eyelids. Then the game became a kind of "tag": guided only by her hearing, the "blind hen" would stretch her arms out and stumble after laughter and shrieks until she reached somebody's shoulder, elbow, back. That's when her punishment ended and somebody else's began.

At the Londres 38 torture house, I became a vibrant eardrum, an amazing blind hen, an expert in decoding—as if it were a grotesque musical score—screams and whispers, silences, heartbeats, blows, creaks, coughs, steps. The world had turned into a living hell with background music.

That's how I knew that Gloria had also been abducted; I heard her curse the soldiers as they dragged her along the hallway. Then they opened the door and with a muffled thud, threw her among the many of us piled up in the dark space. My sense of smell confirmed that it was her: the scent of *Coral Verde* mixed with Gloria's unique body odor that had fascinated me since we were kids.

I felt ill. Had they raided my house and found the notebook hidden in the desk? Had I written something there which could've led them to Gloria?

"Gloria?" I whispered as I tried to quell the urge to vomit.

But she didn't have a chance to respond because the door slammed open once again and Gloria and I were hauled out and taken to the torture chamber.

We were tortured together. I became mute and went back to my underwater world. Gloria cursed them, swore at them, didn't stop fighting for one second. She sang the chorus of "Workers to Power" over and over again, driving the men in charge of the grill crazy.

Their order was simple: "When you're ready to speak, communist whore, lift a finger and I'll turn the electric current off."

My fingers ceased to exist. Gloria's must've acquired a life of their own because every so often they would take the rag out of her mouth, but instead of giving them the information they demanded, she would start singing.

I was returned to the dark space with the rest of the prisoners, but she wasn't. When I was being dragged out of the torture chamber, Gloria wasn't exuding her distinctive scent anymore. She smelled of burnt flesh.

Miss Graciela, my grade three teacher, was obsessed with cleanliness and tidiness. Everything had to be "very clean" and "very tidy." Ears, fingernails, necks, teeth and shoes were the object of daily ocular inspections, together with a quick hand incursion into our smocks' pockets—heaven forbid she might find a pebble picked up on our way back home the day before, or a cookie reserved for the ten o'clock recess. No-no-no. Pockets must be used solely and exclusively for the purpose of putting away our immaculate and evenly folded handkerchiefs, products of our self-denying mothers' hard work. After all, our mothers, with great love and sacrifice, had dedicated many precious hours to the sewing, embroidering, washing and ironing of those handkerchiefs, created with the noble purpose of keeping our cute little noses free of intrusions and covering our mouths when an insolent sneeze or a rude coughing fit forced its way out of our respiratory system. It could very well be that this useful ally of our personal hygiene might sometimes become a receptacle for our physiological activities, but every Señorita's duty was to maintain such attempts against cleanliness and tidiness duly concealed inside the symmetrical folds of our handkerchiefs.

Notebooks and books must be smartly covered with double-sided aluminum paper of different colours, each colour corresponding to a particular subject: blue for Arithmetic, red for Spanish, green for Natural Sciences, brown for History and Geography, yellow for Visual Arts and orange for Calligraphy. On the top right-hand corner of the cover, we must apply a three-by-two black-bordered white label with the name of the subject, our own name, the class we belonged to and the name of the school, all in Gothic letters elegantly scribed with black Indian ink.

The container for school implements—a rectangular wooden case that opened by inserting your thumb nail into the miniscule slot carved into its cover and then sliding it along—must contain no more and no less than two pencils and two white erasers, one pencil sharpener, a small box of twelve pencil-crayons, a compass and a ruler. On Wednesdays, calligraphy day, we must also bring along an inkwell with royal blue Parker ink, a wooden pen and a complete set of interchangeable nibs of different thicknesses, plus three sheets of blotting paper.

Miss Graciela was also the queen of the blackboard. She would write *everything* on that polished, dark surface, starting with the date and the proverb of the day: "Don't leave for tomorrow what you can do today. A closed mouth keeps out the flies. Laziness is the mother of all vices." Next, she'd write the name of the subject at hand, underlined with the corresponding colour of chalk, and then the blackboard would turn into an ocean of round and even white letters, threatening to drown us in so much tidiness and boredom. Everything she wrote must be copied word for word in our scribbling pad and, later on in the afternoon, at home, re-copied in the notebook for the pertinent subject, in blue ink, with titles and subtitles underlined in red.

All these rules must be strictly followed if you didn't want to perish under Miss Graciela's verbal artillery or be trampled by an invasion of bad marks at the end of the term. However, there was one issue that rose above everything else and that could only be compared to one's sublime aspiration to live in our Lord's kingdom forever and ever, an issue that transcended the insignificances of earthly matters and took on a purely celestial quality: the issue of "beautiful handwriting." According to Miss Graciela, a Señorita must not only aspire to have "good handwriting," but also, and much more importantly, to perfect and master the art of "beautiful handwriting." After all, one's handwriting and one's soul were nothing other than facing mirrors that reflected each other for eternity.

When my torturers showed me the pages in the red notebook where they found the information that led them to abduct Gloria, the first thing that came to my mind was, *Oh, no! My handwriting is so ugly!*

Everything was left half-done: the celery salad curling up in a bowl of fresh water; the laundry soaking in the bathtub with *Bio-luvil*; a tapestry I had begun embroidering in the last few weeks; the bed, the warmth of our bodies still imprinted on the mattress, under the tangle of sheets and covers. When the military forced their way into our apartment, they had found an interrupted life, abandoned in a rush.

What time did they arrive? If they got there in the morning, were they blinded by the light rushing in through the living room windows? If they got there at dusk, were they moved by the silhouette of the Andes, jaggedly drawn on the glass, painted in pink?

I don't know what time they got there; all I know is that they did and found the red notebook that Raúl had ordered me to burn, but that I, in the confusion and rush of the morning of September 11, 1973, forgot in the bowels of the mahogany desk.

The mahogany desk: an ample top, eighteen small and six big drawers, eight pigeon holes and a roll-up cover imitating an accordion. It had been our great acquisition when Miguel and I returned to Santiago shortly after getting married in 1968. For days on end we visited all the antique shops on Monjitas Street until we found it, collecting dust in a corner.

With the help of my friend Pastor—an expert in repairing, sanding and varnishing, and a genius in the art of creating secret compartments impossible to find—we returned the mahogany desk to its original majesty while transforming it into a valuable helper, a mute accomplice to our political activities.

However, the fact that I had turned mute was good for nothing when, with a couple of axe blows, the butchers disemboweled our dear mahogany desk and made it speak.

On October 18, 1973, I knew that Miguel was dead.

That day, I heard my torturer confirm the date to his superior. "Of course I know that today is October 18, my captain. Today is my birthday. Thirty-seven years old," he announced proudly.

Then, for a few instants, he pulled off my blindfold and showed me Miguel's violin, intact in its wooden box with red velvet lining. In my heart, I knew that Miguel couldn't live without his violin.

But my mind didn't listen to my heart—it insisted on constructing the fictitious memory of his last journey, from the moment of his abduction to the time of his murder. The versions varied, but somehow, in each one of them, the ending offered room for hope—a window open to the possibility of life.

Some time later, the memory of those invented stories, hope and all, was suddenly and completely shattered. My torturer took my blindfold off again and showed me Miguel's left hand—a bloody mass with black fingers and no fingernails, but with his silver wedding band grafted into his flesh.

In the darkness and the terror of Londres 38, I hid inside myself over and over again, found the fondest moments of my life with Miguel, listened to his violin, his voice, caressed his body, told him stories, sang to him and made lists of the events I would correct, the words I would erase, the ones I hadn't uttered enough times: "I love you, love you, love you" "Your fingers are the curliest and your ears the roundest in the whole wide world" "I'll never fight with you again" "Never again will I say that your violin is good for nothing" "I want to have a child with you" "I'll never cheat on you again."

Antonio Reyes was a poet. He was also a professor of literature, but, above all, he was a poet. In winter, you could see him walking around the university grounds cloaked in a *Mapuche* poncho or a smooth black *castilla wrap*. In summer, he always wore faded blue jeans, a white t-shirt and a pair of Franciscan sandals.

Antonio was not only well-known as a good teacher and poet, but also because he had the disposition to collaborate with his students' social projects. That's why, in November of 1969, it occurred to me that we could invite him to lead a poetry writing workshop at La Esperanza. When I introduced the idea to the weekly assembly, at least fifteen people became interested and I was given the green light to extend the invitation to Antonio.

I found him in his office, surrounded by a scattering of books and papers. He apologized profusely as he cleared a chair and invited me to sit across from him, on the other side of his desk. He listened attentively while I described the *campamento*, explained the literacy campaign and my proposal for a poetry writing workshop; he nodded once, and again, as he scribbled in a notebook with a plaid cover, but he didn't say a word. As I didn't know what else to tell him, I got up and asked him to give me his response the following week.

Without breaking his silence, he got up and left the office with me. We walked towards Macul Avenue and when I was about to say good-bye, he took me by the arm and said, "Let's go for a coffee." He flagged down a bus, we got on and he paid for both tickets. We sat very close together, right behind the driver. Then I remembered that Antonio also had the fame of a Casanova. It was too late. My right thigh, hardly covered with an insolent cotton miniskirt, was already stuck to Antonio's leg, and when I stopped looking obstinately at everything that went by the window and turned my head, I was met by a pair of moss-green eyes that didn't withdraw their gaze for the half hour of the bus ride.

When we got off at Plaza Italia and began to walk with our arms around each other's waists towards Parque Forestal, I had already forgotten that I was a married woman, that Antonio was a married man, that at that precise moment I was supposed to be in my Social Theory class, and that after class Miguel would come for me and we'd go home together; I had forgotten everything. The only thing that mattered was Antonio's hot arm around my waist, his bony right hand holding on to my hip, his breath in my ear, the sweet aroma of his sweat making me dizzy.

For several weeks my heart beat abnormally fast and I lived in a constant state of agitation. Peace could only be found in the little hotel at Parque Forestal. And then, one day, just as if I had been suffering from a bout of a mysterious virus, everything went away and life returned to normal. Somehow, that morning, I looked at Miguel having breakfast across from me and saw him for who he was: my beautiful, darling partner and lover. I walked around the table, put my arms around him and kissed him on the top of the head. It was as if the whole world had come into focus again.

"Are you back?" he asked.

"Yes," I answered.

"And may I ask you where you've been during all these weeks? Because even though you have come home every night, you haven't really been here with me," he pressed.

"Someday I may tell you," I responded hesitantly.

He got up, took me in his arms and carried me to our bed. We made urgent, sweet love, the way we had learned together, forgetting about condoms and precautions. After two months of not getting my period and when I couldn't blame the morning sickness on indigestion anymore, I had to accept that I was pregnant.

How to reconcile my ambitions and desires at age nineteen with a baby? How to continue with my studies while bringing up a child? How to go on with the literacy campaign at *Campamento La Esperanza*?

When I told Miguel about it, he became euphoric. Without stopping to ask what I thought, he began to pace around the living room as he made plans: that year he was finishing his studies, so by the time the baby was born he would stop being on-call and would have a permanent job with the Symphony; we'd move to a little house with a garden; the baby would be a girl and we'd name her Sol, just like me; we'd ask Pastor to make her crib; we'd ask my mom to knit her layette; we'd ask his mom to sew her diapers and shirts; from an early age she'd learn to play the piano, the violin and the guitar. When he was finally finished, I was crying with anxiety.

"What's the matter, my love?" he asked, obviously confused. By now he was sitting beside me on the couch, holding my hand.

"I can't have this baby, Miguel—I just can't..." I responded, resting my head on his shoulder.

"We'll make it work, Sol, you'll see. The university has a great day-care centre, I'll help with the housework. It'll be just fine..." he pressed on, running his fingers through my hair.

"It won't be just fine!" I shouted, standing up. "I won't be able to study, I won't be able to keep on helping at La Esperanza!

Don't you see? I'm nineteen years old, Miguel. We can have tons of babies in a few years, after I finish my career."

I sat down again and tried to put my arms around him, but this time he got up, walked around the coffee table and plonked himself down in the armchair across from me.

"I can't have a baby now!" I repeated, searching his gaze. He stared at me for a few moments, hurt and disappointment in his eyes. "Miguel, please, try to understand..." I begged.

But obviously, he didn't understand. He got up, grabbed his violin and left the house.

Gloria got me the information for a Dr. Marín, a woman who had been stripped of her medical license and position as a surgeon at the José Joaquín Aguirre Hospital when she had been caught performing an abortion in one of the hospital's operating rooms.

Miguel wasn't able to go with me because he had an important exam and Gloria couldn't leave her responsibilities as an intern. Nobody else knew that I was pregnant so, on a hot Thursday afternoon, feeling absolutely alone in the world, I took the bus to La Reina neighbourhood. When that terrible day was finally over and I stumbled out of Dr. Marín's house, I was relieved to discover that Miguel was waiting for me in a taxi around the corner.

For several weeks, we didn't look each other in the eye. We'd talk about everything else, except that. I don't know what he was thinking about. I couldn't get the baby off my mind. Was it a boy or a girl? Who would it have looked like? What colour eyes would it have had? Would it have had its father's long, curly fingers, its mother's dark, straight hair? As I was in quarantine—wasn't supposed to have intercourse for forty days—Miguel and I wouldn't touch, so every night I'd cry myself to sleep on my side of the bed.

When the issue finally came out into the open, we said ugly things to each other. We both felt betrayed: Miguel because I hadn't wanted to have our child, me because he had been blinded by his euphoria about the baby and hadn't been able to appreciate my anxieties and dilemmas.

After weeks of keeping our distance, Miguel and I woke up in the early morning of December 24 sniffing each other out like a pair of curious hounds. Little by little, we drew closer together until we didn't know who was who anymore and sunrise caught us transformed into a bundle of ears and knees, our hands overflowing with skin and hair. Our bodies, wiser and more humble than we, had shown us the way back.

All my life I was attracted to "the other side" of things. As a kid, I had a green duffle coat that my mom made me out of a hand-me-down jacket from aunt Amparo. I loved that coat, not only because it had a hood, wooden buttons in the form of spindles, and cloth loops instead of button holes, but mainly because of its lining. It was made of a green, beige and brown plaid, velvety wool that invited me to dream of faraway countries—places where snowflakes fell gently and quietly, and blonde girls wrapped in duffle-coats just like mine traveled in sleighs drawn by white horses with silver bells on their ears.

When the duffle coat became too small, my mom made me the horrible mohair purple coat, but with the most beautiful lining in the world: a thick, shiny taffeta with an iridescent sheen. I would've loved to wear it inside out and never understood why my mom had made me a piece of clothing that was infinitely lovelier on the inside than on the outside.

My experiences at Londres 38 confirmed that, for us humans, life's most precious things also reside inside, hidden from everybody's eyes. Nothing and nobody would ever be able to strip me of what I carried inside me: my secrets; my memories; my ideals; my principles; my love for Miguel, my family and my friends.

One night, I was moved out of Londres 38. It must've been the middle of the night because not a drop of light filtered through the blindfold. After a ride of at least half an hour, the vehicle came to a stop. I heard the sound of chains and a gate opening, then the driver and passenger got out and slammed their doors. Next thing I knew, my torturer was dragging me out of the back of the truck, his shrill voice grating on my ears.

"We can't make this whore sing, my captain. She's not a big fish, but she's a small fish with information about bigger fish, like the son of a bitch who was a student leader, Allende's friend. We don't know what else to do to her, my captain. I don't feel like eating her up anymore because she doesn't sing, and when they don't sing, I lose my appetite, no matter how tasty these communists may be. Maybe she'll sing for you, my captain... Ha, ha, ha..."

They made me go up a set of long, creaky stairs and then threw me on a hard, damp and cold floor. I was the only one there.

As I sat, my back against a wall, drifting in and out of consciousness, I promised myself that they wouldn't break me; that I wouldn't give them the satisfaction of becoming an informer. I had done enough damage already by not burning my red notebook. Thank goodness there was no information about Raúl in there. I was thrilled to hear that they hadn't found him. But my best friend had been abducted because of my mistake. Where was Gloria now? What were they doing to her? I wouldn't make any more mistakes.

So, I dedicated myself to reliving beautiful moments and experiences in my life. Sometimes these were just sensations and feelings: the crisp fragrance of freshly cut grass at the Valdivia Municipal Stadium; the suppleness of my favourite flannel pajamas; the silvery, perfect voice of Miguel's violin; the simple pleasure of putting a piece of my mom's apple *kuchen* in my mouth; the soul-stirring words and beautiful melody of a Joan Manuel Serrat song.

At other times, complete episodes unfolded over and over again in my mind, like a revolving film—moving images, colour and sound—but even better than a movie, as I would also recall the flavours and odors involved. There were two such episodes that occupied quite a bit of my time, I'm not sure why—perhaps because I remembered them so clearly that I didn't have any problem going over them in great detail; the exercise was effortless. At the drop of a hat, they took me right out of my confinement and into a time and space where I had felt not only utterly free, but immersed in love and beauty, connected to Miguel and to nature. Perhaps most importantly, I felt a special affection for these experiences because on both occasions I had been struck by a feeling of wonderment that had stayed with me through the years.

The first one was an excursion Miguel and I had made to the *cordillera*. A bright Spring morning, Pastor lent us his motorcycle so that we could have a Sunday outing. I was looking forward to riding it myself, but it turned out that the bike was too tall for me. Reluctantly, I moved out of the way so that Miguel could try it. It took him a bit of practice, but soon he was proudly revving up the engine and inviting me to jump on the back seat.

We made our way out of the city. The fields were "embroidered" with flowers—as the National Anthem appropriately describes the Chilean countryside—and the perfume of jasmine and honeysuckle filled the air. As we turned east and began to ride parallel to the Maipo River, the Andes rose impressively into the sky and the road became a zigzagging ribbon. When we got to the summit, we sat on a rock and listened to the wind and the sobering silence for what felt like an eternity.

On the ride back, half way between the top and the base of

the highest peak, I heard an unexpected whisper. I turned my head and saw a gigantic condor flying beside us, wings fully extended, eyes shining like pebbles polished by water, his solemn beak pointing to the ground, a white-feathered tiara adorning his neck. Miguel turned off the engine and for a few moments we coasted down the hill, our precarious balance parallel to the condor's flight, the tip of his right wing brushing our shoulders. I pressed my face against Miguel's back—his heart was pounding as loudly as mine.

The other episode also had to do with an excursion. A few summers earlier, Miguel and I had gone with Raúl to visit his family in the Elqui Valley, a bright green canyon framed by copper-coloured mountains. One afternoon, Miguel and I made our way to Monte Grande, Gabriela Mistral's hometown, and also headquarters of Las Catacumbas *Pisco* Distillery, one of the oldest and most prestigious in the region.

The valley was bursting at the seams; avocados, peaches and apricots were nearly ready to be harvvested and the vineyards stretched out row after row. Through the open window of the rickety bus, we could breathe in the delicious fragrance of the fruit and see the river jumping nimbly between glistening boulders as it made its way towards the ocean.

Don Pancho, the proprietor and an expert in the manufacture of *pisco*, gave us a warm welcome to his distillery and then invited us to join a small group of visitors gathered under an ancient *chañar* tree. We were all curious to learn how it was possible for grapes to yield this transparent and powerful liquor, so different from the wine of the central region.

"That's an ancient secret we will not tell you about," Don Pancho joked.

"Oh come on," a few of us pleaded.

"Okay, but don't tell anybody, promise?" he joked again. "The answer to your question is actually quite simple: *pisco* is like a brandy, the result of a double process. First, the grapes are turned into wine, and then the wine is distilled into *pisco* and aged for a short period of time. You'll see," he assured us as he led the way into the plant.

We walked through the installations, observed the production process and listened to Don Pancho's explanations before he invited us to go into the *catacumbas*, a series of caves carved into the side of the mountain. The space was lit only by a few flickering candles, so it took a while for my eyes to adjust. Only then was I able to see that hundreds of bottles lined the walls and enormous cedar kegs rested on the pressed earth. Also, there was a round table pushed against the back wall and on a shelf right above it sat a human skull.

Holding on to Miguel's hand, I observed the rest of the group and was quick to realize that I wasn't the only one shaking with fear and curiosity. Whose skull was this? What was it doing there?

But nobody uttered a word, and when Don Pancho finally

emerged from the shadows carrying a tray with six small tumblers of *pisco*, nobody dared ask a thing. We toasted to *pisco*, to grapes, to the valley, to life. Then Don Pancho offered a toast to Carmelita, whose phosphorescent whiteness watched us from up above.

"If we don't toast to her, she gets mad," he explained.

We all laughed raucously—as if saying, "What an absurd thing to say!"—but didn't hesitate to join the toast, except for an astronomer from California who, in ungrammatical Spanish pronounced as if it were American English, declared, "Me no. That be very stupid. That very ignorant."

The man had hardly finished speaking when we saw Carmelita dart off the shelf with the speed of a lightening rod and land on the table, her lipless smile facing the scientist.

"You've got to be cautious with the spirits," Don Pancho stated calmly as he picked up the skull, apologized to it and put it back on the shelf.

My reveries in the solitary confinement "cage," as I later learned the prisoners called it, came to an abrupt ending one day when I was dragged out and pushed down the stairs. Once again, I found myself in a torture chamber. There were many more sessions after that first one and every single time I was returned to the cage. The last time, as I made my way up the stairs, I recognized the touch of a guard who stood out from the rest because he always spoke to me softly and guided me instead of pushing or dragging me into or out of the cage. Under my blindfolded eyes, I liked to imagine that he looked like Miguel.

I begged him not to tie my hands; I explained that I couldn't stand the pain on my back and shoulders anymore.

"I have to tie your hands," he responded apologetically. "If I get caught, I'll be in real trouble," he explained.

I had already resigned myself and was offering him my wrists, now behind my back, when I heard him whisper, "I'll tie them in front this time. That won't hurt so much."

"Thanks," I replied sincerely, turning around and raising my arms in front of me.

I sat in my usual corner for a while, but when I realized that I could move my hands towards my mouth, I decided that this was my opportunity to stop the suffering forever. After all, the skin that protects the inside of one's wrists is thin and fragile and mine had already been cut and scraped by the rope. So, I used my teeth to put a halt to my pain.

When I woke up, a pair of woman's arms was rocking me gently while a chorus of whispers tickled my ears.

The guard had found me bleeding and unconscious in the solitary confinement cage and had taken me to the infirmary. From there I had been moved to a cell with fifteen other prisoners. Apparently, the torturers had finally realized that I didn't have the information they needed to find Raúl.

My cellmates took care of me as if I were a newborn baby. They fed me, dressed me, took me to the bathroom. There was another guard that managed to give us an extra piece of bread or a couple of cigarettes once in a while. Never before had it occurred to me that one piece of bread could be divided into sixteen equal parts, but in that cell everything was possible, as it was also possible for me to end up eating the sixteen pieces because I was the weakest.

We would sleep four to a mat, arms and legs entwined, our bodies molded to the others' curves and hollows. If someone woke up in the middle of a nightmare, somebody else was always ready to listen to her, cuddle, rock and calm her down until she went back to sleep. And if someone was invaded by sadness, the rest were there to lift her spirits up.

We spent the time telling each other tales from books and movies, trying to remember all the funny stories and jokes we could, and laughing, in spite of everything and against all odds. When we ran out of books, movies and jokes, we sang and even danced.

One night, as I was lying awake, I heard a man's voice on the other side of the wall. He was singing "Vamos mujer" very softly. I got up and rested my ear against a narrow crack in between two boards and listened.

When the voice died down, I attached my mouth to the crack and whisper-sang "América novia mía."

The voice responded with "Valparaíso."

For a long time we continued to exchange songs, until a guard ordered us to be quiet.

Night after night, the voice kept on singing and telling me novels by Jules Verne, while I responded by reciting Neruda poems and singing everything that came to my mind. We never spoke of our lives or of what we looked like—fat, thin, tall, short. But one day, while I was lining up for the bathroom, I heard the voice a few meters to my right. As I was blindfolded, I couldn't see the carrier of the voice, so I stretched my arms out and, for an instant, my hands interlaced with a cluster of warm and fleshy fingers. The blow of the guard's baton didn't manage to take away the feeling of agitated joy and longing that had lodged itself in my chest.

In that concentration camp, I was in love with three people at the same time: Miguel, the man with the deep voice and the fleshy fingers, and Maria.

Maria was tall and thin and had the most beautiful smile in the world. Her arms brought me back to life after the solitary confinement cage. Not only that, her fingers, expert in massaging my temples and scratching my head, put me to sleep when my body refused to come out of the state of alert the torturers had left it in.

I loved my friend's singular way of being there, no conditions, no questions asked. I loved the surrender of her sleeping body molded to the curve of my back, the weight of her arm on my waist, the warmth of her intermittent breath in my ear. When I left that cell, Maria gave me her wool sweater because she knew that I was terrified of the cold, one of my worst enemies in solitary confinement.

A couple of weeks earlier I had mentioned to my cellmates that I hadn't menstruated for a long time. They assured me that a lot of them had the same problem—those kinds of irregularities were normal given the extreme circumstances we were living through. But one day I woke up overtaken by nausea. I was taken to the infirmary and the doctor confirmed the unthinkable: I was pregnant.

That same day, I was moved. While a guard handcuffed my wrists and plastered my eyes with a blindfold, my *compañeras* filled my pockets with pieces of bread and bade me farewell by singing at the top of their lungs, "I would like to have wings so that I could fly, cross the space in freedom, like the birds, in freedom..."

Soledad

After we buried Andresito, Isabel, Carlos and I left for Santiago. I plucked a few things from the mess in my house and put them in a suitcase: photo albums, a few samples of my watercolour and pottery creations, Andresito's soccer jersey, the sky blue dress Sol wore for the Youth Orchestra concerts, the *Imperial 62* cookbook with my winning recipe in it, the handkerchief I embroidered for Andrés when he turned twenty, and a few clothes of mine.

Mrs. Zoraida offered to get rid of the debris, repair the damage and return the house to the landlord. She was also kind enough to drive us to the bus station. That was the last time I saw her.

Our search for Sol, Miguel and Gloria began the same morning we got to Santiago: Monday, September 23, 1973, the day my son would've turned thirty years old.

Isabel's sister was there to greet her and Carlos, and my friend Rina was waiting for me. We agreed that we shouldn't even go near *Campamento* Che Guevara as most likely it had been taken over by the military. Similarly, Rina warned us not to go to our children's homes—she had known of cases in which soldiers had been waiting at the political prisoners' houses, so as to bust their relatives and friends as well. We decided to start with the kids' places of work. Rina and Isabel's sister offered to take our bags to their respective places, I went straight to the Municipal Theatre and then the Women's Centre, and the Díaz's left for José Joaquín Aguirre Hospital.

When we met for lunch, neither they nor I had been at all successful; the Women's Centre was shut down, the theatre was closed and at the hospital they had insisted that Gloria hadn't been to work since the day of the coup.

Day after day, we continued doing our rounds, sometimes together, other times separately. We went to every police station, army barracks, hospital and clinic in Santiago and the surrounding suburbs. Progressive members of several churches had formed the Committee for Peace, which documented human rights violations, helped people find their imprisoned relatives and presented cases to the courts. At some point they sent us to the National Stadium, and for many days we kept on returning and waiting in endless lines that never led anywhere.

Then, in January of 1974, we heard about a concentration camp on Departamental Avenue, near Vicuña Mackenna Street: Tres Álamos.

There we went, day after day, but Sol, Miguel and Gloria's names didn't show up on the prisoners' list. One morning, a couple of women waiting in line took pity on us and suggested that we tell the guards that we were relatives of theirs; that's how we managed to get in during visiting hours. We spread the word about our loved ones and several prisoners confirmed that Gloria and Miguel had been at the National Stadium for a while and that Gloria and Sol had also been seen in the torture house at 38 Londres Street.

We couldn't get any more information about Gloria, but I was assured that Sol had also been seen at the Villa Grimaldi concentration camp. About Miguel, we were told that he had been taken out of the National Stadium with a big group of prisoners.

Then, one afternoon in early February, a young woman told me that Sol was alive in that very place, but in a different building called Cuatro Álamos. A few days later, my daughter's name showed up on the prisoners' list and the following afternoon I was allowed to spend time with her in the visitors' shed—a makeshift wood frame with a canvas roof and a dirt floor, metal folding chairs piled up on one side. As I took in the grim scenery and tried to imagine what the prisoners' cells looked like, I noticed that several people had already grabbed a couple of chairs, so I proceeded to do the same.

I found a free space and sat down to wait. My mind was blank, but my heart was racing; I had been told that Sol was alive, but I wouldn't believe it until I saw her with my own eyes. After a few minutes I heard steps behind me. A line of a dozen or so women was approaching the shed, one guard at the front and another one at the end of the line. I didn't recognize my daughter until she was standing right in front of me. She was a bundle of skin and bones, had no eyebrows or eyelashes and was missing big patches of hair on her head. I covered her with kisses, cuddled her in my arms and caressed her scrawny body. We held on to each other, sobbing, until she was able to get her voice back and told me that most likely Miguel was dead and she suspected that Gloria was too. Then I had no choice but tell her about her brother, Tito and Miss Blanca.

My daughter crumpled in my arms. She didn't shed one tear, but began to shiver and went completely limp. In a panic, I cried out for help. A couple of Sol's cellmates were close by visiting with their own loved ones and didn't hesitate to take charge of the situation. By now, a guard had come up and was demanding to know what the problem was, but Sol's friends assured him that everything was fine as they took Sol's arms, wrapped them across their shoulders and basically dragged her limp body out of the shed. As they were leaving, they promised me that Sol would be all right, that they would take care of her. I was still in shock but managed to hand them the package with provisions I had brought along, which had already been inspected by the guards at the gate.

Religiously, every Wednesday and Sunday, Isabel, Carlos and I went to visit Sol. Little by little, we saw her get better, put a bit of meat on her bones, recover a small dose of joy. Prisoners were allowed to do crafts at Tres Álamos, so we began to bring her the materials she needed to make her embroidered tapestries and we were also able to take in a guitar and other instruments so that she could distract herself by singing with her fellow prisoners.

One of those afternoons, she asked me if I would take a message to somebody "in the outside." In a whisper, she explained, "It involves some risk, but not much—the message will be in code and you'll just have to leave it in a particular place; you won't even have to meet the person."

I was puzzled and my face must have shown it, because my daughter continued, "Mom, there are *compañeros* who are organizing a resistance movement to the dictatorship, we need to keep in touch with them."

"Sol!" I called out, a little bit too loudly. I hastily lowered my voice to a whisper, my mouth to her ear. "What if you get caught? They'll kill you this time!"

She held me tight for a few moments before she went on, "I won't get caught, mom. There's nothing to get caught about. Not yet and not here." She took my hand in hers. "Mom, it's the least we can do. Think about it. It's okay if you don't want to do it, but you know what? Many of the visitors that you see here today are helping us," she added. Then, with smiling eyes, she uttered the punch line: "Señora Isabel and Don Carlos are involved."

On the bus back, I observed Isabel and Carlos as they sat very close together, holding on to each other in spite of the summer heat. They must've been devastated inside—there were no signs of Gloria showing up— but they were always in good spirits. Not only that, they had supported me unconditionally for months on end. When we got downtown, I asked them to join me for a cup of tea at the Paula. There, I broached the issue of "helping" the political prisoners communicate with their comrades in the city.

Isabel repeated Sol's words: "It's the least we can do."

Carlos went even further: "Helping to bring down the dictatorship is the *only* thing we can do. We can't sit idly while Pinochet and his goons kill and plunder as they wish."

I told them about my fears; I didn't want my daughter to go through any more suffering, never mind get killed.

They reassured me. "That's unlikely to happen, Soledad," Isabel explained. "The movement is just beginning and communications have more to do with political positions than with concrete actions."

"How do you know?" I asked her suspiciously.

She blushed and averted her gaze.

Leaning over the table, Carlos responded, "We're active in the movement, Soledad. We joined a while back."

It made sense to me. They had been strong Allende supporters and now their daughter had disappeared. Maybe they were right. Maybe we could help end the horror. Besides, Sol would most certainly continue participating with or without my help. She had always been like that: when she set her mind to something, there was no way to stop her.

I became an expert in invisible writing, secret storage places, blind meetings, security measures and all the tricks needed to fool the military. I took on my duties with dedication and enthusiasm. I was proud of myself. Sol was proud of me.

A couple of months later we learned that my daughter had been accused of being a terrorist because of her connections to *Campamento* Che Guevara. She would have to face a military tribunal and, according to the lawyers at the Committee for Peace, most likely she'd be sentenced to at least twenty years in jail.

By now she was six months pregnant, so I presented an official request to have her imprisonment exchanged for exile.

After many comings and goings, interviews and paperwork, I managed to talk to the Cultural Attaché of the Canadian Embassy. He treated me with utmost respect, listened to me attentively and then proceeded to guide me through the whole process of asking for refugee status for my daughter, her baby and myself. He even took it upon himself to obtain the permit for Sol to leave Chile. That's how an agreement with the military "authorities" was reached: as soon as the baby was born, we would leave for Vancouver, Canada.

Sol

I was pregnant. I ascertained the date of my last period, counted the days over and over again, reviewed my last few weeks with Miguel and every time I came to the same conclusion: the child was not Miguel's, but my torturer's. How could new life be conceived under such horrific circumstances? How could I bear a child whose father was a psychopath and a rapist? First, I was in shock. Then, I convinced myself, and told everybody, that the baby was Miguel's.

I was now at Tres Álamos concentration camp, where life had taken on the semblance of normalcy. We weren't blindfolded anymore, so time ceased to be chaotic; no more endless nights giving way to short explosions of light. At long last, the orderly passing of the hours brought back the comings and goings of the sun, the moon and the stars.

We were given food on a regular basis, so the bread that my cellmates had put in my pockets at Villa Grimaldi became food for the soul instead. Following my new friends' example, I turned them into small figurines, which I then powdered with plaster scratched off the ceiling, sprinkled with freckles of blue ink and added to the collection that ornamented our drab cell.

At Tres Álamos we were also permitted to have visitors.

The first time I saw my mom, it took me a while to recognize her. Her face seemed to be crooked, as if someone had pushed her forehead in one direction and her chin in the other. She also looked much thinner and older than I remembered. We held each other for a long time and then she told me about my brother's murder. I wanted to die. Why hadn't I died instead? Why hadn't I died already? By all accounts, I should've been dead by then. But, for some inexplicable reason, I had survived horrendous torture and my own attempt to commit suicide. Not only that, I was now carrying a new life inside me. What was the matter with me?

Again, my cellmates didn't let me die. They would tickle me until I opened my mouth and then manage to feed me water and milk with a dropper. They took turns keeping me company, telling me stories, singing me *tonadas*, *cuecas* and rock'n rolls, giving me back rubs and taking me to the bathroom.

Then, one day, a winged little horse threw my womb and my heart into disarray with its galloping pirouettes. It was true; I did have a human being inside me. My astonishment was such that I sat up and announced, "I'm getting up."

Would my daughter look like me or Miguel? Would she have his curly fingers and rounded ears? Would she have my fleshy lips and black hair? Would she like to play the violin or the piano? Somehow, I was convinced that the baby would be a girl and decided to call her Tania, after the heroic guerrilla that fought alongside Che Guevara in Bolivia.

Once in a while the face of my torturer would flash in front of my eyes, the way I had seen it the couple of times he took the blindfold off me. But, as soon as the image took shape, I made sure to erase it and replace it with Miguel's. Miguel was my daughter's father.

When word about my pregnancy got around, many prisoners began to dedicate time to the baby: cutting out and painting little wooden animals, sewing batiste shirts, knitting shawls and sweaters, booties and toques. A *compañero* called Julio spent hours putting together, polishing and painting a royal-blue trunk with the name "Tania" carved on its cover.

I started to embroider my most joyous tapestries ever: children playing Ring-a-ring-a-roses on pastures dotted with multicoloured flowers; red-roofed adobe houses beside a serpentine river, the snow-capped Andes in the background; white-sand beaches sprinkled with shells, the sunlight shimmering on the turquoise ocean....

And then one day, out of nowhere, I began to embroider a set of green eyes in every one of my tapestries. In some, they were watching vigilantly from a corner, in others, they had a piercing light to them and took centre stage, or looked at me from behind a tree. They were my torturer's eyes.

When my friends asked me about them, I just smiled and said, "I always wanted to have green eyes myself, so perhaps this is my way of wishing them on my daughter."

At Tres Álamos, our days were filled with multiple activities. In addition to being allowed to do arts and crafts, we had a choir, a folk singing ensemble, a theatre group and a dance troupe. Our productions and recitals were attended not only by all the prisoners, but also by the guards. We became experts in double meanings and insinuations, social and political messages that were clear and veiled at the same time. After every presentation, our task was to strike up a conversation with one of the soldiers that had shown a special interest in the performance. Our goal was to "conscientize" the guards, to have them question the country's current situation and their own role in it. After all, most of them were young men from working class or *campesino* families with no better options in life than to become soldiers.

But that was not our only political activity; we also developed extensive contacts with the underground resistance movement. My mom, Gloria's mom and dad, as well as the relatives and friends of many other prisoners, became important links to the outside. They would take our coded messages and bring back our *compañeros'* missives written on the inside of canned food labels, or in invisible ink on a clean shirt. Their messages would inform us of political parties getting reorganized, present analyses and propose strategies, and let us know that there were groups researching and denouncing human rights violations.

Our comrades in the resistance urged us to eat as much as we could, exercise and keep our minds active. They also encouraged us to strengthen our work on the soldiers. There was hope that the military would split, as it was becoming more and more clear that Pinochet was hoarding all power for himself; if the Air Force and the Navy rebelled, perhaps our movement could spur a popular insurrection.

At the same time, sectors of the political right and the Christian Democrats had changed their tune: they weren't happy with the military take-over anymore, as they had come to realize that the armed forces would not call on them to govern the country. Would they be able to persuade the United States to stop supporting Pinochet and get behind them instead? How could our movement capitalize on such developments?

Our discussions would go on for hours, in whispers, in small groups of two or three people at a time. After reaching our conclusions, we would encode them and write them with lemon juice on pieces of paper that then would contain a harmless letter to a friend or relative. When our comrades in the outside applied a hot iron to the paper, they were able to read our hidden words.

The satisfaction of fooling the military was the source of conspiratorial smiles, tacit understandings and even a sort of happiness. But inside, I was shattered, just like I suspect every other prisoner was, only we didn't talk about it; we all played at pretending to be whole and strong. My body hurt, I suffered from a chronic headache, but worst of all, I was permeated by a deep sadness.

Sometimes I would force myself to believe that everybody I loved was still alive, that what had happened was actually a big lie, a kind of prank that life had pulled on me, just to test me. Any time now, very soon, life would say, "Okay, the exam is over. You passed with flying colours! You can leave this place now because Miguel, your brother, Gloria, Tito Ramírez, Miss Blanca, everybody is waiting for you!"

Often, this illusion kept me going. When it stopped working, I would invent my future.

I would be walking along Providencia Avenue on a beautiful summer evening. I would've regained enough weight to look attractive again and I'd be wearing a red sun dress and jute sandals. Tania would be in her stroller, gurgling and smiling at all the passersby. Then, a beautiful young man—who invariably ended up looking like Miguel—would approach me and ask for directions. As the place that he was looking for was nearby, I would offer to walk him there. As we talked, we became more and more attracted to each other and decided to meet again. After several dates—in these fantasies Tania was always in her stroller, behaving like an angel—we would realize not only that we had fallen in love with each other, but that we were both involved in the underground resistance to the dictatorship. We were ecstatic, made passionate love in a park, behind a tree, and lived happily ever after.

Often enough, though, reality hit me, and hit me hard: Miguel was most likely dead, my brother was dead, my friends were dead, I was pregnant with my torturer's baby and the future was a huge black hole. How much longer would I be in the concentration camp? Where would I deliver my daughter? Would I be allowed to keep her with me after her birth? Would she be normal, after all that had been done to me? Would I be able to love her? What if she looked like my torturer? Would I hate her then?

I didn't really know the meaning of the word "hate." Some of my fellow prisoners talked quite a bit about hatred and revenge, but, for some reason, I didn't feel any of that. I didn't hate the men who had caused me so much pain, I didn't hate Miguel's or my brother's murderers, Pinochet and his cohorts... I wasn't sure what I felt for them. Contempt? Anger? Disgust? I was afraid that my baby's birth would add the word "hatred" to my emotional vocabulary.

As I became healthier and put on some weight, my aches and pains began to subside. My hair was growing back, I had fingernails, eyebrows and eyelashes once again, and my belly was starting to show. There were no mirrors in any of the prisons where I had been, so I had lost all awareness of my looks; actually, for the longest time, I wasn't interested in knowing how I looked. But as I felt my body changing, I became curious.

One of those days, an Amnesty International delegation came to visit the camp. The group was fairly large and there was a photographer among them. I approached her and asked her to take a picture of me. She snapped several shots and then agreed to call my mom and pass on a copy of the photographs to her. When my mom came to visit the following Sunday, she brought them along. I couldn't believe my eyes: I looked like a scarecrow with a little balloon sticking out halfway down its body. My oversized clothing resembled a sack of potatoes on my scrawny frame, my face was bony and sunken, my lips, narrow and tight.

I looked at the pictures for a long time, as if they were of somebody else, a woman that I had known a long time ago, but who was now estranged from me. In my mind, I continued to see myself the way I had once been: healthy, with a mane of shiny black hair, full lips and lively eyes. I couldn't reconcile the image that I carried inside me with the one in the photographs. Why had this been done to me? Why had I survived?

That night I had a dream: It was a big house full of people. There was supposed to be a baby somewhere—a baby who had been decapitated inside her mother's womb. You could hear her crying. I ran around, looking for her, and some women told me that the baby was in the bathtub. I found her underwater, her head separate from her body. She was green-grey in colour and, even though it was underwater, the head was crying.

I was alarmed at people's indifference about the baby; they continued talking as if nothing were happening. As I took her out of the bathtub, the bathroom and hallway floor flooded with water. I pressed on the baby's back to let the water inside her come out and then tried to mop up the floor with a towel, but to no avail.

A moment later, my mom took the baby's head and body in her arms and cuddled and rocked them. She said that she was going to help me put them back together again, not to worry, that everything was going to be all right.

I woke up feeling at peace: I realized that the real prank that life was pulling on me, the test I was supposed to pass, was to give birth to the torturer's daughter and bring her up to be a good person. I wouldn't do it alone; my mother would help me. Together, we would not only pick up the pieces and restore our own lives, but also nurture a loving and respectful human being: a girl, and then a woman, who would take after Miguel, Andresito, Gloria and the rest of our dear, dear dead. That would be our revenge, our retribution.

In April of 1974, giving in to international pressure, the dictatorship began to allow political prisoners to leave Chile. Mexico, Argentina, Sweden, France, Italy and Canada were among the countries that had offered to take refugees in. The position of many of us at Tres Álamos was that we should do our best to be released from the camp, stay in our homeland and join the underground resistance. When it became clear that a number of us were in prison for the long haul, we encouraged each other to apply for the penalty of exile instead.

One of the prisoner's relatives had brought us a shortwave radio a few weeks before and, depending on the guard on duty, we were allowed to listen to it at night. We convinced him that all we wanted was to enjoy Argentinean tango shows, but instead tuned into Radio Moscow's *¡Escucha, Chile!*—"Listen, Chile!"—a nightly program in the voices of Volodia Teitelbom, a Chilean journalist, writer and former senator now living in the Soviet Union, and Katia Olevskaia, a lively Spanish-speaking Russian announcer. The guard's only condition was that we turn the volume as low as possible and have the lights off. We would thank him profusely and comply with no objections whatsoever. Then we would huddle together, our heads pressed to the small black box, and listen to the words through the creaks and squeaks of the magnetic waves.

¡Escucha, Chile! played music by Víctor Jara, Quilapayún, Inti Illimani, Violeta, Isabel and Angel Parra, and also provided a comprehensive newsreel about the situation in our country: the ongoing human rights violations, the work of the Committee for Peace, the deep and drastic changes to the economy undertaken by Pinochet, the abject poverty that was plaguing large sectors of the population... Often, the newscast also included information about the activities of the international campaign that had been organized in solidarity with the resistance movement inside Chile. We knew, then, that if we were to leave, there would be work awaiting us in our host country.

The "Elders' Circle," a group composed of the wisest and most dignified prisoners we had elected as our leaders, insisted that I go into exile.

"We have to make sure that the new life that we've stolen from death, your daughter Tania's life, carries on and develops under the best possible conditions," *compañero* Ramón, the circle's spokesperson, said in his most solemn of voices.

The truth is that I didn't want to leave. I wanted to remain in Chile, perhaps go back to Valdivia, or maybe go live in a completely different place. How long would the dictatorship last? Everything indicated that sooner rather than later, Pinochet would fall. At Tres Álamos we were hopeful, but our isolation had filled us with excessive optimism.

One Wednesday in May, my mom announced that we would be going to Canada. A few of my prisoner friends had been recently informed that they'd be going to Sweden and I had mused about the idea of joining them there, but it turned out that we would be going to Canada instead, as the Canadian Embassy had been the only one to offer us refugee status so far.

I knew that Canada was just north of the United States, but that was about it. Was it as far up as Sweden? Was it as cold as Sweden? If I had gone to Sweden, perhaps I would've bumped into Ingmar Bergman and Liv Ullman walking down a Stockholm street, or perhaps I would've met the actress whose toes were kissed by her lover in the film *My Beloved John*. But Vancouver, Canada? What was there in Vancouver to look forward to? Nothing that I was aware of.

At first I was overwhelmed by anxiety, but after a while I decided that perhaps this was the best thing that could happen to us: a clean start in a completely new place. We would make our home in a city we didn't know anything about and where nobody knew anything about us.

The morning of June 15, my daughter announced her arrival. My cellmates helped me to get ready and the whole concentration camp bade me farewell, singing "Negro José." My friends and I were not the only ones to cry, tears were also streaming down the face of the private that helped me to get the blue trunk into the military vehicle that took me to the hospital.

I gave birth at the *Asistencia Pública* under the care of a kind midwife while two armed soldiers kept guard at the door. My mom wasn't allowed to be there, but it didn't matter because I felt her presence beside me all along, together with the rest of my dear ones.

The contractions made me scream and yelp, not so much from the pain itself as from a pulsating feeling of utter wonder. These spasms were completely different from the torment I had suffered in the torture chamber; now, my body was aflame with raw energy. Burning lava was pushing its way through the crater in between my legs. This was life demanding that I unzip, that I open up and let myself go.

My daughter, a slippery, tiny human being, burst into the world still attached to my insides by a mucky, greenish rope. There she was, at long last, my winged little fish, my conspiratorial, intimate Pegasus.

"It's a *mujercita*, a little woman!" the midwife announced as she proceeded to cut the umbilical cord and place the baby on my chest.

"I know. Her name is Tania," I told her.

I felt the slight weight and the warmth of my daughter's body on me, caressed the sticky brush of her hair, explored her froggy legs, counted her miniature toes and whispered in her ear, "My name is Sol Martínez and I'm your mother. Your father is Miguel Rivera, principal violinist of Chile's Symphony Orchestra. That's the absolute truth. And another truth: we both love you more than anything else in the world."

A couple of days later, my mom and the Canadian Cultural Attaché came to pick us up. I was worried about Tania's trunk.

"What if the military don't let us take it?" I asked him.

"Don't worry," he responded. Then he added something that I found both ironic and utterly funny: "All your luggage is part of our diplomatic bag."

A blue, wooden diplomatic bag, full of baby clothes and toys made by political prisoners, I thought as I smiled back at him.

Strands of clouds floating in the sky, the sound of traffic pecking at my ears, the sudden flight of a flock of birds—everything made me weep on our way to the airport. My mom was sitting beside me with Tania in her arms, and from our position in the back seat I wanted to stretch my hand out and run my fingers through the golden curls that rested on the Canadian diplomat's head, felt like caressing the right earlobe of the uniformed chauffeur. Everything had become a source of pleasure, a happening, a reason to be alive.

It had rained earlier in the day and the trees, buildings, cars and buses lit up with the jagged reflection of a diamond as they traveled past my window. I turned around to steal a last glance at the Andes. There they were, towering over the city, their imposing height now painted in the usual pinks and lilacs of the late afternoon.

From the airplane window, I saw my country vanish behind the clouds, a stroke of earth hardly discernible between the *cordillera* and the frothy blue of the Pacific Ocean. Only then did I really grasp what was happening: I was leaving everything I knew. What lay ahead? A city called Vancouver in a country called Canada. A question mark. A hole filled with hope.

Vancouver, Canada

1974 – 1998

Soledad

Sol, Tania and I landed in Vancouver on Tuesday, June 18, 1974. Sol had not only survived nine months of torture houses and concentration camps, but had also given birth to a beautiful little girl. It had taken me months to complete all the paper work, but finally we had been allowed to leave Chile, that long and narrow strip of land I had loved with patriotic fervor for most of my life, but had come to despise since the military coup of September 11, 1973.

Yet, as much as I wanted to pretend that I didn't care about Chile anymore, it didn't take me long to realize that when you leave your country behind, you don't really leave your country behind. It haunts you, it teases you, it plays tricks on you; it shows up at every corner, in every street; in the wind, in the clouds. It doesn't leave you alone. Your past life plays in your head over and over again, like a movie that you already know by heart, but cannot stop watching.

A few days after we landed in Canada, Sol told me about the baby's father. We were staying at the Cove Motor Inn, a place right on English Bay which is now an expensive tourist resort, but back then didn't even amount to a one-star hotel. It was run by the Canadian government, exclusively for newly arrived immigrants and refugees.

Two things stand out in my mind from our time there: the stench that seemed to permeate everything—a combination of greasy spoon restaurant and body odour—and the odd feeling of numbness that had taken over my whole being. Nothing mattered. Nothing stirred me, not even the baby. I attended to her, just like Sol did, but I didn't love her. I didn't even find her cute or ugly. I didn't feel anything for my daughter, either, but what was even worse, I didn't care.

Sometimes I wondered if I was actually dead and I would literally pinch myself to make sure that I still had a body.

The room we were assigned looked onto the street and had two single beds, a crib, a bathroom, and a kitchenette with a two-burner stove-top and a small fridge. Mr. Johnson, the official who had welcomed us at the airport and taken us to the hotel, had put a few snacks in the fridge and provided us with food vouchers, but it took days for Sol and me to start eating. I don't think we even went out of the room for at least a week.

One of those nights, as I was looking out the window at the empty, lonely street, I heard Sol get up and walk towards me.

"The baby is not Miguel's," I heard her say.

I didn't respond—I was quite absorbed by the shimmering,

wet asphalt—but she continued.

"The baby's father is my torturer."

I heard the words, but they didn't make any sense to me. *What did she say? What does she mean?* I thought as I turned to look at my daughter.

Tears were streaming down Sol's face. I hugged her and rocked her in my arms while I repeated, "It's okay, my darling, it's okay," but I might as well have been a robot because I went through those motions and uttered those words without feeling a thing.

Nothing was said about the baby's father until many weeks later, when we had already moved to a basement suite on Thirty-seventh Avenue, near Main Street.

By then Sol's English had been assessed as "adequate," so she was working as a janitor at the Toronto Dominion Bank downtown, and I was taking an English course at Vancouver Community College. As my classes went from nine to three and Sol's job didn't start until five, we took turns looking after Tania.

Sol would come home close to midnight, so I would wait up for her with a hot cup of tea and a little treat, and we would talk for a while before going to bed.

One night, Sol brought up the issue of Tania's father again.

I was busying myself with the teapot, my back to my daughter, when I heard her say, "Mom, you have never said anything about Tania's father... You haven't told me how you feel about it... about

Miguel not being her biological father."

It was as if, all of a sudden, somebody had taken me by the shoulders and shaken me with such force that everything inside me began to crack and spin, my shattered insides pushing outwards at the speed of light. I felt my body explode. I screamed so loudly that Tania woke up. A few minutes later, the upstairs neighbours knocked on our door, wanting to know if burglars had broken into our suite.

I heard myself wail and grunt, swear and roar, as I threw every single plate, glass and cup in our kitchen cupboard against the wall.

When I finished, all I managed to do was laugh like a mad woman at the chaos I had caused: pieces of glass and china all over the floor, a crying baby in my daughter's arms, and an older couple looking absolutely ludicrous in their slippers and pajamas, their hair in disarray and their mouths uttering sounds in a language I couldn't understand.

After that night, everything began to hurt. If it wasn't my head, it was my back; if it wasn't my back, it was my hips; if it wasn't my hips, it was my shoulders, or my legs, or my feet. But what hurt the most was my chest, as if something dark and hideous, slimy and foul-smelling had exchanged places with my heart. It took me a while, but eventually I realized that "the thing," as I started calling it, was nothing other than hatred.

I hated Pinochet. I hated my son's murderer. I hated my sister for having turned my daughter in. I hated my daughter's torturer.

I hated my daughter for giving birth to the torturer's baby and I hated baby Tania. Above all, I hated myself for not having known to live life to the fullest when I was young; for not having accepted and loved my son for who he was; for having disapproved of my children's political views; for not having appreciated what I had. I hated myself for being alive, and for not having the guts to end it and leave this world once and for all.

But, even though I was drenched with hatred, there was a part of me that couldn't help noticing that Sol seemed to be at peace with herself. She doted on her baby and never complained about anything. She went to great lengths to cheer me up and to make life more pleasant for me. She would help me with my ESL homework, show up with little presents, offer me back rubs... All to no avail. I was utterly unhappy.

In the fall of 1974, my daughter was accepted as a graduate student at the University of British Columbia; that changed our lives completely. We moved to a unit in the student-housing complex, a cozy little house that felt like a mansion compared to the basement suite on Thirty-seventh Avenue, and we both began to see a psychologist through the Family Services Department of the university. Her name was Megan.

Little by little, I found the courage to tell Megan everything that had happened to us and she helped me to work through my pain. For the first time in more than a year, I was able to mourn my losses: Andresito, Miguel, my country, my friends, even my sister. I had tried hard to put Amparo out of my mind, but the hatred I felt for her wouldn't make room for oblivion. Megan made me realize that "forgetting" about her was not an option, that my mind and my heart would always remember her.

"Why don't you tell me what you like about her," she suggested.

"There's nothing I like about her—I don't even know her anymore," I answered, feeling my blood begin to boil.

"Did you like her before she turned your daughter in to the military?" she asked now.

"I'm not sure... I still loved her, but she had changed a lot, she had turned into a self-righteous, greedy woman, her stores and her money were the only important things in her life," I responded.

"What did you like about her before she became wealthy?" Megan pressed on.

In my mind's eye I could see Amparo the way she was as a young woman—warm, affectionate, cheerful—but also rebellious and strong-minded. I had to smile as I recalled how she drove my parents crazy; she always answered back in her own cocky way, something I would've never dared to do. Then I saw her as a small girl, her pudgy little body clad in a red swimming suit, her hair flying in the breeze as she skipped along on our way to the beach.

"You're smiling," Megan pointed out.

I told her what was on my mind, about our daily excursions to the beach with our grandmother.

"Where was that?" she wanted to know.

"In Arica, the northernmost city in Chile, we lived there when we were little," I explained.

Megan urged me to tell her about the excursions. "They sound like fun!" she exclaimed as she sat back in her chair, getting ready to listen.

So, I told her.

Every day, early in the morning, our grandma Carmen used to take me and Amparo fishing. We'd settle on the rocks with a line in our hands for what seemed like an eternity, waiting for the fish to bite. My sister and I never caught anything, but our grandma was an expert and would get a ton of smelts just like that. Once her basket was full, we'd get in the ocean and play in the waves. After a while we'd walk back home, singing and dancing to the rhythm of our own voices. By then, our parents were up; my mom had made coffee, got fresh bread from the bakery and set the table. Grandma would go straight into the kitchen to prepare the fish while Amparo and I were sent off to wash and dress ourselves. Then, our mom would braid our hair and finally we'd all sit at the table to enjoy the fried smelts with bread and butter.

Megan waited for a few moments before she spoke. "Soledad," she started, "those are wonderful, wonderful memories. I'm sure there are many more. Find them. Unbury them. Remember the sister you loved," she pleaded. "Even though she did something awful, she's still the same person you grew up with."

Megan also helped me to understand my sister's extraordinary accomplishments. She was a single woman in a male-dominated society, but that hadn't stopped her from becoming a very successful business woman.

"Yeah," I acknowledged, "obviously that must've taken a lot of perseverance and courage."

"And a lot of pushing and shoving. Even ruthlessness," she added.

I had to agree. Amparo had become ruthless.

"She obviously couldn't allow anything or anyone to undo what she had accomplished with so much effort," Megan suggested.

"To the extent of turning in her own niece?" I cried out, getting up from my chair and pacing around the room.

Megan got up and walked towards me. She put her hand on my shoulder before she spoke.

"Soledad, I'm not trying to justify what she did. What she did is unthinkable, abhorrent. I'm just trying to understand why she might've done it," she explained calmly.

But I never understood. I continued to unbury memories of our childhood and youth together, but could never come close to comprehending Amparo's actions on the day of the coup. Perhaps I didn't want to; I don't know. What I do know is that, with Megan's help, I was able to come to terms with my past, remember the people I loved, the places I had left behind, the colours and aromas of my previous life. It hurt, but there was love in my hurt. Most important of all, "the thing," the hatred in my chest, started to shrink.

I planted a garden in our little backyard and began to make pottery and paint watercolours again. Once in a while, I would pack myself a picnic, walk down to Spanish Banks, and spend the afternoon there with my clipboard, paints and brushes. I loved depicting English Bay: the buildings with their hundreds of wide-open eyes, and the mountains with their green forests and snow-capped peaks as the perfect backdrop. After a while, I also discovered the beauty in the huge logs strewn around the beach and, in the spring, when all Vancouver plants and trees seemed to explode with colour, I began to concentrate on the cherry blossoms, the rhododendrons, the camellias.

By then, Sol had several Chilean and Canadian friends and had helped to organize a committee in support of the resistance movement in our country. In between classes, political work and Tania, she was always on the go, but seemed content.

In September of 1975, fifteen months after our arrival in Vancouver, I became involved in the solidarity movement for the first time. In Santiago, I had served as a link between the political prisoners and members of the underground resistance, but since coming to Canada, I hadn't done anything against the dictatorship. Then, that year, when Sol and her friends organized a *peña* to commemorate the anniversary of the military coup, I offered to help.

My daughter was delighted and suggested that I be in charge of the *empanada*-making—after all, I had been a pastry-making teacher in Chile and I did make delicious *empanadas*, she argued. That's how I became the official, undisputed *empanada* maker in the community.

Our *peñas* attracted hundreds of people: Canadians of all ancestries, members of other immigrant groups, adults, youth and children. Chilean exiles participated and cooperated in myriad ways: singing the songs that were banned in Chile, performing folk dances, designing posters, preparing the hall, cleaning up. I had a team of men who did the shopping for the *empanadas* and a group of ladies who helped me make them.

The children also collaborated, decorating the space with their artwork and singing the songs that we taught them in the Spanish and Chilean culture classes we held at Douglas Park Community Centre on Saturday mornings.

That's how, little by little, with the help of my counselor and my community, I recovered my desire to live.

Around that time, one of Sol's professors offered me a job as her maid. I had graduated with honours from my English course, but I knew that most likely I would never be able to find work as a pastry-making teacher in Vancouver—I'd be required to have a Canadian teaching certificate, something that would take years and bundles of money to get. So, when Dr. Cohen offered me the opportunity, I took it.

The Cohens lived near Dunbar Street and Forty-first Avenue

in a huge, three-storey house with a beautiful garden in front, and two garages and a big yard in the back.

When I saw the house and found out that there were four children in the family, I prepared myself to work like a horse, but it turned out that there were machines to do everything—something I welcomed with great relief.

At the beginning I worked Mondays, Wednesdays and Fridays, but when Dr. Cohen realized that I was also an excellent cook, she asked me to work every day so that, in addition to doing the cleaning and taking care of the clothes, I could also prepare the family's dinner.

The Cohens' house was beautifully furnished and decorated, but what I loved the most were the bed sheets. In Chile, bed sheets had always been white and since coming to Canada we had been using second hand hospital sheets that had been given to us by an organization that helped refugees, but in this house, for the first time, I saw sheets in all kinds of colours and with a variety of motifs. The children's had miniature animals, balls, toys or flowers, and the adults' were striped or had geometric designs. So, when Dr. Cohen paid me for my first two weeks of work, I took the bus and went straight to The Bay to buy us new sheets: lime green with colourful flowers for Tania's crib, striped ones in different hues of yellow and orange for Sol, and checkered ones in aquamarine and blue for me.

I worked at Dr. Cohen's for more than six years, until the family left Vancouver and went to live in Los Angeles. Next, I began to supply La Quena Coffee House, our Latin American gathering place on Commercial Drive, with *empanadas* and cakes; that's how I continued to contribute to our household's finances until Sol got a well-paying job as a social worker and insisted that I slow down and spend more time making pottery and painting watercolours. By then I was already a "senior citizen," as people sixty-five years of age and older are called here, and started collecting my well-deserved government pension.

Now, I'm seventy-three years old and I will die before I turn seventy-four.

Dr. Feder broke the news to me yesterday. He didn't say it like that, but clearly, I will die soon. I have terminal cancer of the bones. The doctor suggested that I undergo chemotherapy and radiation treatment, but I declined. I don't want to end up looking like a soccer ball, my face swollen and full of spots, not a strand of hair on my head. I'd rather carry on with my life as normally as possible during the few months I have left.

I will die. Period. If I still believed in heaven and hell, I could find solace in thinking that I will go to heaven where I will have the joy of joining my son forever and ever. Most likely, I would also find Andrés, Miguel, Miss Blanca, Tito Ramírez and Gloria there. I'm sure I would go to heaven because I've never done any harm to anyone, although I must confess that it hasn't been for a lack of desire. But, as I don't believe in God or anything related to God anymore, all I know is that my spirit will stay alive in the memory of those who love me and whom I love: my daughter Sol, my granddaughter Tania and my friends.

I never thought I would live this long, but I'm glad I did: I lived to hear about Augusto Pinochet's imprisonment in England. Maybe the number one beast, the supreme master of all the torturers and murderers, will be tried and convicted for his crimes. Perhaps, justice will be done.

We celebrated for hours at the Russian Hall, singing, dancing, eating, drinking wine... It had been years since I'd last seen some of the Chileans who showed up and I had a hard time recognizing them, as I'm sure they had a hard time recognizing me. They all look ancient—the men, gray-haired and pot-bellied, and the women, plump, their hair dyed all sorts of gaudy colours and their faces evidently crisscrossed with wrinkles in spite of their attempt to hide them under a thick layer of make-up. I don't know why people have so much trouble accepting that they're getting old.

I'm also glad I lived this long so that I could witness Tania grow up to become the beautiful and generous young woman she is—an accomplished artist and an excellent hockey player, a coach and a mentor to little girls and an art therapist for teenagers in trouble with the law.

When, at age five, Tania announced that she wanted to play hockey, I almost had a heart attack. Hockey? A girl playing hockey?

But she was determined. She had got the idea at school, where the boys would wear Vancouver Canucks jerseys and talk endlessly about hockey.

By then Sol had graduated from university and we had moved to Mariposa Housing Co-op on Commercial Drive. So, on a Saturday morning, the three of us made our way to Britannia Community Centre and signed Tania up on the "Atom" team.

There was a swap meet at the rink that day, so we got her equipment secondhand for a greatly reduced price. Our little girl was ecstatic; as soon as we got home she wanted to try her helmet, the enormous shoulder and shin pads, the oversized jersey, the tiny skates. I burst out laughing when I saw the garter belt she had to wear to hold her wool hockey socks up and I laughed even harder when Sol explained that male hockey players also wear a garter belt.

When Tania wasn't playing hockey or going to school, she was drawing or painting. Our walls were always plastered with her portraits of Miguel, Andresito, Andrés, her pictures of the Andes, the Calle-Calle River, our house in Valdivia... She loved to listen to Sol's and my stories about Chile and then begged for more.

But, I must admit that she wasn't always the perfect little girl. Actually, as a teenager, she was obnoxious, stubborn and rebellious—even more so than Sol had been at that age. She was hardly ever home and, when she happened to be, she hid in her bedroom, listened to rock music at full blast and talked on the phone for hours on end.

She was friends with two Canadian girls who lived in our building and the three of them would go out dressed like slobs and looking like zombies—a thick layer of white paste on their faces and black lines around their eyes. One of those girls had dyed her hair purple and, one day, Tania announced that she was going to tint her own hair blue.

"I'm just letting you guys know so that you don't have a heart attack the next time you see me," she said nonchalantly as she opened the fridge, took out a soda and walked out of the kitchen towards her room.

Sol and I looked at each other with our mouths open.

"Tania, come here!" Sol ordered.

But the earsplitting slam-bang of my granddaughter's music was already making the whole house boom and shake.

The next day I made a point of parking myself in the hallway, near the front door, so that I could catch Tania on her way out to school. She was wearing a black outfit that even the poorest of the poor would've been embarrassed to be seen in: pants with slashes and rips all over, hiking boots that had never been near a tin of shoe polish and an oversized, shapeless sweater that made her look like a scarecrow.

She was so self-absorbed in those days that when she saw me standing by the door like a statue clad in a housecoat, she didn't find it odd at all.

"Excuse me, grandma," she said politely as she reached for the deadbolt.

"Not so fast, young lady," I replied firmly. Then I commanded my voice to turn softer. "I need to talk to you, my queen," I said, attempting to find her gaze.

She kept eluding my eyes.

"Tania! Look at me!" I finally shouted.

She did.

"You have beautiful, beautiful hair, my queen. Don't spoil it—those chemicals are terrible, they'll turn your hair to straw... Blue straw to boot," I said as gently as I could.

"I have to get to school, grandma," she offered for an answer as she tried to reach for the deadbolt once again.

I remained firmly in front of the door. "My queen, you don't have to be like those friends of yours... Let them look ugly and stupid if they want to. Don't follow their lead so blindly. You have enough brains to choose for yourself, you know that."

She stood still, her head lowered. Then she responded, "I'll think about it grandma."

I gave her a peck on the cheek and moved out of the way.

Tania did not dye her hair blue after all. She remained hard-headed and obnoxious for a couple of years, but, little by little, her rebelliousness began to fade away. By then she had started to dress like a normal human being and had new friends—nice, regular-looking kids that she invited home after school.

In Chile, I had sewn out of need—store-bought clothes were outrageously expensive—but here in Canada, I began doing it for pleasure. I still remember an outfit I made for Tania when she turned fifteen: a pair of black and white plaid pants with a narrow cuff and a collarless, double-breasted white blouse with three-quarter length sleeves. They had been featured as the latest fashion in Vogue Magazine, so my granddaughter was ecstatic when she opened my present and saw her new outfit. It fit her perfectly and made her look like a movie star.

Another good reason to have lived this long is that I got to meet Sadu's family. Sadu is a computer animator and has been Tania's boyfriend for almost a year now; a good-looking, thoughtful boy of Indian descent, but who could very well pass for a Chilean: slim, neither tall nor short, black hair, dark skin and brown eyes.

The family lives in Burnaby, in a huge house with a beautiful, manicured garden. The house itself is also very nice and elegant—Persian rugs, antique furniture and Indian art pieces on the walls. Resting on the sofa and armchairs, there were some cushions that really caught my eye. They had designs which at first I thought had been created with sequins, but then realized that what I had taken for sequins were actually tiny mirrors attached to the cloth with flat-loop stitch. I can't even begin to imagine the amount of work involved!

This was the first time I tried Indian food, even though Sol and Tania love it and have invited me many times to join them at a restaurant they frequent in Gastown. The truth is that I seldom enjoy eating outside of my own home. Undoubtedly, once in a while it *is* nice to sit comfortably and be waited on, but generally speaking, I prefer my own cooking.

All the dishes at Sadu's house were delicious—very savoury and, in some cases, quite spicy. They reminded me of the food from the north of Chile, prepared with all kinds of hot peppers and condiments.

Sadu's dad is a professor of Punjabi language and literature at the university and his mom is a lawyer. They were very well informed about Chile and the gentleman even showed us an anthology of Pablo Neruda's poetry translated into Punjabi. It made me feel very proud. The mother gave us her opinion about Pinochet's case—she thinks there are more than enough grounds to extradite and try him for crimes against humanity.

We talked about all kinds of subjects: Canadian politics and hockey; Chilean soccer; Indian cricket; this, that and the other. What we didn't talk about was my illness, even though I know that they know about it and that was the reason why they invited us over now and not later: because I'm going to die and they wanted to meet me before I leave the planet. That made me sad. Since people learned about it, my condition has become a sort of mute, gigantic shadow that follows me everywhere. Now I'm treated differently. "Do you need this? Do you need that? Are you feeling okay? Are you comfortable? Are you sure I can't get you anything?" everybody insists. *Yes. How about a brand new life—an easy one this time, please,* I feel like saying. But of course I don't.

I must admit that I do feel sorry for Sol and Tania. They are devastated by the news of my cancer. They dote on me as if I were the Queen of England. I can't stand it. I've had to get mad at them a couple of times because they really get on my nerves, but then they cry, and I cry and it's all a big drama.

Tania is the more emotional one of the two. I had to chuckle a few days ago—she got mad at me for having cancer!

"Why didn't you take good care of yourself, grandma?" she yelled. I had asked her to come into my room so that she could choose the watercolours and pottery pieces she wants for herself.

"What do you mean, my queen?" I asked, feeling quite confused.

"Well... You're too young to die! If you had exercised and eaten organic food, most likely you wouldn't have got this horrible illness!" she responded as she examined one of my watercolours.

I chuckled, walked up to her and took her in my arms. "My queen, I'm not too young to die. *Your dad* was too young to die. *My son* was too young to die. If you consider everything I lived through, I've had a very long life." I whispered in her ear.

She sobbed in my arms for a while.

"I don't want you to die, grandma," she said finally as she wiped her face with the back of her hands.

"I know, I know. But you have to let me go, my queen. I'm ready... You will let me go, right?" I asked her now, taking her by the shoulders and looking into those beautiful green eyes of hers.

She nodded.

Most of the time, Sol tries to put on a strong face, to show me that she's prepared for my imminent death. But I know her better than that; she gets overly talkative and her voice goes way up when she's pretending to be tough. She's taken it upon herself to do a lot of the housework, but the poor thing is terrible at it. She takes a couple of steps this way and another couple of steps the other way with the vacuum cleaner and that's it. "Okay, all right, all done!" she exclaims cheerfully while I shudder at the dust balls under the table.

But, at this point in life, who cares about a few dust balls? I don't. What I do care about is dying in peace and I think I've got that covered. I've done my share: I've loved my daughter and granddaughter with all my heart and I've tried my best to be a good human being.

I even got to have a very good relationship with Sol, something that before the coup I never thought would be possible. When my daughter was a teenager and then a young woman, seldom were we able to communicate in a meaningful way. She didn't want to hear my advice about anything and, later on, our opposing political views pushed us even further apart.

The coup changed all that. In the face of pain and despair, we became close and didn't hesitate to show our love and affection for each other during our visits at the concentration camp. But it was here in Canada that we were finally able to talk, to express our feelings and thoughts not only as mother and daughter, but also as friends, parents to little Tania, and, eventually, as "conspirators."

One stormy night, after having mulled it over for quite a while, I mustered the courage to tell her about the numbness and the pain that had taken hold of me for months on end when we had first got to Vancouver, about "the thing" that had lodged in my chest, my regrets and renewed desire to live. I apologized for not having understood her when she was younger, for having rejected her values and beliefs.

She apologized to me for not having been a more thoughtful daughter, more attentive to my needs, more sympathetic to my loneliness following Andrés' death, more understanding of the challenges of having a gay son.

Our nightly conversations became a sort of a ritual. After putting Tania to bed, we would sit at the kitchen table to drink a cup of tea and talk. We told and retold each other our respective sagas in the aftermath of the coup, as we recalled more and more details. We cried and laughed together.

And then, one night, I confided that I envied her apparent contentment.

"How come you seem to be at peace with yourself? Aren't you sad? Aren't you angry? Don't you hate your torturer?" I asked.

My daughter smiled at me and responded, "I don't know for sure. I guess my ideals helped me to live through the horrible things that were done to me... Also, somehow, I do understand why the dictatorship had to torture and kill people like Miguel, Andresito and Gloria, had to torture people like me. What they really wanted was to kill our ideals; of course they didn't succeed. But I think that the most important reason for my contentment is Tania. I decided to put aside my own pain so that I could offer Tania the best of myself."

With a quivering voice, I confessed to her that for a long time I hadn't felt anything for the baby and had even come to hate her as much as I hated everybody else, including myself.

"I don't blame you," Sol replied as she took my hand. "I know, I know... How do you bring yourself to love the torturer's daughter?" she mused. "I will tell you my secret."

That's when she let me in on her "conspiracy." She related how she had decided to take revenge on the dictatorship by bringing up Tania to be a good person—to be Miguel's daughter, not the torturer's.

"It's about retribution," she stated, her voice, loud, her touch on my hand, firm. "This is our justice, mom; there will be no other justice. Andresito's murderer and my torturer will never be tried, our friends' executioners will never be tried, who knows who is responsible for Miguel and Gloria's disappearances. Pinochet has been detained in London, but I bet you that sooner rather than later he will let go, he'll die of old age and never be tried. Tania is our revenge, our justice."

We made a pact: we would never tell anyone about Tania's biological father and we would outdo ourselves to bring up the girl to be an exemplary human being.

By the time Sol and I had this conversation, I had already fallen in love with my granddaughter and took great pleasure in pampering her. How not to love her pudgy little legs, her beautiful green eyes, her silky dark hair, her wavy mouth and turned-up nose? How not to adore her husky voice and fiery spirit?

The morning after I made the pact with Sol, I woke up thinking that Tania was the queen of our lives; she would have a life of happiness and peace, as Gabriela Mistral had wished for herself and her friends in her poem "We Would All Be Queens."

In those verses, the Nobel laureate reminisces about her childhood in the Elqui Valley and about three girls with whom she used to play: Rosalía, Efigenia and Soledad. As they climbed the mountains, ran about the orchards and swam in the river, the four friends would muse about their future and talk about the life of gratification and joy they would all achieve, their dreams and hopes fulfilled forever; they would all be queens:

Todas íbamos a ser reinas

We would all be queens
We said it in a trance and believed it to be true
We would all be queens
And our kingdoms would be vast...
Have fruits, trees of milk, trees of bread...
We would all be queens and truly reign

The first time I read the poem, I was elated to see that one of Gabriela's friends was called Soledad. As I grew older and came to understand that those girls' dreams had never been fulfilled, I wondered about what the future had in store for me. I was so determined to be happy! I was so convinced that I would be happy, that I would become a queen!

But, just like the Soledad in the poem, destiny had a different plan for me.

How could I have ever imagined that this plan would include Tania—Sol and her torturer's daughter? Had destiny conspired with a ruthless, soulless dictatorship to cause us even more pain and despair? Was destiny's ambition to create a human being that would take after a psychopath and a rapist?

If it was, destiny failed and Tania, Sol and I succeeded.

Tania became a queen.

We got our retribution.

I can die in peace.

Vancouver and Chile

1985-1986

Sol

At the end of October, 1985, I agreed to join Operación Aconcagua.

It had been a luminous, blue day and from the confines of my office I had been admiring the crisp colours of the autumn leaves as they danced outside my window. Tania was eleven years old and my mom, sixty. My daughter was an exemplary student, a talented artist and hockey player, but, most importantly, a sociable and good-hearted little girl. My mom made decent money supplying La Quena Coffee House with baked goods, and appeared content and satisfied with her life.

I had a good, meaningful job working with immigrant women, but I wasn't satisfied with *my* life. Something was sorely missing. It wasn't love; it had taken me years, but I had finally fallen in love with Martin, a Social Studies teacher and union leader, originally from Toronto, who had been an active participant in the solidarity movement with Chile from the very beginning.

When we first met, I couldn't understand Martin's interest in me. I still hadn't gotten over Miguel and the ghosts of my beloved dead ones haunted me day and night. I was obsessed with death and the dead.

But Martin listened to my stories. He let me ramble as he anointed my deformed and parched nipples with flax seed oil, offered me a bowl of his Manhattan-style clam chowder, brushed my hair, guided me through the nooks and crannies of a Vancouver that I would've never discovered on my own. That's how I learned to enjoy tofu and purple eggplant hot-pot at The Green Door, savour a cappuccino at Café Italia, figure out how old the gigantic cedars at Stanley Park are...

Martin gave me back my curiosity about life. With him, life stopped being just memories, dreams and nightmares; I began to enjoy the here and now. Through his hands, I felt the suppleness of my own skin once again, the curve of my neck, the humidity of my desires. Martin confirmed something that I had doubted for a long time: I was alive.

On October 10, 1985, I got a call from Mariana, one of the leaders of the solidarity movement with the Chilean resistance. She wanted to meet with Martin and me for a coffee. That evening, the three of us sat around a table at Café Continental. I was nervous, as I didn't know what to expect—there was a certain solemnity to the occasion. No preliminary joking around this time, no small talk. Mariana went straight to the point.

"Combatants from both inside and outside Chile are being recruited for an important armed operation. Would you two be willing to take part?" she asked point blank.

Martin and I looked at each other. He was obviously taken aback as much as I was.

Mariana didn't wait for an answer. "In case you're wondering, you will have to live underground for close to a year prior to the operation and indefinitely afterwards, depending on the circumstances. And the work itself will be very meticulous, even boring. Mainly, it'll involve researching places, people's routines... Providing logistical support—safe houses, vehicles, that kind of thing," she explained, looking at both of us over the rim of her glasses which were now resting on the tip of her nose. "Nothing heroic, but still risky," she added, pushing her glasses back up.

Now she *did* wait for a reaction.

Martin was quick and adamant. "I'm in," he declared.

"Good," Mariana responded, nodding.

Then she turned to me. "What about you, Sol?"

I wanted to say Yes, but couldn't. I had to think about it, talk it over with my mother, decide whether or not I was prepared to leave Tania behind.

"You'll have to give me a few days to make up my mind. You know I have a daughter..." I reminded her.

"Yes, of course," she replied. "Please get back to me in the next couple of days, okay?" she requested, getting up and starting to put her coat on.

"Wait," Martin called out.

Mariana sat down again.

"Please tell us more," he pleaded. "Can you tell us about the operation itself?" he inquired, searching Mariana's eyes.

"No, I can't," she responded calmly. "I don't know what the operation is about and I don't want to know either. The less we all know, the better. I've just been directed to ask you two to participate and to explain in general terms the conditions and the kind of work you'll be doing," she clarified.

That night, I sat on my daughter's bed for a long time as I watched her sleep and attempted to come to terms with Mariana's proposal. Tania had turned out to be everything I had hoped for and more. My mom and I had been amply rewarded for our efforts; so far, we had gotten the retribution we had striven for.

For years, I had believed that this would be enough to satisfy my desire for justice. Tania had come to represent the better world I had dreamed of as a young woman; she embodied the peace, balance and beauty contained in the word "justice".

But as time went on and the dictatorship in Chile became more and more entrenched, I began to feel a desperate urge to fight more actively for the social justice I had envisioned for my country when I was young: an end to abject poverty, the right to a healthy life, to education, to freedom. I yearned to see the Señoras Guillerminas of Chile building their own, dignified homes once again; reading world literature; writing poetry; witnessing their kids develop as worthy human beings with a future of hope ahead of them. All along, I had been a tireless participant in the solidarity movement in Vancouver, but that work—while important and worthwhile in itself—just seemed to whet my ambition to become more involved. I wanted to be part of the underground armed resistance to the dictatorship inside Chile. Now the opportunity had presented itself but, while I was excited, I couldn't imagine spending a long time away from Tania. And what if I never came back? I couldn't bear the thought of her pain.

I knew that Chile was going through a critical period: from 1983 on, the resistance movement had become much more open and massive and the regime had responded with brutal repression. At the same time, Pinochet had been making efforts to change his public image, to give the impression of being more open and tolerant while, in reality, his 1980 constitution had ensured that his economic and political model would dominate Chile for a long time. Now the resistance movement needed to intensify its work, trigger a radical change, avert the prospects of a watered-down transformation into a pseudo-democracy. I had been offered the opportunity to take an active part in that revolutionary work and had to decide whether I would say Yes or No.

I explained my dilemma to my mom. She was in the kitchen, chopping onions for that evening's stew. She stopped and listened to me attentively, then she rinsed her hands, wiped them on the front of her apron and invited me join her at the table. She sat very straight, looking ahead of her, past me; then she looked out the window and, finally, directly at me.

"You have to go, Sol. Tania will be fine. I will take good care of her," she stated resolutely.

"But I promised myself that I would be a good mother to her, that I would be there for her," I responded, choking back the tears. "How can I be a good mother if I leave her?" I cried out, and started to sob.

My mom got up and came around the table. She held my head against her stomach. I could smell the piquancy of the onions in her apron. Then she crouched down and cupped my face with her hands.

"Sol, my darling daughter, life *is* messy and confusing, you know that. We say one thing, but without even realizing it, do the opposite. We think we'll be able to do this, that or the other, only to find out down the road that we just can't, that things have changed. Things do change. Besides, you have been a good mother. You *have* been there for Tania. Now you are faced with a hard choice, but at least it's an honourable one. You wouldn't be leaving her for some stupid, selfish reason... Besides, Tania's almost twelve, she'll be fine. She'll miss you, but she'll be fine," she contended.

"*Ay!* My knees are killing me," she complained.

She got up, walked back to the counter and resumed the chopping. "If *I* were young and was asked, I would go," she declared. "And if I had the wherewithal, I would kill my son's murderer, your torturer *and* Pinochet with my own hands," she added as she worked the knife with an extra dose of zeal.

"It's not about revenge, mom; it's about justice," I replied.

"I know, I know," she mumbled as she tossed the onions into the pot.

The next day I let Mariana know that I would join the operation.

Martin and I arrived in Santiago on January 14, 1986, disguised as Mr. and Mrs. Gordon, a professional couple taking a leave of absence from their well-paid Canadian jobs in order to experience life in Chile. Martin's documentation indicated that he had been born in Vancouver, while mine stated that I had arrived there from my native Chile in 1972. The implication was that I was the daughter of a well-to-do couple that had left the country escaping the socialist policies of Salvador Allende.

We rented a house on a tree-lined street near Providencia Avenue, right in the heart of the city. As stereotypical Canadians, we were pleasant and courteous to our neighbours, but kept mainly to ourselves; as stereotypical residents of a middle-class sector of Santiago, we had a maid, Eliana, and a gardener, José, both of whom were in fact members of the resistance movement. The four of us formed one of the cells in charge of logistical support for the operation. Eliana was our leader and our connection to the upper echelons of the organization.

Eliana was a tall, dark, not-so-young woman with a sharp memory and a logical mind. Once a week we would sit down to go over our research. Martin, José and I had to consult the pages and pages of notes we had taken during our excursions, but Eliana related her findings from sheer memory as she drew diagrams and charts on a piece of paper. She listened attentively to each one of our reports, scribbled a few hasty words, and at the end of the session summarized everybody's research and drew general conclusions while sketching another set of diagrams and charts. I will never forget Eliana's drawings: cryptic words enclosed in perfect squares and circles connected by arrows going in different directions. I never understood them, but it was obvious that she wasn't making them for us, but rather for herself; she needed to draw so as to have a clear picture of her conclusions in her own mind.

I never warmed up to Eliana. I admired her immensely, but found her reserved beyond the call of duty. Obviously, I knew that we couldn't talk about anything remotely personal, but what about a little bit of camaraderie, of joking around? I thought it was quite amusing, for example, that I had to dress like a stuck-up Señora, something I had never done in my life, while she arrived looking like the perfect maid—shabby coat, flat, lumpy shoes and a bun on top of her head. But we never connected at that level. We just worked together.

José, on the other hand, was a warm, jovial little guy who didn't hesitate to tell a joke, give a hug, and talk a mile a minute about everything and anything, from the state of the world to the eating habits of chimpanzees. He would arrive in a beat-up pick-up truck overflowing with hoes, spades, rakes, and all kinds of garden-related implements, clad in coveralls and a straw hat. He would call Martin *gringuito* which, according to Eliana, was "incorrect" because we were not supposed to comment on our comrades' origins. But, even though Martin spoke very good Spanish, it was obvious that he was from an English-speaking country, so José would just roll his eyes and keep calling Martin *gringuito*, in spite of Eliana's disapproval.

I never knew if Eliana and José had partners and children. I often wondered about it as I spent more and more time in their company. What were they like in their regular world? What did they do for a living? I had the strong feeling that Eliana was a loner. I couldn't imagine her in love, vulnerable, in an intimate relationship. My picture of José, on the other hand, was as the head of a big, boisterous family; I imagined him surrounded by children, going to see a Colo-Colo game with his friends, making *empanadas* for Sunday's lunch. Actually, one particularly hot day in late February, he did show up with delicious *empanadas* for everyone.

Experiencing life underground as Martin's partner was a real blessing. We could talk about our families and friends, and reminisce together about life in Vancouver. I don't know how I would've fared if I hadn't had that outlet. Nobody else knew about Tania, but I could entrust Martin with my fears and dreams, my anxiety, my feelings of guilt. He understood how much I missed her, how hard it was to be away from her. Furthermore, and perhaps most importantly, he would comfort me with kisses and cuddles.

At the same time, he would confess his feelings of inadequacy to me, explain the difficulties he had understanding Chilean cultural norms, discuss the challenges of having to operate in a language that he didn't feel completely comfortable in. I had never imagined that Martin could feel unsure of himself—he had always appeared like a kind of superman to me. In Vancouver he had helped me to overcome my traumas. In Santiago, our relationship became more balanced as I also had the opportunity to provide him with support.

Our cell's first task was to do a thorough exploration of the valley of the Aconcagua river —a canyon just north-east of Santiago. After a few months, we got to know the area thoroughly: every inch and turn of the highway and the exact location and orientation of every bridge; traffic patterns on different days and at all times; what you could see and not see from every vantage point; all the villages and their layouts; every establishment, their hours of operation and type of clientele.

Life underground, away from my daughter, my mother and my regular life, was like a black tunnel sporadically sprinkled with splashes of colour and a bright, beautiful light at its very end. As time went on, I had come to believe not only that we would survive the operation, but also that we would be successful. However, that light, that goal, was far away and while every day of meticulous, unheroic tasks took us closer and closer to it, a good deal of my thoughts and dreams were devoted to Tania.

I would constantly look at my watch and figure out what time it was in Vancouver so that I could picture my daughter going through her daily and weekly routines. Now, she was on her way to her hockey practice. Now, she was at school. Was she doing Math or Reading? Now she was at her weekly painting class at Emily Carr Institute. Now, she was having dinner with my mom. Now, she was watching cartoons on television. Now, she was going to bed...

In addition to my mom, there were a few comrades who knew about the real purpose of our trip to Chile, as they had become our "rearguard"—the people in charge of raising the funds needed to carry out our work. But the story we told Tania and the rest of our friends before leaving Vancouver, was that I had been asked to work with women's groups in the *barrios*, under the auspices of the Vicariate of Solidarity. The sacrifice of being apart from each other for about a year would be worth it, as many, many people would benefit from my knowledge and experience.

As I perused maps of the Aconcagua Valley and drove our SUV up and down the canyon making notes of everything I saw, I wondered about my alleged reason to have come back to Chile. I asked myself how real the need for my expertise really was. Perhaps, once we got to the end of the tunnel, once we got to the bright beautiful light I envisioned in my head and were living in the "new" future, there would be an opportunity for me to make a contribution as a social worker and not as a combatant.

As far as Martin was concerned, he had always wanted to come to Chile, particularly after so many years of anti-dictatorial solidarity work in Vancouver. So, his part of the story came naturally: he would take advantage of this opportunity to join me and, once in Santiago, he would look for a job teaching English.

Once a week I would post a letter to my daughter and my mom, and once a month I would call them collect from a pay phone. As their letters to me had to follow a circuitous path, sometimes I would get them weeks and even months late. At least we had our monthly telephone conversations in which I spoke enthusiastically about a series of fictitious events—just as I did in my letters—and Tania and my mother updated me on their lives in Vancouver.

While it took me days to recover from those calls, they also kept me going. Things were under control; Tania was fine; my mom was fine; Martin and I were fine; our tasks were moving along; the light at the end of the tunnel appeared closer.

At the beginning of August we rented a house in the town of Cerro Colorado, right at the entrance to the canyon, which became the operation's headquarters. The grounds were extensive and, in addition to the mansion-like main dwelling, there was a swimming pool, a tennis court, ample gardens and a coach house. As important as its size and versatility, the property was in a secluded spot and was encircled by a tall, electrified wall.

Our explanation to the landlord was that Martin was a Canadian United Church minister who would be offering Bible study seminars to groups of young people for the next few months. The man was delighted. Not only would he be renting the house to a trustworthy couple, but he would also be paid in dollars.

The first one to come to see the place was Alejandra, the *compañera* in charge of all logistical support; then, Jorge showed up—the top leader for the whole operation. Laura, the physical training instructor, dropped by next and, finally, Mauricio, who looked after the weapons and came to check on dry and safe storage spaces.

These visits would break the monotony of our days and add a splash of colour to "life in the tunnel," as I had come to call it. I found it both extraordinary and ironic that each one of our lives depended on the others' loyalty and efficiency, even though we had never met before and knew nothing about one another. So, I would observe my comrades' features, their ways of carrying themselves, the light in their eyes, their smiles, and try to connect them to somebody I knew and loved. Alejandra, for example, reminded me of Maria—the beautiful woman who had brought me back to life at Cuatro Álamos concentration camp; Jorge's honey eyes were very much like my brother Andresito's; Laura was tall, blonde and blue-eyed, just like my friend Silvia. Mauricio was the exception. I didn't have to wonder about trusting or not trusting him and I didn't have to think of anybody else when I met him. Mauricio had been an important part of my youth.

The day I opened the gate for Mauricio, I had to cover my mouth with my hand, so as not to yell out his real name: Carloncho! We lingered in a tight embrace as we whispered greetings in each other's ears. He wanted to know how my mom was.

"Don't tell me anything else, *compañera* Rosa," he added, as he perceived that I was struggling with my urge to fill him in on the details of our lives. "I just want to know how she is."

"She's great, she's just fine," I responded, wiping off the tears.

Nobody else in the organization ever learned that Carloncho and I had known each other as kids. Not even Martin. There was no need to tell them, as the information we had on each other's lives was old and of no consequence to our current situation. During the many months that we worked together, Carloncho and I mentioned our days in Valdivia only once.

"I was truly in love with your brother, you know," he whispered, as we stacked boxes of bullets in one of the bedrooms' closets.

"I know... and he loved you too," I responded with a knot in my throat. Then, I uttered the words I had never said while my brother was still alive. "I'm sorry about that day in the kitchen... When I called you faggots and threw the cast iron pan at the two of you..."

He laughed wholeheartedly. "You were something to reckon with, *compañera* Rosa, something to reckon with..." Then he turned, looked at me in the eye and stated in a hushed, but clear, voice, "You were just a kid, Sol, just a kid. You have nothing to be sorry about."

Was he still in the closet? Did he have a new partner? I was dying to know more about Carloncho's life as I was also dying to tell him about Tania, our years in Canada. But I knew better. Besides, it wouldn't have worked anyway, as I was sure he would've stopped me in my tracks and scolded me with a wagging finger. So, we only discussed business, just like we did with the rest of the group, but there was a silent complicity between the two of us, an intimate comfort in knowing that we shared a common history and were both seeking justice at the same time, in the same place.

At the end of August, Jorge, Mauricio, Alejandra, Laura, Eliana and José came to stay with us in Cerro Colorado. Jorge, Mauricio and Alejandra would be part of the operation; Laura would continue to work on maintaining everybody's physical fitness; and Eliana and José would collaborate more closely with Martin and me on the now urgent logistical tasks: renting several vehicles, preparing the house and getting enough supplies to lodge and feed a large group of people, buying the clothes that the combatants would wear during and after the operation, ensuring that the underground clinic that had been set up in Santiago in order to treat possible casualties was ready to go, and completing the plans for the group's retreat.

The first of September, the rest of the combatants arrived. They were dressed in youthful outfits and carried bibles, hymnals and guitars in their hands. When we first rented the house, we had placed a beautiful bronze cross on the gate and hung a small church bell from one of the beams in the front porch. Now that all the "students" had arrived, the bell served the dual purpose of having the neighbours believe that we were, indeed, holding Bible study seminars and announcing the beginning of different activities throughout the day: wake-up time; morning work-out; change of guard; "mass," which would always end with loud religious singing; breakfast; "study sessions," which had to do with going over every detail of the operation; and so on. Most of the evenings were spent playing ping-pong or chess.

For most of that week, Eliana, José, Martin and I were checking on security houses, collecting travel documents, verifying escape routes...

The excitement and the tension among all of us were evident. We were almost at the end of the tunnel. Having a good night of rest became difficult. The collective amount of adrenaline in our bodies must have been enormous. In the middle of the night, the place resembled more a haunted house than military headquarters—ghosts meandering around in silence. Unable to sleep, a few of us would sit in the kitchen, in the dark, and sip on a cup of tea without uttering a word. Others would just continue to wander, incapable of staying put.

The afternoon of Saturday, September 6, Alejandra ordered everybody into the living room. It was a cool, foggy day and I remember thinking, as I wrapped myself in a shawl and sat in one of the armchairs, *This is it. In a few hours it will be all over.*

Jorge was the last one to come in. He looked at all of us with his honey-coloured eyes, smiled, and then spoke, his voice calm, but firm. "Brothers and sisters, the moment we have all been awaiting is upon us. Tomorrow, at around six fifteen in the evening, we will have the honour of carrying out justice on behalf of all of those who have been murdered and those who have suffered under the ruthless rule of the dictatorship. Tomorrow, Augusto

272

Pinochet will be travelling back to Santiago from his weekend house in the town of Mirador. It will be our task to eliminate him. We will execute the tyrant."

The air in the room became thick with emotion. My own chest was about to explode, as images of my dear dead and disappeared galloped through my mind: Miguel, Andresito, Gloria, Tito, Miss Blanca, Señora Guillermina, Don Arnulfo, Nicolasa... Then I thought about my mom, about Tania; about how my daughter had been conceived and my determination to bring her up to be a good person. Now we were about to achieve a broader, more collective kind of justice; one that would trigger irreversible social and political changes.

That night, Martin and I made urgent love and fell asleep in each other's arms. When I awoke, the sun was streaming into the room. Spring had finally arrived. It was six fifteen in the morning. Only twelve more hours until Chile's reality took a drastic change.

Little by little, the house came alive. At eight o'clock I rang the bell and by nine we were all singing "A Mighty Fortress is my God" at the top of our lungs. The day dragged on. The cooking team made *cazuela* and tomato salad, but nobody had much of an appetite.

In the afternoon, each contingent retired to a separate room to go over their strategy, check their weapons one last time and get dressed for the operation; they would be wearing street clothes with sweat suits over top. That way, when the operation was finished, they could remove the sweat suits and be ready to retreat looking like regular people.

Martin, Eliana, José and I collected our belongings and loaded them into our respective vehicles. Then we cleaned the house and the grounds, put the garbage in José's truck and got ready to take our leave.

At six o'clock, the weapons were loaded, the drivers were behind their wheels and the rest of the combatants were lining up in the hallway, waiting to jump into their corresponding vehicles. Martin was at the gate, ready to open it. I was standing by the telephone. The call from the *compañera* who had been watching the road from her second-story room at Hostería Juanita in the town of San Patricio, up the canyon, came in at exactly six fifteen. Pinochet's convoy was on its way.

When I hung up the phone, I turned to see everyone looking at me expectantly. "The tyrant is coming," I stated in a strong, clear voice. Everybody ran to their vehicles and, in a flash, they were gone. Martin jumped into the driver's seat of our car and drove out. I closed the gate, got in, and we were off to the Santiago international airport.

For a few minutes, we drove in absolute silence. My heart was pounding in my chest, my throat, my temples and inside my ears. I breathed in deeply and told myself to stay calm. Everything would be all right. Everything had been taken care of. The operation would be successful. But my mind was racing: had our comrades already intercepted Pinochet's convoy? Was there a battle going on at this very moment? Would regular radio programming be interrupted by an urgent news flash? I turned the radio on.

"Turn the radio off," Martin ordered in a hoarse, low voice. "You're forgetting our plan. Turn the radio off and concentrate on what we have to do. It's not over yet. We have to get to the airport and make that plane."

He was right. The orders were to not seek information about the operation until we were out of the country. That way, we could continue to play our roles in the calmest way possible. Besides, whatever happened was now out of our hands. We had done everything that had been required of us and the time had come to focus on our own retreat.

The trip between Cerro Colorado and the Santiago airport took forever. The fifty minute drive felt like hours. Nothing appeared out of the ordinary. Life in the outskirts of Santiago went on as usual.

We got to the airport, returned the rented car and proceeded to the main terminal. As soon as we went in, we saw groups of people gathered in front of television monitors, uttering hushed expressions of astonishment. The operation had taken place and the news was out.

I did my best to keep my mind blank and, as we walked towards the Iberia desk, began to talk sprightly to Martin about the excitement of travelling to Spain in September, now that the European summer was coming to an end and all the tourists had gone home.

"It'll just be the *madrileños* and us," I declared as I offered Martin a big smile.

As a response, he put his arm around my shoulder, squeezed it, and smiled back.

We were playing our well-rehearsed roles as a fairly affluent foreign couple in our mid-thirties; the roles that had allowed us to perform our underground activities undetected. We were dressed in designer clothes and carried our belonging in expensive luggage. There was nothing suspicious about us whatsoever.

By now people in line were talking about the operation, but we continued to appear disinterested, absorbed in our own little world. When we got to the desk, we presented our tickets and passports and, in no time, had checked our luggage and were holding our boarding passes on our way to the gate. We made it through the immigration wicket with no glitches and proceeded to the waiting room.

There, it became impossible not to pay attention to what was happening. The announcer on the television screen repeated the news of the operation against Pinochet's convoy in the Aconcagua Valley, while explaining that there were no images available at this time, as the road to the canyon had been closed and the media was not allowed in. Similarly, it was not yet clear what the results of the operation were.

As soon as we sat down, the woman next to me leaned over and half-whispered while pointing at the television, "There was a terrorist attempt on President Pinochet's life."

I faked surprise and disgust, turned to Martin and repeated the woman's words in English.

"Oh my God!" shouted Martin, as he got up and joined the group gathered in front of the monitor.

That night, we left Santiago without knowing the results of the operation. The next morning, when we got to Madrid, we found out that Pinochet had not been killed. Five of his bodyguards had, but the rocket directed at his car had not exploded. The dictator had escaped unscathed. There had been no casualties among our *compañeros* and none of them had been caught. They had all escaped unharmed. A state of siege had been declared and poor neighbourhoods were being raided and combed for subversive elements. Many people, among them leaders of anti-dictatorial organizations, had been incarcerated. Later on, we would also learn that in the middle of the night, four unarmed leftists, including journalist José Carrasco, had been kidnapped from their respective homes and murdered, their bruised and bullet-ridden bodies left in public places for everybody to see the next morning.

I have a vague recollection of the next five weeks as we pretended to be tourists in Spain and France. These were countries I had always yearned to visit, but, under the circumstances, all I wanted was something impossible to achieve: to go back to the house in Cerro Colorado and get together with the rest of my *compañeros* and *compañeras* so that we could talk about what had happened and find out exactly what had gone wrong.

Where were they now? According to our plans, most would be leaving the city the very evening of the operations, just like us, while a few would be staying in Santiago under cover. It was a relief to hear that nobody had been hurt and that the arrangements made by our cell had been successful, but what was foremost in Martin's and my minds was the fact that the goal of the operation, the elimination of Augusto Pinochet, had not been achieved. We had failed. Now, the dictator had more excuses than ever to use extreme repression, play victim and entrench himself even more doggedly in his seat of power.

Bits and pieces of the operation unfolded in the newscasts as the days went by, but it was difficult to figure out what the truth was. Why had the rocket aimed at Pinochet not exploded? Mauricio, who had been in charge of looking after the weapons, must've been devastated. But then, other reports didn't blame the weapons themselves, only the fact that they had not been used properly—that particular bazooka had been fired at too short a range, thus preventing the rocket's internal mechanism from falling into place and exploding.

While most of Pinochet's bodyguards had been slow to respond to the attack and, in many cases, had even attempted to escape by rolling off the road and down the hill, the dictator's personal chauffeur had been quick and efficient: in a flash he had backed up, turned the car around and started driving back towards Mirador. Our comrades had attacked the car at close range but, given that it was bulletproof, the ammunition had just bounced off.

Among the many disappointing reports, there was one that gave me and Martin a good laugh. Our comrades had actually fooled the police and the military during their escape, at the end of the operation. They had pretended to be members of Pinochet's secret police by placing flashing emergency lights and sirens on the roofs of their cars and pointing rifles through the open windows, in a military fashion. When the police saw them coming, they didn't hesitate to lift the barriers so that they could go through. In the meantime, dozens of military vehicles were driving in the opposite direction, up the canyon, towards the spot of the attack. As the "secret police" convoy continued its race towards Santiago at a hundred and fifty kilometers an hour, these vehicles moved to the shoulder of the road so as not to slow them down.

We got back to Vancouver on Thanksgiving Day. It was a beautiful, autumn morning and the streets were virtually empty as we rode in a taxi into town. The mountains, the forests, the humid air, the Fraser River, the ocean, the city—everything had a sense of calm and order that I hadn't experienced in ten months of life underground. Finally, I was home.

I couldn't wait to see my daughter and my mom. While I was away, Tania had turned twelve. How much had she grown? What did she look like now? I hadn't been able to phone or send a letter since the beginning of September and knew that my mom must be worried. But I had warned her that there would be times when communication would not be possible and had left a few undated letters with her—a couple of pages containing fluffy, general stories that she could show Tania in cases like this.

Now, at long last, I would be able to hug my girl and my mother.

As Martin had moved out of his apartment before going to Chile, I invited him to stay with us until he got back to work and rented a new place. So, that morning of October 14, when my mother opened the door, we were both standing there, expectantly. My mom almost had a heart attack. She screamed so loudly that in no time Tania was also at the door, her eyes and mouth wide open in astonishment. We all laughed, cried, kissed, hugged, looked at each other, laughed some more, cried some more, hugged some more.

That evening, we celebrated our return with a delicious turkey dinner. A few friends came over and, as expected, they wanted to know everything about our ten months in Chile, including, of course, the attempt against Pinochet's life. I told my fictitious stories about working with women's groups and Martin his, as an English teacher, and we both pretended to know very little about the Aconcagua Valley event. All we did was narrate the bits and pieces of news we had gathered along the way, which were basically the same as what had been broadcast in Canada. At least we didn't have to fake our disappointment at the failed operation, as everybody around the table kept lamenting the fact that everything had gone so well, except for the key component.

By then photographs of the rear window of Pinochet's car—the spot where the rocket had landed but not exploded—had made it around the world. According to the dictator, if you looked at the marks in a particular way, you could see the picture of the Virgin of Perpetual Help, which meant that *she* had saved his life; obviously, a miracle had taken place.

"Amazing!" our friend Teresa exclaimed, as we were still laughing at Pinochet's explanation for his escape. "The opiate of the people is also the opiate of the tyrant," she added echoing Marx's remarks regarding the role of religion in keeping the masses sedated. "Pinochet's obviously delusional. The miracle here is not that he survived the attempt against his life, but that the operation actually took place; that a few armed guerrillas were able to attack his convoy, kill five and wound two of his own personal guards. We're talking about the cream of the crop here—men who were hand-picked from one of the most disciplined and ruthless armies in the world! Men who were trained to defend the dictator with their own lives! *They*, and not the virgin, were supposed to protect him! And what did they do? Nothing! Isn't that astonishing? They didn't respond! On the contrary, they tried to escape by rolling down the hill!" she laughed. "Never mind the rocket that didn't explode! Of course it's too bad that the ultimate goal of the operation failed, but we have to keep things in perspective. The real losers here are Pinochet and the Chilean army. Mark my words. *Va a caer.* He will fall."

While I agreed with Teresa on an intellectual level, I felt emotionally exhausted and defeated. A month later, my feelings of failure were compounded by the latest news: five *compañeros* who had participated in the operation had been taken prisoner. As we had expected and planned for, the military had discovered the house in Cerro Colorado. What we hadn't expected was that there they would find a bottle of Coke with a fingerprint on it. It had taken two months to match that fingerprint with one that the secret police had on record. It corresponded to a *compañero* who had been a suspect in a previous armed operation. The information he had provided under severe torture had led the military to other four combatants.

Where had they found that bottle? How could that be? José, Eliana, Martin and I had cleaned the house and the grounds meticulously before leaving and José had taken all the garbage with him. Martin and I talked about it to no end, but couldn't figure it out. At some point he let go of it, but I couldn't. That bottle of Coke haunted me. I couldn't stop thinking about it; I even dreamed about it. How could it be that we hadn't seen it? I became obsessed.

Then, I realized that this was just a different version of what had happened with my red notebook. Not destroying that notebook, as I should have before going out that morning, had given the military the information that had led them to find, abduct, torture and disappear my friend Gloria. I would never know where in the Cerro Colorado house they had found the bottle with the fingerprint. As four of us had been responsible for cleaning four different parts of the house, there was a twenty-five percent chance that I'd been the one to leave the bottle behind.

But, all the same, I felt one hundred percent accountable and ashamed.

I became completely despondent. My daughter was my only source of contentedness. By then Martin had rented his own place and was busy with his teaching and union activities. We saw each other less and less, became distant, emotionally disconnected. He refused to talk about Chile, kept repeating that it was time to move on, to forget about what had happened and just live in the present, plan for the future. But I was stuck in the past. I couldn't get our time in Chile off my mind.

The night before the operation, I had asked Martin why he had become so involved in the Chilean struggle. After all, he was Canadian-Canadian and, as far as I could see, he had no emotional attachment to Chile.

"At first I became involved strictly for political reasons. I supported Allende's Peaceful Road to Socialism wholeheartedly. I still believe in socialism, my sweetheart," he explained as we lay on our bed, thinking about the next day. "Allende's experiment was the first of its kind and I was hopeful, just like many others around the world were hopeful," he continued, caressing my hair. "But you already know that, I don't have to explain all that again, do I?" he asked rhetorically. "So, joining the anti-dictatorial movement in Vancouver came naturally," he added as he circled my face with his right index finger. "But then you arrived—you, with your haunting eyes, your mane of black hair, your blue trunk, your stories, and your mother and baby in tow. I fell in love with you and there you have it! That's when my emotional involvement with Chile began!" he concluded playfully as he hugged me tightly.

Now, a bit over two months later, Martin and I were falling out of love. We didn't yearn to be together anymore. We didn't get excited to hear the other one's voice over the phone. Actually, whenever we held a conversation, it resembled a couple of parallel lines, doomed to never connect. It was as if we didn't have anything in common anymore. What had happened? I don't know. The time that had elapsed between the operation and the news of our comrades being caught felt like years. We had gone from ten months of a difficult but optimistic life underground in Chile to feeling completely dejected as we "cooled down" through five snail-paced, endless weeks of life underground in Europe. Now we were home, leading regular lives, but I carried a huge tangle of new memories and pain inside.

The next ones to fall were the *compañeros* and *compañeras* who had set up the clandestine clinic in Santiago. The following year, Jorge and Alejandra, our top leaders, were killed in cold blood together with ten other members of the resistance movement in what became known as the Corpus Christi Massacre. This is what the Chilean military were good at: apprehending their opponents in the middle of the night, dragging them out of their homes, tying their hands, beating them brutally, rendering them defenseless and then riddling them with bullets. They had not been able to kill or wound any of them in battle, so they were now hunting and assassinating them in the most cowardly fashion.

My work with immigrant women became burdensome. I felt

drained, devoid of the emotional strength required for the job. My mom insisted that I needed a vacation.

"Go away on holidays—take a rest for once in your life!" she prescribed.

I resisted. My clients needed my help. But finally, I had to acknowledge that I was in no shape to help others. I had to help myself first.

I took a leave of absence and went to Mexico for a couple of weeks. It was good to feel the sun on my skin, swim in the ocean, read innocuous mysteries, go for walks on the beach, visit the art galleries around town, stroll up and down the *Malecón* along with hundreds of people...

I protected my anonymity. Politely, but surely, I steered away from engaging in conversation. I didn't want to have to explain who I was, where I was from, what I did. For the first time in many years I felt light, carefree; for two weeks I didn't have to be a mother, a daughter, a social worker or a combatant. I was just another tourist having a holiday in a beautiful, warm place.

Before leaving Vancouver I had gone to the bookstore to find some reading material, but, without even realizing it, I had found myself in front of piles and piles of assorted notebooks displayed on a table in the centre of the store: small and large, fat and thin, with striped and flowery covers, black, blue and green... And then, I saw it—one red notebook hidden at the bottom of a pile. My heart started to race and I was tempted to turn around and walk away, but next thing I knew, I was pulling it out from underneath the pile. It looked almost exactly like the one I had had in Chile: small, fairly thick, and with a smooth red vinyl surface. I thumbed through its blank pages; saw myself jotting down the name of the restaurant where I had agreed to meet Gloria for lunch on Saturday, September 15, 1973. It was a small place with a peculiar name on a very short, obscure street just outside the downtown core.

I stood there holding the notebook for what felt like an eternity. Finally, I walked up to the cashier and paid for it.

In Puerto Vallarta, it took me a few days to take it out of the suitcase. I wasn't sure why I had bought it, why I had taken it with me to Mexico. But, one evening, in the solitude of my hotel room, I began to write.

G, I jotted down first.

Next to it I wrote, *-1 – Sat. - Heretford – Ariztía.*

Until that moment, I didn't know that the names of the restaurant and the street were imprinted on my mind.

My hand moved to the next line.

Gloria, you went to the restaurant that Saturday.

My hand kept moving down, line after line.

You wanted to find out how Miguel and I were doing. Let us know you were okay.

We had already been abducted, Gloria.

I had been tortured, but I didn't talk; didn't tell them about our lunch date.

Our house was raided.

They found my notebook—the red one, remember?

I should've burnt it before I left the house the morning of the eleventh, but I was too scattered and panicky—I forgot about the notebook.

I had jotted down the time and place of our meeting on a margin, alongside a grocery shopping list.

I got up. Paced around the room. Sat down again and kept on writing.

I should've been the one to die, not you, Gloria.

You were my best friend.

I admired you.

You were smart.

You were gutsy.

You were funny.

Gloria, I love you.

Gloria, please forgive me.

For the first time since her disappearance, I allowed myself to say those words, to write them down two, three times.

Gloria, please forgive me.

Then, I began to recall and describe Gloria's face, eyes, hands, hair, body; her invincible spirit, her sense of humour, her playfulness, her optimism, her contagious laughter—everything about her—down to the tiniest detail. I let myself feel the warmth of our friendship. I gave myself permission to remember and put into words the stories of our youth.

It was six in the morning when I stopped writing. I walked out onto the balcony and rested my hands on the railing. The ocean stretched out like a diamond-studded skin in the rising light. I listened to the pulse of the waves and the chirps and trills of the birds; breathed in the limpid, fresh air.

My mom was right. Life is made of contradictions. Sometimes, our minds and bodies don't align—our mind tells us to do one thing, but our body decides to do the exact opposite. Other times, we just can't muster the courage to "walk the talk." Often, our feelings betray us, don't allow us to think straight, to do the right thing. And, of course, we make mistakes. I thought I had learned from the mistake that had cost my best friend's life. But then, I had been part of the foursome responsible for another fatal error: the coke bottle with a fingerprint on it left behind in the Cerro Colorado house.

I went back inside.

Will I ever be able to forgive myself? I wrote.

The next afternoon, as I stood at the edge of the water, watching the parasailers up in the sky, I was approached by yet another vendor. At first I kept repeating "No, gracias, no gracias," but then I heard him say the word "dolphins."

"Dolphins? There are dolphins out there?" I asked skeptically as I turned to face him, my right hand over my eyes and my left one stretched out, pointing at the water.

"Sí, Señora. And if you're lucky, they'll come out and you'll catch sight of them," he assured me.

I had always been fascinated by dolphins, but hadn't had a chance to see them in the wild, so that evening I joined a handful of tourists in what was presented as "a sunset sailing excursion."

The boat turned out to be more striking than I expected—a giant, multicoloured sail billowing out in the wind over a beautiful, elongated white body.

The captain and his assistant welcomed us warmly as they handed out lifejackets and helped us on to the deck. We were directed to sit in small steamer chairs and make ourselves comfortable.

Shortly thereafter, we began to sail out into the setting sun, a brass-coloured ball floating in the haze over the horizon. The silhouette of the mountains embracing the bay was still visible, a dark backdrop to the sprawling city. The calm, indigo water had become a reflector of the dying light while, behind us, our passage left a wake of sparkling white froth. The wind was on our backs, pushing the boat gently farther and farther away from the coast.

I took in the scene—its sheer beauty, its extraordinary sense of peace. And then I saw them: a pod of dolphins jumping in and out of the water right next to me. I gasped in wonder as I pointed insistently with my right index finger to call the other passengers' attention. Then, somebody else pointed at the other side of the boat, another one in front of us, behind us, as far as the eye could see. There were dolphins everywhere, hundreds of them, leaping, dancing, doing somersaults, smiling, chirping, whistling... We were in their midst, enveloped in their joy and love of life. They stayed with us for a long time. By now the sun had finished plunging into the ocean, but the dolphins kept on playing in the gathering dusk. Then, as suddenly as they had appeared, they were gone.

Nobody said a word. I saw an older couple reach for each other's hands; a young man wipe tears off his face. I was smiling to myself.

"Gloria," I whispered, "you haven't changed one little bit."

The first night I was back in Vancouver, the baby that I had dreamed about at Tres Álamos concentration camp showed up in my sleep again. This time, her head and body were not separated and she appeared healthy and content. I was rocking her in my arms when a man in a white smock opened the door and came into the room. Then, I realized that there was a bathtub filled with water right beside me. In a kind voice, the man ordered me to put the baby in the tub.

"You have to," he said. "You just have to," he repeated.

"I will," I responded calmly, because I knew that either outcome would be positive. If the baby didn't drown, she would grow up to have a meaningful life; if she did drown, her spirit would give life to others. I knelt on the floor and gently laid her down at the bottom of the tub.

Still kneeling, I waited, my eyes fixed on the baby. It didn't take long for her to come up to the surface, breathing normally and offering me a wide, toothless smile. I picked her up and held her against my breast. Only then did I realize how much I had wanted the baby to live. I had accepted the fact that she might die so as to give life to others, but her staying alive filled me with joy and relief. The serenity I had felt before putting the baby in the water was now replaced by an outburst of emotion. I was laughing and crying as I examined her face; I stretched my arms out so that I could look over her small body and ensure that all of her was intact.

Just like at Tres Álamos, I woke up feeling at peace with myself. Not only that: in the days and weeks to come, I began to feel as if my eyes had finally turned outwards, beyond my recollections of Chile, past my own and my family's little world.

While I continued to support the resistance movement in my native country, I also started to embrace other causes; I collaborated with a magazine published by a collective of immigrant women in Vancouver and became a volunteer literacy tutor at the Carnegie Community Centre in the impoverished Downtown East Side of the city.

In the nineties, I didn't hesitate to join the Anti-Globalization movement in response to the unbridled power of multinational corporations around the world. By then the dictatorship in Chile had been replaced by a lukewarm democracy—not what we had fought so hard for, but a welcome change nonetheless.

The new millennium brought about devastating developments. Thousands of people were killed at the World Trade Centre in New York. Afghanistan and Iraq were invaded by the United States with the help of Canada and other countries. Hundreds of thousands were killed in civil wars in Africa. Thousands also died in tsunamis and earthquakes around the globe.

But not all was bad news. In Latin America, progressive governments were elected in several places, including Evo Morales in Bolivia—the first indigenous president in the history of that nation. In Argentina, following a catastrophic meltdown, workers took over and began to run the factories that their bosses had abandoned. The Landless Workers Movement was able to bring Agrarian Reform to the forefront of Brazilian politics. There was a lot to be proud of and I found ways to support these initiatives. But, actually, most of my time and energy were taken by my professional work.

Over the years, funding to social programs had been drastically cut while more and more immigrant women needed assistance. So, I began to take a more active role in my union: pushing for renewed funding, denouncing the privatization of the public sector, pressing for affordable housing and day care programs demanding better services for immigrants. It was hard but necessary work.

Finally, I had learned how to live in the here and now.

Then, one day, I got a phone call from Gloria's parents in Santiago. A mass grave had been found just outside the Pisagua cemetery in the Atacama Desert. There was reason to believe that Miguel's remains might be buried there.

Chile
January—February, 2011

Sol

Cars honk; bells ring; dogs bark; children sing; voices offer their hellos, their good-byes. I open my eyes and find myself in the semi-darkness of a bedroom. It takes me a moment to remember that I'm in the city of love, the city of terror. I jump out of bed and open the window. Santiago pours in like the haunting song of a mermaid. I cannot help but surrender to her appeal. How to resist the dry and warm air of this summer morning, the height of the snow-capped Andes, the aroma of the blooming honeysuckle, the luminous purple of the jacarandas?

Santiago is beautiful. In my daily walks I've been rediscovering the city's treasures: centenary buildings with red-tiled roofs; thick adobe walls and interior courtyards where a grape-vine twines itself around a wooden arbour; cobblestoned streets bordered by gigantic *ceibo* trees; old *plazas* where dark-skinned children with huge, rosy cheeks play *ronda* or swing to and fro accompanied by giggles and squeaks.

So many forgotten sounds! When I came back clandestinely,

in 1986, Santiago was still a whispering city, its hushed din punctured by sporadic street demonstrations against the dictatorship. Today, it has recovered its tongue. There go the organ-grinders of Parque Forestal, the street vendors offering Band-Aids, chewing gum, sugar-covered *berlines*, sewing needles, handkerchiefs, roasted peanuts, caramel-filled *barquillos*, peaches, ice-cream, lottery tickets, newspapers and magazines. There goes the boom of the cannon announcing noon-hour from Santa Lucía Hill.

My ears have been savouring the sing-song of Chilean Spanish, its quick tempo. I haven't hesitated to follow suit and now I can hear myself speak in my most Chilean of voices to the person sitting next to me on the bus or admiring shoes in the Falabella store window on Ahumada Street. I catch myself complementing conversations with that peculiar fluttering of hands and eyelashes, that propensity to laughter, that wanting to talk to everybody about everything, all at once. In Canada, I have a foreign accent. Here, I have an accent, but it's just like everybody else's.

My daughter is far away. Vancouver is far away.

Commercial Drive. That's my neighbourhood, the one I've come to love, I tell myself. But my body doesn't respond. What my body wants is to submerge itself in this "Chileanness"; it wants to eat its fill of *hayuya* buns, avocados, *lúcuma* ice-cream, *burrito* bean stew, corn casserole, *cazuela* soup with tasty chunks of beef and fresh veggies, cheese-filled *empanadas*, juicy *chirimoyas* and watermelons, *manjar*—the ambrosial concoction made of creamy milk and sugar—the flavours and aromas of my childhood and youth. My body wants to convince me that I haven't changed and that the country hasn't changed.

But it has changed. And I have changed. Every time I get on the modern and impeccably clean subway train, terror lodges in my throat once again as I wonder, *How many of these men and women were informers, torturers, collaborators? How many made false accusations in order to save their own skin? How many covered their ears and eyes so as not to hear, not to see? How many would support the persecution and the massacre once again?*

But then, as I look around and attempt to see through those inscrutable faces, I also ask myself, *How many of these men and women had their dreams and part of their lives amputated on September 11, 1973? How many participated in the resistance movement to the dictatorship? Who is who?*

January 6

In the next few weeks, I'll travel north to identify Miguel's remains—if they are, indeed, Miguel's remains. According to reports by different commissions and data collected by the Association of Relatives of Disappeared Political Prisoners, several witnesses have placed him at the Pisagua concentration camp around the time he went missing in October of that terrible year. That would mean that he wasn't killed in Santiago, as I had believed all along, but rather moved to Pisagua and killed there. Most likely, by then his hand had already been amputated. How did he survive the trip?

299

Every time I go to the office of the Association, I can feel the presence of thousands of spirits wandering around and I can even see Miguel, hanging by the door with his curly fingers, hair shooting up, and that face of a naughty boy that accompanied him even in the most solemn of moments. My hair is almost fully grey now; my face, crisscrossed by wrinkles, darkened by shadows. Miguel will continue to be young as long as somebody remembers him.

I'm staying with Señora Rina, my mom's friend. She welcomed me with open arms and continues to shower me with her kindness. She has taken it upon herself to offer me abundant Chilean specialties and if I continue to eat the way I've been eating so far, I'll be rolling back up to Canada. Thank goodness my long walks must be having some effect, because I can still get into my clothes. Also, I already found a beautiful spot to jog: a smooth dirt trail along the park that borders the Mapocho River. The river is as ugly as I remember it from the times of my youth: a trickle of chocolate-coloured water skipping over boulders and rocks. At least now it's not carrying mutilated corpses, as it did after the coup. The park, on the other hand, is gorgeous and steeped in the exquisite aroma of honeysuckle.

Señora Isabel and Don Carlos, Gloria's parents, are also happy to have me in Santiago. I see them almost daily at the premises of the Association of Relatives of Disappeared Political Prisoners. From the moment I knew I would be coming to Chile, I've been pondering over whether or not to tell them I'm responsible for Gloria's abduction. I still haven't made up my mind. Perhaps

I would feel relieved after confessing my mistake to them, but would they feel any better? I don't know.

January 7

Today I took the bus to Peñalolén to have *onces* with Señora Isabel and Don Carlos. Their little house is beautiful: adobe walls, terracotta floors, large windows looking out on the city below and a courtyard bursting with flowers. There are photographs of Gloria everywhere, her childhood and youth omnipresent, a conspicuous reminder of a life cut short by savagery.

We had just finished our tea and *hayuyas* when I heard Señora Isabel say, "We finally found out where and when Gloria was abducted."

I felt my blood drop to my feet.

"It's okay, *mijita*," Don Carlos comforted me while patting my hand. "It's better to know than not to know," he added.

"Along the years we presented many petitions for a writ of habeas corpus,' with no results at all. But, two years ago, two witnesses came forward," Señora Isabel went on.

"Restaurante Heretford on Ariztía Street," I mumbled, as I lowered my head and tears began to stream down my face.

"Sol, darling, what did you say?" Señora Isabel asked as she got up, walked around the table and put her arms around me.

"Restaurante Heretford on Ariztía Street," I repeated, and then continued, "they found my notebook... I had jotted down the place and time where Gloria and I would meet that Saturday, four days after the coup."

"Ay, mijita por Dios!" Señora Isabel cried out as she rocked me in her arms.

Now Don Carlos was beside me as well. "No, Sol, no!" he said in a hoarse voice as he bent down and cupped my face in his hands. Then, as he looked me in the eye, he said in a loud, clear voice, "Sol, that's not where they abducted her."

"But, they showed me the notebook, the page where I had written ..." I uttered in disbelief.

Señora Isabel was in a huff. "It shouldn't surprise me, after everything we've learned about their tactics," she said finally. This time, she made me look at her in the eye. "Sol, they abducted her on that Saturday, but not from the restaurant where you say you were supposed to meet her. Actually, she wasn't even near there. She was crossing the Alameda at the corner of Cummings Street," she disclosed, calmer now, as she took my hands in hers.

"But, why... Why did they show me?" I asked, shaking my head.

"Because they wanted to break you. They knew that Gloria was your best friend. If they made you believe that you were responsible for her abduction, maybe you would break down and give them the information they were after," Don Carlos explained pacing around the room.

"As you well know, *mijita*, they would do *anything* to pull information out of people. Demoralizing the prisoners was just one of their tactics," Señora Isabel added.

For a few moments, I couldn't move. I just sat there while Gloria's parents patted my hair, stroked my back, planted kisses on my cheeks.

Then I felt a wave of rage surge up from my gut.

"I hate them!" I yelled, getting up. "Fucking assholes! Beasts!" I heard myself shout as I punched the wall.

Next thing I knew, I was half-sitting, half-lying on the couch. Don Carlos was wiping the sweat off my forehead while Señora Isabel attended to my bleeding hand.

"Sol, *mijita*, don't give in to their ploys, don't let yourself feel hatred," she urged. "You were strong enough to survive, to bring up a beautiful girl, to have a life driven by love. Don't let them get you now," she added, a sad smile on her face.

"Isabel is right, Sol. You have every right to be angry, but don't let hatred take hold of you now," Don Carlos insisted.

They're right. They didn't break me thirty-six years ago and I won't let them break me now.

Gloria, I can't even begin to tell you how relieved I am to know that I didn't turn you in. I had gotten used to living with the burden of my guilt. What will life be like without it? I just have to make sure not to replace it with a bundle of hatred.

January 11

Today I went to the Santiago Cemetery with Señora Rina to see the monument erected in honour of those who disappeared and were executed during the dictatorship. It's an imposing stone wall on which thousands of names have been engraved in alphabetical order, including the well-known heroes like Salvador Allende, Víctor Jara and Miguel Enríquez, as well as the anonymous dreamers and combatants like our Miguel, Gloria, Señora Guillermina and Don Arnulfo. I also found Raúl, Pastor and Nicolasa on the list; for all these years I had held on to the hope that they had survived. I felt a strong urge to scream. To scream until I had no voice left. But of course I didn't. I just sobbed on Señora Rina's shoulder for a few minutes. Then, we took the bus and went to the Fuente Alemana for a *lomito con palta*—a pork and avocado sandwich—and a mug of draft beer.

Miguel loved *lomitos con palta*, so every time we had a bit of extra money we'd go to the Fuente Alemana for our special banquet, served by Juanita or Bertita, our favourite waitresses. They were utterly amused by the sight of Miguel always carrying his violin under his arm, rain or shine, and every time they saw us they'd ask if the violin also shared our bed at night.

One of those times, Juanita and Bertita asked Miguel to play something for them. As Miguel was shy, it took him a while to make up his mind, but finally, persuaded not only by them, but also by all the patrons, he got up and played a piece from one of Paganini's caprices. The Fuente Alemana, which was a constant whirl of activity, became absolutely silent and still, while Miguel's violin playing filled the space with ethereal beauty.

Juanita and Bertita are still working there. I recognized them right away. They didn't recognize me. Better that way.

January 13

I went for a walk on San Cristóbal Hill and, on the way back, without even realizing it, I found myself ringing my aunt Amparo's doorbell. I was taken aback by the peeling paint on the outside walls, the neglected garden—everything dry and weeded over. An elderly nurse dressed in white, fully made-up and with a tall hairdo resurrected from the sixties, opened the door.

"I'm here to see Señorita Amparo," I heard myself say.

"Señorita Amparo is very ill and does not receive visitors," he declared in a high-pitched, staccato voice as she proceeded to close the door in my face.

I held the door open with my stretched-out hand as I explained that I am Señorita Amparo's only niece.

She scrutinized me from top to bottom and asked me to wait. When she came back, she had a bunch of keys in her hand. In silence, she showed me in and asked me to sit in the living room—

the same maroon velvet armchair of 1973, the same furniture of thirty-odd years ago, but frayed and shabby now; a sour, putrid smell floated through the air.

The nurse came back a few minutes later, sat in front of me and explained that my aunt has been in a catatonic state for a year and a half. Apparently, for quite a long time she had been behaving in strange ways—didn't fulfill her financial obligations, mistreated her servants, hardly ever showed up at her stores, seemed to be completely absent-minded, became deaf and mute for days on end. Then, she started to stay in bed with no explanation whatsoever, until one day she never got up again, not even to go to the bathroom.

The parish priest at La Merced, where she attended daily mass, had taken charge of her affairs because my aunt had willed all her assets to that parish. The church's financial advisors had already liquidated her stores and were now preparing to sell her house and move my aunt to a seniors' home.

I don't know what kind of a face I made because when the nurse finished her explanations, she looked at me compassionately, patted my shoulder and assured me that Señorita Amparo "is not suffering" and "is not experiencing any kind of pain." As we climbed the stairs to the second floor, I told her that I lived abroad and hadn't seen my aunt for more than thirty years. "Then brace yourself, my darling," she responded.

How to brace yourself for such a spectacle? My aunt Amparo a small bundle of skin and bones, all eyes, not a single strand of hair on her head, was half-sitting, half-lying in an enormous bed with an ancient flowery cotton quilt, surrounded by stuffed animals of all sizes: big dogs, small dogs, bears, tigers, kitty cats, big kangaroos with little kangaroos stuck in their tummies, monkeys, panthers, zebras, frogs, lizards, and even caterpillars and snakes.

I took her hand in mine, kissed it, and told her in between sobs that I forgave her, that obviously she could've never imagined the cruelty of the military. My aunt just looked at me with her fixed, wide eyes, like the eyes of the porcelain dolls she used to give me when I was a small girl. And when I turned around to leave the room, she let out a gigantic belch.

January 16

I went to the National Stadium with Señora Isabel and Don Carlos. The excuse was a Colo-Colo soccer game, but the real reason was to be there, where Gloria and Miguel were detained almost at the same time. Did they see each other, sitting on the bleachers, freezing to death, their faces black and blue, their tortured bodies filthy and ill-smelling?

It's hard to imagine that this hub of sports enthusiasm was once the dictatorship's largest concentration camp. Between September and November of 1973, over forty thousand political prisoners were held here, among them many foreigners, including three Canadians.

In 1962, the National Stadium was the main venue for the soccer World Cup, stage to many feats by the Chilean team and to enthusiastic demonstrations of patriotic pride by their fans. In Valdivia, we listened to every Chile game on the radio, cheered our team along, celebrated its victories and cried over its losses. This was the stadium where Chile earned third place and tens of thousands sang the national anthem at the top of their lungs: "¡O el asilo contra la opresión!"—"Oh shelter from oppression!" Yet, this was the place where, in 1973, people had been tortured, killed and made to disappear.

Today, nothing reveals that truth: not one drop of leftover blood, not one pair of petrified eyes, not one scream of terror intermingled with the roar of the thousands of voices cheering on their teams. The horror of those months in 1973 has been buried forever beneath the fervent passion for soccer.

Perhaps, sheltered by the deafening racket, the souls of those who died there still wander around, on the bleachers, where so many years ago, jabbed by military boots and machine guns, they waited for their turn to be tortured. Perhaps, the Colo-Colo dressing room is not only the Colo-Colo dressing room. Perhaps in that very room, those castigated souls dress and undress over and over again, put on and take off the blackened human rags that the military "disappeared" in an attempt to make their own barbarism disappear.

January 18

I'm on my way back to Valdivia, the city of my birth, childhood and adolescence. The lights of the oncoming vehicles pierce the darkness and skip from window to window, leaving behind a trail of memories from my former life. Life before the arrival of fear and hatred. The life of my first world.

January 20

This morning I went to the market by the river and ate some sea urchins in their shell with a good dose of lemon juice. How many years since my last taste of sea urchins? Too many to count. Then I picked up a big bag of roasted hazelnuts and headed for the cemetery.

It took me a while to find the graves, hidden by a tangle of overgrown weeds. Besides, the rain and the passing of time have managed to wear down the names on the headstones. I paid a few pesos to a boy who offered to do a bit of weeding while I went back to the front gate to buy some flowers. When I got back, he was waiting for me with a big smile on his face, as if saying, "Look at the great job I did." And, actually, he had managed to get rid of practically all the weeds and had given the graves a good wash.

I arranged the flowers and sat down on a bench right across from the tombs.

The only time I had been to the cemetery before today—or any cemetery, for that matter—was for my dad's funeral, and that day has always been hazy in my mind. I tried to recall it again this morning, but couldn't; all I got was a blur. I sat on the bench for a few minutes, looking at the two slabs of stone that conceal the remains of those who once were my father and my brother, but didn't feel any emotion. It was as if they weren't there.

"Where are you two?" I whispered.

I left the graveyard. Just as I was getting downtown, it started to drizzle, so I found shelter at the entrance to the post office. I was contemplating the green filigree of the lime trees in the square, the street lamps, the gazebo fluttering with pigeons, when, all of a sudden, a huge bolt of lightning crisscrossed the sky, and the Valdivia rain, hasty and joyful, began to fall in buckets. Instinctively, I covered my ears with the palms of my hands and while I waited for the roll of thunder to arrive I saw, yes, I saw my dad and my brother running across the street, my dad in his pearl-grey suit and sky-blue shirt and my brother in his school uniform. The air smelled of firewood and smoke.

January 23

The Commercial High School, my dear old school, has become a mass of cement that takes up almost half a block. Though only a couple of hours have passed since I stood looking at the building, I have managed to forget all the details and now I can only conjure up a grey smudge. On top of that smudge, my memory

310

continues to paint the old garden, the simple wood structures and the yellow house with solid oak windows and doors at the corner of Pérez Rosales Avenue and Yerbas Buenas Street.

This morning, when I turned around to steal a last glance at San Francisco Church, kitty-corner from the school, the din of voices escaping from the open windows set a sudden ambush on me. Boots, smocks, notebooks, ribbons—broken, fleeting images—galloped in front of my eyes and then vanished as quickly as they had appeared.

January 24

The *pension* where I'm staying is on General Lagos Street, almost right across from the Conservatory where, for so many years, I took piano and musical theory lessons; where I met Miguel. The *pension* is a typical Valdivia house: old, big, and with wood-burning stoves in every room.

From my lace-curtained window I can see the garden and the front door of the Conservatory. This afternoon I spent quite a while watching the kids going in and out. Some were carrying their school bags; others, their instruments: violins, cellos, and even wind instruments. In my time, wind instruments were not taught at the Conservatory. Other than that, things don't seem to have changed much.

As I watched the kids, I began to think that sometimes life's rhythm is slow, cadenced, like an andante or an adagio. Other times, it seems to take on the flow of a speeding train, like an allegro. How many notes, how many silences, can be accommodated in one bar? How many sorrows and joys fit in one afternoon, one morning?

January 26

My last day in Valdivia. This morning I went to the Municipal Stadium where our school's track and field team used to practice and compete. On the way back I stopped to take a look at our old house on Esmeralda Street, but it's not there anymore; instead, I found a hideous apartment building. Then I crossed the river to Teja Island and looked for my friend Silvia's house, but it, also, is gone. At least the structure that took its place is beautiful—a museum and art gallery made of cedar and glass.

When I returned, I went to Café Palace for a *completo*—a Chilean-style hotdog—and wrote a postcard to Silvia, who has been living in Germany since 1974. I told her that her house and my house don't exist anymore, that the Stadium is the same and smells of freshly-cut grass, the Commercial High School is completely changed and Café Palace continues to serve as delicious and slippery hotdogs as ever. Most importantly, the Calle-Calle River is exactly the same.

The river. Blue, prudent, infinite time. Today's water is not the same as yesterday's and will not be tomorrow's. Other water will shelter fish and plants, kiss the underside of barges and boats. A different time will continue its silent passage, until some day nature or men decide to throw everything into disarray once again.

There are no traces of the 1960 earthquake, tidal wave and flood; no cues to remind us that the military threw dozens of mutilated corpses into the water after the 1973 coup. But the river remembers. The river saw everything with its waking eyes. The river observes and listens, protects the secrets it has been entrusted with, the truths it has been offered.

January 27

The bus is approaching Santiago. The sun has just appeared from behind the Andes and, all of a sudden, as if by magic, the landscape has lit up. The vineyards are heavy with ripe fruit and dozens of clay ovens greet me like Señoras in full skirts, their smoky forelocks pointing to the sky and their bulky bellies ready to give birth to the daily bread: flat, round, puffy, chewy, firm... Clay ovens: paunchy pots planted in front of the *campesinos'* little houses, zealous caretakers of the central region's countryside.

January 29

The trip north has been set for February second. Last night I phoned Alfonso, Miguel's brother in Temuco, and it turns out that he also wants to go. He'll take the bus up to Santiago and from here we'll all go on with Señora Isabel and Don Carlos, in their little car.

"*Mijita, por Dios,* we wouldn't dream of letting you go to Pisaua all by yourself!" Señora Isabel exclaimed when I told them about the trip.

"I won't be by myself—Miguel's brother will be going too," I clarified.

"Then it'll be four of us in the car," Don Carlos concluded.

"It's a very long trip, it'll be exhausting, you don't have to go, you know... Alfonso and I can take the bus," I insisted.

But they wouldn't hear of it. They wanted to go and reassured me that they would be fine; that though they both look very old on the outside, they feel young and healthy on the inside.

January 30

Today I went to Maipú with Señora Rina to have lunch at her daughter's house. Eliana is an elementary school teacher, has been married for twenty-five years and has three kids in university. Her husband must have a good job at the Bank of Santander because obviously they lead a comfortable life.

For a long time, I hadn't felt envious—envious of somebody else's life. I was envious of Eliana's country house, her apparently healthy and carefree children, her solvent and solid looking husband; envious of the "stable" and "normal" life I never had.

We drank a few *pisco-sours* and ate a delicious Chilean style barbecue accompanied by typical salads and sprinkled with plenty of red wine. We even had an afternoon nap and then *onces*

For a few hours I believed I was happy.

I could've opted for a life of comfort, followed in my aunt's footsteps or chosen a lucrative career. Who would I have become then? A successful businesswoman? A renowned lawyer? Would I have married an entrepreneur or a famous surgeon? Would I have been an exemplary wife and mother in one of those mansions you can see behind electrified fences in the wealthy neighbourhoods of Santiago? Would I have been right-wing or a humanitarian liberal? Would I have played bridge and tennis with my friends in a private club on a Sunday afternoon? Would I have had maids in charge of the kitchen, the cleaning and the kids? Would I have been happy?

January 31

In two days we leave for Iquique and Pisagua. Alfonso, Miguel's brother, arrived yesterday from Temuco. He showed me pictures of his sisters and their respective families, of his own children, his wife—a good looking bunch. But he looks old, thin and worn. He's a chain smoker and his hands shake every time he tries to light a cigarette. He told me he has never recovered from the torture, from the time he spent in jail after the coup, the long years of the dictatorship, Miguel's disappearance, the family's suffering, having to assume responsibility for his sisters after his parents' premature deaths. So much bitterness, so much hatred in his voice! I asked him if he had looked for help, seen a therapist.

"Seeing a therapist helped me and my mom immensely," I told him.

He laughed, said that he had neither the time nor the money for those kinds of "luxuries."

"Those are not 'luxuries,' Alfonso. In our cases, they're a basic necessity," I shot back.

"And besides, you don't need money to get help," I went on. "Just being part of a group of people who have shared similar circumstances can help too," I offered, and proceeded to explain that, for Gloria's parents, their work with the Association of Relatives of the Disappeared Political Prisoners had been very healing.

"I don't know, Sol. The torture happened such a long time ago I wouldn't even know where to start telling somebody about it. I haven't even told my wife..." he confessed.

It didn't surprise me. I knew of plenty of cases in which survivors of torture had never talked to anyone about their experience I gave him a tight hug.

"Maybe that would be a good start," I suggested.

"I'll give it a try," he promised.

February 1

Today, those of us going north had a meeting with two of the forensic scientists that have been working on the exhumation. They informed us that their colleagues at Northern University have already moved the remains from Pisagua to their labs in Iquique, where they have begun their analyses. Each corpse was found inside a burlap sack. This, in addition to the dryness and composition of the soil, helped to preserve the bodies almost intact.

There are fourteen of us—mothers, fathers, brothers, sisters, children and partners of disappeared prisoners. There was a mixture of sadness and quiet excitement in the air, as I'm sure we were all asking ourselves the same questions: what if we find them? What if we don't?

February 4

Today we made it as far as Copiapó, an oasis in the middle of the desert. We ate at a little restaurant across from Plaza Prat and then went for a walk on Matta Avenue, a beautiful boulevard bordered by gigantic trees.

We're staying at a lodge with an altar to Virgin Carmen in the front yard and a portrait of Augusto Pinochet in the living-room. Pía, the owner, must've been a toddler at the time of the coup. Where does her adoration for the dictator stem from?

I was staring at Pinochet's picture when I heard her say, "So, you're a Canadian citizen! How old were you when you went to live in Canada?"

"Oh, I was very, very young," I answered offhandedly, as if to say, "Who cares about me when there's such an important figure on your wall?"

She finished registering us in an enormous, old-fashioned log-book, and then stood up, walked around to the front of her desk and started a long-winded speech. Obviously, she had taken it upon herself to "educate" me.

"The *caballero*, the 'gentleman'—may he rest in peace—was Chile's saviour, you know. He liberated our homeland from the grip of the Marxist hordes, but international communism is still set on lying about him. The truth is that he sacrificed his life for our country and we Chileans know that General Augusto Pinochet is the most illustrious and distinguished president we have ever had."

She said all this while pointing to the dictator's photograph on the wall with her chin, patting her pregnant belly with her left hand and crossing herself with her right.

I just nodded and smiled.

At this point, Señora Isabel was able to get a word in edgewise and asked if we could be shown to our rooms. Without responding, Pía went behind her desk again, got a few keys out of a drawer and began to walk down the hallway

Thank goodness she shut up, I thought. But actually, she wasn't finished.

"Aren't you glad that Michelle Bachelet is not the president anymore? Everybody knows that she's just another communist in disguise. She should've been eliminated while she was in prison after the 'military pronouncement,' together with her father and all the rest of them. That's what I think. General Pinochet's biggest mistake was not to kill them all at once."

By now she had unlocked our rooms, so I stepped into mine and quickly closed the door behind me. I was sweating and my heart was racing.

How does a country continue living when a good chunk of the population thinks and feels like that?

February 5

I've been reading about the history of this place. Since I was a kid I've been fascinated by the Atacama Desert, "the driest environment in the world," but never took the time or made the effort to learn more about it. It took the prospect of finding Miguel's remains to finally motivate me to find out about its history. I had no idea, for example, that this desert is home to the Chinchorro mummies, the oldest and best preserved in the world. And while I did know that this was part of the Inca Empire at the time of the Spanish conquest, I hadn't heard about the crucial role that the dead played in the culture of the peoples of the region.

The Inca believed that death was the beginning of the most important phase in people's lives: the transformation of human beings into an eternal source of wisdom. That's why they treated their dead with the utmost respect, making sure they were kept well dressed and adequately supplied with coca leaves and *chicha,* maize liquor. When the Spaniards realized this, they carried out a ruthless campaign of desecration of the Inca graves, punishing with torture—and even death—anyone who attempted to protect them.

Some authors claim that more than the appropriation of the land, this is what consummated the conquest. Perhaps we are a bit like the Inca—cannot and will not forgive Pinochet for violating the bodies of our dear ones and then making them disappear

Tonight we stopped in Quillagua, a beautiful town in the Loa Valley. The owner of this lodge turned out to be the opposite of Pía and also quite curious. When we said we needed three separate rooms, she didn't hesitate to ask how we are related to each other, then she went on to inquire about the purpose of our trip. We remained silent for a few instants, but then Señora Isabel explained that we're on our way to Pisagua; that my husband disappeared a few weeks after the 1973 coup and his body may be in a common grave that was found there. The poor lady's eyes filled with tears and, after giving us all a tight hug, she invited us into her kitchen and served us a delicious dinner, free of charge

February 6

This afternoon we finally made it to Pisagua.

Pisagua: the fishing village with the infamous concentration camp first used by President Gabriel González Videla in the late forties and early fifties. Back then, the government's agenda was to exterminate two "abhorrent" and "dangerous" groups: communists and homosexuals. Who was the cruel, young Army Captain in charge of the prison at the time? Augusto Pinochet.

I didn't know about this piece of the puzzle until a few weeks ago, when Señora Isabel and Don Carlos told me about it. It makes sense—the dictator didn't crop out of nowhere, after all. His training as a tyrant and a murderer had begun decades before the coup.

The road to Pisagua is treacherous and some sections border an abrupt cliff; no wonder there are quite a few crosses along the way—modest memorials to the victims of accidents. Fortunately, we didn't have any mishaps.

In spite of the clear sky and the brilliant, blue ocean, the town appears depressed, somewhat decrepit: many ramshackle, abandoned houses and a few beautiful old buildings, but most of them in urgent need of a coat of paint. It's hard to imagine the prosperous Pisagua of the 1800's, when it was one of the main ports in the region.

We parked the car in front of the Municipal Theatre and began our search for the concentration camp and the common grave.

There were people sitting on chairs outside their doors, watching their kids play in the street or just passing the time. After a few inquiries, we made it to the prison.

I had already seen pictures, read descriptions of the three-storey building, its cells, the barbed wire fence that encloses the premises... But nothing had prepared me for the experience of standing in front of the place where hundreds and hundreds of prisoners were confined in the most appalling conditions; where Miguel also was mistreated and tormented.

I was overtaken by waves of anxiety and sorrow, panic and grief. I couldn't imagine, didn't want to imagine, Miguel's last weeks of life in this horrible building. He must've suffered unfathomable pain here. How had he managed with his amputated limb? Had his stump got infected? Had he received any kind of medical care?

"Cry, my darling, cry," I heard Señora Isabel whisper in my ear as she enveloped me in a tight hug. After a few moments we opened our arms and invited Alfonso and Don Carlos to join us. It was good to feel their emotions blending with mine, to take comfort in our four-way embrace.

The common grave is next to the cemetery, in a flat area bordering the town.

The site is cordoned off as the scientists need to continue the excavation in case they find further evidence hidden in the soil. Fortunately, though, we were able to get quite close and took a good look at it. It's larger than I imagined—at least ten metres

322

long and two or three wide. It's also deep, which makes sense, given that it accommodated layer after layer of bodies, twenty in total.

It's been said that Pisagua is a cemetery with an ocean view. On this narrow stretch of land, wedged between the Coastal Range and the Pacific Ocean, the dead of all the civilizations that inhabited the region have been preserved by the dryness of the sand. It's not surprising, then, that there are more dead than living bodies in Pisagua today.

For the longest time, the fishermen who live here insisted that they'd seen some twenty-odd men rise from the earth and walk along the edge of the cemetery. What set these spirits apart was that they were dressed in rags, had their hands tied, were blindfolded and appeared to be wounded, unlike the other souls that frequently emerge from their burial sites and wander around the port.

Pinochet, fully convinced of holding the absolute truth, didn't count on the omniscience of the souls and believed that he could hide the mutilated bodies of his victims forever. But our dead rose from their secret graves to denounce the injustice of their murders, to call us to their side.

We came to meet them. The night opened up its luminous map. The gigantic birds and shamans tattooed on the sides of the mountains showed us the way. And the Atacama Desert, the monumental, the implacable, the eternal, opened up to offer us the bodies of our beloved.

February 10

We've been in Iquique for three days, waiting, and finally today were notified that Miguel's body has been identified. Tomorrow, Alfonso and I will be allowed to see him.

February 11

Miguel
curly fingers
bewildered hair
rounded ears
skin of a peach
smile of a naughty boy

Miguel
tortured and massacred

Miguel
flesh blackened and fissured
bones splintered
organs pierced by bullets

Miguel
in rags and barefoot

Miguel
emerging

sweetly   quietly
like a flower in the desert
You're here

Aquí
Presente

Friend
lover
compañero

You're here
and with the certainty
of your parched body
the screaming silence
of your two absences:
your left hand and your violin
Gone

Desaparecidos

Forever

February 15

This afternoon, we spread a handful of Miguel's ashes over the
secret mass grave where he was found. Alfonso will take a good
portion with him; today he told me that years ago the Riveras

decided that when Miguel's body was found, his ashes would be sprinkled on the waters of the Chanleufú River, one of his favourite places when he was growing up.

I'll take the rest to Canada. Miguel would've never imagined that part of his body and soul would travel so far away from where he was born, but the dictatorship made sure we'd end up scattered around the world and now Vancouver is home to his daughter and his *compañera*.

February 23

I'm on my way back to Vancouver. Señora Rina, Señora Isabel and Don Carlos, plus several of my new friends from the Association of Relatives of the Disappeared Political Prisoners came to the airport to say good-bye. Last night, Señora Isabel brought me the placard with Miguel's picture, the one we used at a demonstration outside the Supreme Court building. I had left it as a memento for the Association, but my friends insisted that I should take it with me.

In this picture, Miguel is playing with the Symphony; his violin rests on his shoulder, the fingers in his left hand are dancing on the neck of the instrument, his right hand holds the bow. He's smiling and his eyes are half-open, as if he were dreaming.

Now I'm glad I'm taking the placard home with me. This is the way I want to remember Miguel. I will never forget the sight of his remains—the astonishment and pain imprinted on his face his dry, blackened skin; his shrunken body... No. I will not let my mind forget that sight. But my heart will carry the image on the placard: Miguel *entero*. All of Miguel. Miguel, the violinist. Miguel, the dreamer.

Vancouver, Canada
September, 2011

Tania

One bright morning in July, we took the ferry to Vancouver
Island, three cars and twelve people in total: Ayanna, my friend
since I was fifteen, her partner Tom and their two kids; my hockey buddies Kathy, Joyce and Lian; my mami's friends Megan and
Teresa; Sadu and me. We spent a good part of the crossing on
the outside decks, basking in the breathtaking spectacle of water,
mountains and sky, and looking for migrating whales. At one
point, the captain announced that a pod of orcas was visible from
the left side of the ship, but by the time we got there, they were
gone. Obviously, the kids were very disappointed and didn't let
up until we promised to take them on a whale-watching expedi-
tion out of Tofino in the next couple of days.

Dwayne and his sister were waiting for us at the Nanaimo
terminal. I hadn't seen my friend in years, since he moved back
to Port Hardy after graduating from the Emily Carr Institute for
Art and Design. He's put on some weight, but otherwise looks
exactly the same: a thick brush of black hair on his head and a
wide, toothy smile on his face. He's his band's chief now—a position of honour, power and responsibility—but that doesn't seem

to have gone to his head; he continues to be the humble, gentle Dwayne of our days at Britannia High School.

Back in February, when my mami came back from Chile, we decided that, come summer, we'd go to Pacific Rim National Park on the west coast of Vancouver Island and spread Miguel's ashes there. But my mami didn't live long enough to be part of the excursion. The cancer of the bones that struck her so suddenly ravaged her body quickly and she passed away on June fifteenth, the same day that the Vancouver Canucks lost the game for the Stanley Cup. She was sixty-one years old.

Unlike my grandma, who wished for her ashes to be buried in a small urn-plot at Mountain View Cemetery in Vancouver, my mami asked that hers be offered to the Pacific Ocean, together with Miguel's. So, after picking up Dwayne and his sister in Nanaimo, we began our drive across the island through a lush, never-ending forest of ancient fir, spruce and cedar. We had to stop twice: once to make sure we didn't hurt a family of black tailed deer that was eating ferns by the road, and again to let a mama black bear and her cub cross to the other side. They certainly took their time and the cub even stopped to have a good look and a sniff at the idling cars.

"A good sign," Dwayne whispered.

"For us, 'bear' represents strength and wisdom," his sister explained.

"'Bear' also carries the teachings of our ancestors," Dwayne added.

When I had phoned Dwayne a couple of weeks earlier to invite him to join us in the spreading of my mami's and Miguel's ashes, he hadn't hesitated to accept.

"It'll be an honour," he said. Then offered, "I can ask my sister Fay to come along— she's a shaman and I'm sure she'll be happy to help put your mom and dad's spirits to rest."

Fay turned out to be a wonderful cook, as well. While the rest of us pitched the tents and organized the campsite, she took it upon herself to build a fire and cook a wholesome smoked salmon stew.

After dinner, we took off for the seashore. Everybody offered to help me carry the urns with my parents' ashes, but I insisted on taking them myself. I put them in my bag and held them close to my chest. This was my last chance to be close to my mami's body, to feel the weight of Miguel's remains; the father I never met.

The beach stretched out mile after mile—a shimmering, golden surface in the setting sun—and the fierce, open ocean roared like a pack of a thousand lions. In the dying light, the forest became a multitude of ghostly figures swaying in the wind.

A few surfers were still riding the waves, their dark silhouettes balancing on the frothy crests. People of all ages were walking, running, flying kites, playing ball. But the immensity and majesty of the landscape was such that, in the distance, everybody looked tiny and insignificant.

We collected armloads of driftwood and, in no time, had a

strong bonfire going, right on the edge of the ebbing tide. Fay asked us to stand in a semicircle, following the curve of the fire. While Dwayne helped her to drape her traditional button blanket over her shoulders and then put on his own ceremonial mask, I placed both urns on the sand, between our bodies and the rustling flames.

On either side of us, facing the water, Dwayne and Fay began to summon the spirits that would guide my mami's and Miguel's in their last journey. Dwayne held his hand-drum high. A beating heart and a wailing voice rose over the roar of the ocean. Fay joined in with her own voice and the jangling of her rattles. After a few minutes, they urged us to come together in a dance around the fire and the urns. I don't know how long we were dancing and chanting. At times, I felt like I was floating in the wind; at others, I was engulfed by the blazing flames, tumbling in the crashing waves or perched like a bird on one of the gigantic trees.

As the dancing subsided, Dwayne and Fay guided us to stand side by side at the edge of the ocean. Dwayne positioned himself at one end of the line and Fay at the other, each holding an urn. They were the first ones to take a handful of ashes and offer it to the wind. The urns made their way up and down the line, until all the ashes were gone. My parents were finally free. They had joined the spirit world.

My exhibition and performance piece entitled "Retribution" opened to the public a week ago.

The first part is made up of a stainless steel frame in the form of a maze. This frame supports panels of white silk on which I printed black and white photographs portraying the history of my family. Some are simple and direct; others, juxtapositions that in some cases are enhanced by my own illustrations, sketched in charcoal. For example, in one of them I'm sitting on Miguel's lap as he plays with the Santiago Symphony, and in another one I'm playing soccer with my uncle Andresito and the Unión Juvenil boys; my grandfather, Andrés, is in his coaching uniform on the sidelines and my mami and grandma are sitting on the bleachers, cheering us on.

I had great fun working on this piece—going through photo albums, deciding which pictures to use just the way they are and which to combine; printing them on the silk panels and then deciding where to add my own drawings. Going to Dressew, the fabric store on Hastings Street, to find the silk was also quite the adventure: tons of different knits, thicknesses, widths and even shades of white to choose from. It made me think of my grandmother back in the nineteen forties, when she would go to her favourite Santiago store to get fabric for her embroidery projects and home-made dresses. Making the stainless steel frame proved to be more trying, though. Fortunately, I found an excellent metal worker on Granville Island and, with his help, it turned out perfect.

When the spectators come out of the silk maze, they enter a square room. Immediately to the left, on the floor and against the wall, is my blue chest, filled with the gifts that the political

335

prisoners at Tres Álamos concentration camp made for us during my mom's pregnancy. On that same wall I rested the placard with Miguel's picture and hung my mami's tapestries. On the opposite wall, I placed my grandma's pottery pieces and watercolours. The back corners of the space are occupied by two seamstress mannequins: one wearing my uncle Andresito's soccer jersey and the other, the sky blue dress that my mami wore for the Youth Orchestra concerts.

Against the back wall and in the middle of the room, I attempt to reproduce the kitchen of the little house on Esmeralda Street in Valdivia: a wood stove enameled in black, a wooden cupboard and a pinewood table, covered with a red and white checkered oilcloth and surrounded by stools. On top of the table you can see my grandmother's *Imperial 62* recipe book, photo albums, the journal that my mami kept when she returned to Chile and my grandfather Andrés' embroidered handkerchief stretched out on a circular needlepoint frame.

Even though I didn't really have to do any "work" per se, this part of the exhibition was the most difficult to put together since each piece is charged with so much history—so much living and dying. I had a few good cries as I washed and ironed my uncle Andresito's soccer jersey. In the photographs, he appears content and self-confident, but I can't imagine how hard it must've been to be gay in the Chile of the nineteen sixties and seventies, not even accepted by his own mother. I know that after his murder my grandma realized her mistake, but he didn't have a chance to hear about her change of heart. My mami's dress looks s small on the mannequin that I had a good cry about her too; hard to picture my mother as an innocent, young girl, completely unaware of the hardships life had in store for her. But I also had to smile, thinking about how precocious she was—falling in love with Miguel at age twelve and playing in the Youth Orchestra.

Going through my old blue chest was particularly painful. I hadn't opened it in years and was taken aback by its screeching hinges and the strong smell of cedar from the many chips that my grandmother put inside to preserve the clothes. I fingered the miniature batiste shirts, held the supple little sweaters, toques and booties to my cheek, admired the colourful wooden toys and wrapped myself in the knitted blankets. I laid everything on the floor and examined the chest itself, its deep, smooth cavity, the copper hinges, lock and handles, rusted now after so many years, the bright, royal blue paint, which somehow has remained intact, the rounded cover with the word "Tania" carved in big, cursive letters on its very top. I read my name several times before I mustered the courage to run my fingers over it. Only then was I able to let myself feel the horror of my mother's ordeal, consider the likelihood of being the torturer's daughter.

If Marcelino Romero is indeed my father, did I inherit his socio-pathic traits? Does any part of me carry his contempt for human be-ings? I delved inside myself as I traced my name on top of the chest. Clearly, the answer is No. For thirty-six years I have been decent human being and have no intentions of changing. My life has been driven by love, not hatred.

I got up and paced around the room. Now, my heart was thumping and my mind, racing.

We all have the capacity for kindness and cruelty. Marcelino Romero chose cruelty. My mother and grandmother chose kindness. It doesn't really matter whether Marcelino Romero is my biological father or not. What matters is that I'm not at all like him. If my mama actually knew that she had given birth to the torturer's daughter and then shared her secret with my grandmother, the two of them avenged Romero and his masters only too well. They didn't fall in the trap that the dictatorship set up for them. They didn't let hatred take over their spirits. I'm sure they must've felt hatred at some point or another— who wouldn't, given their circumstances? But they made a choice and decided to opt for love and hope, regardless of who my biological father may be. That's how they achieved justice. I am their retribution.

I went to my bedroom, took Judge Arturo Leiva's letter out of my dresser's bottom drawer and read it for the last time. Then walked into the living room. We hadn't used the fireplace for couple of months, but the usual box of matches was still on the mantle. It didn't take long for the paper to burn, for the ashes to mix with the mound of cinders at the bottom of the hearth.

"Miguel is my father," I said to the dead letter in a firm, loud voice.

For two hours a day, between four and six in the afternoon, I make and serve *onces* in this room. It's a performance of sorts, which invites the spectators to participate in one of my family's—

and all Chileans'—daily rituals. The performance begins with my arrival carrying a cloth bag containing a tin of Nescafé, another of sweetened condensed milk, *hayuyas*, butter, cooked ham and cheese. Then I put my purchases on the table, start the fire, open the cupboard, take out what I need and proceed to make an apple *kuchen*.

Every afternoon, when I go to the Latin Market before heading for the gallery, I try to imagine that I'm my mami as a girl, or my grandmother as a young woman, going to the Ideal bakery to get the usual *hayuyas* and then to Nilo Delicatessen for everything else.

After I put the *kuchen* in the oven, I sit down to do what I have loved doing since I was a little girl: sketch in my journal. In the meantime, the room has warmed up, a sweet and sticky aroma has begun to fill the air and the spectators have started to congregate. Then, I take the *kuchen* out of the oven, set the table and serve *onces*.

Generally the ritual begins in silence, but, little by little, people start to ask questions about my family, Chile and the installation itself. Some leaf through the photo albums and mom's journal, or examine the handkerchief; others skim the recipe book. Sometimes lively discussions evolve about politics, immigration, abuse, wars and other catastrophes around the world.

And then, sometimes people are more interested about me personally. A couple of days ago a young man asked me if I had ever gone back to Chile.

"No, I haven't," I had to admit, "but I left when I was only two days old, so for me it would be like going for the first time."

"How come you haven't gone?" he wanted to know.

His question gave me pause.

"Well, I've been busy living my life here—after all, this is where I'm really from—and, I guess I also had to work through a few things first..." I responded as I smiled and pointed to the exhibition. "But now I feel ready... Now I know that I want to go I will go. Soon," I added, speaking to myself more than to him.

When the spectators leave this room, they enter my world—the section of the exhibition where I present the Canada I know and belong to.

In the last six months, as I tried to decide which pieces to show I looked over and over again at everything I have produced along the years—sketches, drawings, collages, portraits, landscapes cityscapes, photographs, computer generated pieces. Many depic the people and the places I love: my family, my friends, Commer cial Drive, the North Shore mountains, Stanley Park, the wes side beaches, the city's skyline... Quite a few illustrate the beaut and skill of the game of hockey, our national sport. But man also portray those aspects of the country that don't appear in th pristine, innocuous postcards of Canada, that are certainly no included in the statement "the best country in the world," as th official propaganda claims, that don't belong in the land of mil and honey that expectant immigrants dream about.

I have dozens of pieces of the Vancouver where steel and glass skyscrapers collide with infested rooming houses, of homeless people sleeping in the streets, of junkies getting their fixes in back allies, of men lost in skid-row, of desperate looking women and children lining up outside a food bank, of anti-globalization and anti-racism demonstrations, of protests against clear-cutting...

I also found a few pieces of immigrants doing menial jobs. One of these is of an older South Asian man mopping the floors at Pacific Mall. I was intrigued by the contrast between his upper-class appearance and the job he was doing, so I approached him and asked if I could make a couple of sketches of him as he worked. He was hesitant.

"I don't know—this is embarrassing," he answered while pointing to the mop. "I was an engineer in Sri Lanka," he explained, blushing.

"My mom was a social worker in Chile, but when we first got here she had to clean buildings for quite a while and then go back to university to have her degree validated," I offered. "And, my grandma was a pastry-making teacher, but she ended up working as a maid for many, many years. She used to say that any kind of work is honourable."

The man smiled and extended his hand. I shook it.

"My name is Kasun," he stated proudly.

"I'm Tania," I responded.

"Please go ahead," he said, referring to my sketching, and went back to work.

So, the selection of pieces I decided to hang in the exhibition attempts to convey a Canada which is both beautiful and ugly, rich and poor, openhanded and greedy, joyous and sullen. A Canada that smells of fresh bread, car exhaust, salt and cedar and sounds like an ocean, the rustling of leaves, the beating of drums and the sing-song of a hundred different languages spoken at the same time.

I called this section *Qenple,* a Salish word meaning "we" and "us," which Dwayne offered to me as a gift to the project.

The inaugural piece is a totem pole carved by the kids who attended summer camp at Britannia Community Centre this year. Dwayne was kind enough to leave his obligations in Port Hardy behind and come to Vancouver to guide the kids through their work. He even brought with him the enormous red cedar stump they used—a work of art in itself, even before it became the breathtaking, monumental figure that welcomes the spectators to *Qenple.* As important as its beauty, though, are the stories that the kids carved on the wood relating memorable events in their own lives and the lives of their communities, exploring their varied ancestries and, above all, expressing the pride they take in who they are.

Next, the spectators enter a room where my work is exhibited on the walls and objects loaned to the project by my friends and their families are displayed in four glass cases in the centre of the room: Ayanna's mom's *diriic,* her Somali wedding dress; a quilt made by Kathy's Mennonite grandmother; Joyce's "button-box"—a beat-up, mother-of-pearl accordion— and an IRA poster with a Bobby Sands' quote, both of which she inherited from her Irish grandfather; and a head-tax certificate presented to Lian's Chinese great-grandfather in 1918.

The final section of the exhibition consists of one large acrylic painting that the spectators see point blank as they walk out of Qenple. It's a portrait of Paloma, the daughter I'm pregnant with.

I broke the news to my mami two days before she died. At first she was dumbfounded.

"Does Sadu know?" she asked, finally.

"Of course, mami! We planned it together, you know?"

"Ay mijita, my lovely kitty-cat, that's wonderful, wonderful news!" she exclaimed, opening her arms. I sat on her bed and hugged her. She was just skin and bones by then but all I could feel was the suppleness and warmth of the body I had known my whole life.

I kissed her on the forehead and then walked towards the window. The chestnut trees that line our street looked like apparitions, their fresh, green leaves concealing their imposing skeletons after months and months of standing naked in the cold. Life and death—the perpetual cycle of transformation and renewal, I thought.

When I turned around, a tear was trickling down my mother's face.

"She'll be as beautiful a human being as you are," she stated.

In my portrait, Paloma is beautiful. She has Sadu's dark complexion, Miguel's small, rounded ears and thick eyebrows, my mami's black, straight hair and fleshy mouth, my grandma's upturned nose, and my own green eyes. Most importantly, she looks happy. She is happy.

As the spectators take in Paloma's portrait, they hear a poem that Sadu wrote and then recorded accompanied by his tabla drum:

we journey from life to life
overflowing with
words   images
flutters   hearths   yearnings

we turn corners
cross thresholds
contrive

fresh
futures

I welcome the new, open threshold and the fresh future that life has set out in front of me. I look over my shoulder and I see them all behind me—my ancestors, my mentors, the companions that have guided me this far and will continue to point me in the direction of decency and integrity. I look ahead and I can see glimpses of the world that so many have strived for long and hard: a world made by and for *qenple*, by and for all of us. A world that we can truly call ours.

Afterword

Que vivan los estudiantes	Long live the students
Jardín de las alegrías	Gardens of joy
Son aves que no se asustan	Birds who aren't afraid
De animal ni policía...	Of neither animals nor policemen...

Violeta Parra—1960

As I complete revisions on *Retribution*, Chilean university and secondary students have taken to the streets by the hundreds of thousands. They have engaged art, theatre, dance, music and poetry to denounce the current educational system and demand the reinstatement of public education as a right guaranteed by the state.

In 1981, the Augusto Pinochet dictatorship imposed a reform that turned education into a commodity to be purchased and sold, to speculate with and profit from. Thirty years later, the students have said "Enough" and are calling for free-of-charge and good quality education for all. In doing so, they have also brought to the forefront the injustices inherent to Chile's entire economic model and the inadequacies and limitations of the country's democracy—twenty-two years after the end of the dictatorship the nation is still being governed by the 1980 Pinochet Constitution.

The participants and leaders of this vibrant movement are

very young. They were born in the late 1980's—at least fifteen years after the coup of 1973—when mounting international and internal pressure finally forced Pinochet to call a plebiscite and then an election. However, these youngsters' bravery and ability to articulate the country's plights and calls for change speak of a political savvy well beyond their years.

Witness Camila Vallejo, the twenty-three year old at the helm of the movement, whose calm, yet strong stance, in addition to her eloquence, beauty and exceptional leadership qualities have sparked robust reactions. On the one hand, she has won the respect and admiration of millions of her compatriots and much of the national and international press has spoken glowingly of her abilities. On the other hand, right-wing politicians and members of the Chilean business class would do anything to get rid of her. So much so, that Tatiana Acuña, a high-ranking official in the Sebastián Piñera government, wrote on her Twitter account: "If you kill the bitch, you kill the uprising"—a threat on Camila's life which cost Acuña her job and also lead Chile's Supreme Court to place the student leader under police surveillance.

I find it serendipitous that as this book is about to be released, students have once again become the protagonists of Chilean history.

Retribution is a work of fiction—a product of my imagination. However, the overall story is based on historical events that I witnessed or participated in. The student movement of the 1960's and 70's is an example of one such development. Today, when I watch and listen to Camila Vallejo, her fellow leaders in the uprising and the hundreds of thousands of students who have taken to the streets, I feel an intense kinship with all of them. As well, I cannot but believe that their know-how and dedication is rooted in the long history of struggle of Chilean students and is the result of the seeds sown by all those who came before.

I'm happy that in a humble way *Retribution* pays tribute to the Chilean students of the past and in doing so, to those of today.

¡Que vivan los estudiantes! Long Live the Students!

Vancouver, September 4, 2011

Glossary

Alameda Boulevard: In Chile, *"La Alameda"* is the short form to refer to Alameda Bernardo O'Higgins, the main artery that crosses
Santiago in an east-west direction. Historically, this boulevard has
been the gathering place for all kinds of celebrations and protests.
In his last speech, Salvador Allende said: "... sooner rather than later
free men will open these great alamedas again and walk towards the
construction of a better society."

Aquí: Here.

Araucaria: Monkey-puzzle tree.

Asistencia Pública: Public Emergency Unit.

Barquillo: Large wafer rolled into the shape of a tube.

Barrio: Neighbourhood.

Berlín (pl. *berlines*): Large, round fried pastry sprinkled with sugar.

Bioluvil: Brand name of a laundry detergent.

Bolero: Slow-tempo, melodic Spanish and Latin American musical
form and dance, usually with romantic lyrics.

Burrito beans: Grey-coloured beans. Also known as Tórtola beans.

Campamento: Shanty town. In Chile, in the early 1970's, the term evolved to describe a permanent community usually built by the dwellers themselves on the grounds of their former shanty town.

Campesino: Country-side worker.

Carbonada: Chilean soup made of small cubes of beef and assorted vegetables.

Castilla wrap: A poncho made of thick, long-haired, black wool.

Cazuela: Chilean soup made with chicken, beef or pork ribs, potatoes, squash, carrots and green beans.

Ceibo: South American tree with bright crimson flowers, also known as cockspur coral tree.

Chañar: Small deciduous tree also known as *kumbaru* and Chilean green wood.

Chanco cheese: Chilean white cheese.

Chirimoya: A large, oval fruit with dark green skin and white, creamy flesh native to the Andean valleys.

Citroneta: A small, inexpensive Citroen car popular in Chile during the 1960's and 70's.

Compañero/compañera: Comrade, companion.

Completo: Chilean-style hotdog topped with mayonnaise, mustard, avocado, sauerkraut and tomatoes.

Coral Verde: Brand name of a popular Chilean cologne.

Cordillera: Mountain range. In Chile, it is used as a short term to refer to the Andes.

Crudo: Tartar steak sandwich.

Cueca: Chilean traditional musical form and also the country's national dance.

El Mercurio: Conservative Chilean daily. Founded in 1827, it is the longest running newspaper in Spanish language in the world. In the early 1970's it received CIA funding to undermine the Salvador Allende government and create the conditions for a military coup.

Entero: Whole.

Gringo: Native of the United States, Canada or Northern and Eastern Europe

Ginguito: Little *gringo*.

Hayuya: Chilean flat, round bread.

Huaso: Chilean cowboy.

Kuchen: German word for "cake," adopted in the South of Chile to describe a fruit cake.

Lavanda Atkinson: Brand name of a popular Chilean cologne.

Liquidámbar: Redgum or sweetgum tree.

Lomito con palta: Chilean sandwich made with pork loin and avocado

Lúcuma: A green, pear-shaped semi-tropical fruit native to the Andean region. In Chile, *lúcuma's* fibrous, yellow flesh is used mainly to make ice cream and cake fillings.

Machista: Male chauvinist.

Madrileño/madrileña: Native of Madrid.

Malecón: A pedestrian walkway by the sea. Also used to refer to a pier.

Manjar: Caramel-like pastry filling made of milk and sugar.

Mapuche: Indigenous nation of south-central Chile and south-western Argentina.

María Cenicienta Cookbook: A popular compilation of Chilean recipes originally published by María Cenicienta in 1900 and reprinted many times up to the 1960's.

Mate: A tea-like drink made from the dried leaves of the South American yerba *mate* shrub. Generally, *mate* is consumed with friends from a shared hollow calabash gourd. The infusion is drunk through a *bombilla*, a metal straw whose submerged end is flared and has small holes, thus acting like a sieve.

Mijita, por Dios: For God's sake, my little daughter.

Onces or Once: Chilean term for "tea time," a meal traditionally taken between 5:00 and 7:00 PM, consisting of tea or coffee, bread, ham and cheese, and pastries.

Plan Z: According to the military, a plan devised by Salvador Allende's supporters to assume control of Chile's democratic institutions in anticipation of a likely take-over by the country's armed forces. The alleged knowledge of this plan was used by Augusto Pinochet as a justification for the coup d'état of September 11, 1973.

Peña: A social gathering with music and food.

Pisco: Chilean and Peruvian brandy-like alcoholic beverage made from grapes.

Pisco sour: Apéritif containing *pisco*, lemon and lime juice, sugar and egg white.

Plaza: Square.

Presente: Present.

Ronda: Ring-a-ring-a-roses.

Tonada: Chilean traditional musical form with lyrics related to rural settings.

Torreón: Watchtower. In Valdivia, two such constructions were built by the Spanish colonial government during the 1700's to safeguard the entrances to the city and defend it from attacks by the *Mapuche*. Now they sit well inside the city and have been preserved as historical monuments.

The following materials were particularly helpful in informing the novel:

Print and virtual publications: *El infierno* (Luz Arce); *Report of the Chilean Commission on Truth and Reconciliation* (Raúl Retigg et al); *Historia no oficial del Frente Patriótico* (Manuel Rodríguez); *Trauma—Explorations in Memory* (Cathy Caruth et al); *Inca Cosmology and The Human Body* (Constance Classen); *Vida, pasión y muerte en Pisagua* (Bernardo Guerrero Jiménez et al); *Archivos de la Agrupación de Familiares de Detenidos Desaparecidos; Revista Ecran; Wisdom of the Elders—Native Traditions on the Northwest Coast* (Ruth Kirk); *Salish Dictionary* and other publications of the Salish Language Institute; various Chilean and Canadian newspapers and magazines.

Paintings, tapestries, collages, installations, sculpture and photography by: Alejandra Aguirre, Judith Currely-Summer, Robert Davidson, Cora Li-Leger, Don Li-Leger, Paula Luttringer, Sally Mankus, Violeta Parra, Bill Reid, Marianna Schmidt and Valentina Vega.

Films: *Campamento* (Tom Cohen, Richard Pearce and Leon Janey), *La Flaca Alejandra* (Carmen Castillo and Guy Girarard), *La Batalla de Chile* (Patricio Guzmán), *Estadio Nacional* (Carmen Luz arot) and *Villa Grimaldi—Archeology of Memory* (Quique Cruz and Marilyn Mulford).

Music: Various albums by Johann Sebastian Bach, Joseph Haydn, Ilapu, Inti Illiminani, Víctor Jara, Patricio Manns, Nicolo Paganini, Angel Parra, Isabel Parra, Violeta Parra, Quilapayún, Osvaldo Rodríguez and Pyotor Ilych Tchaikovsky.

Acknowledgments

Retribution is the result of many years of research, writing and rewriting. Most of this endeavour was solitary. However, I would not have been able to complete the novel without the generous assistance of dozens of people and a few institutions, both in Chile and Canada. I'm indebted to them all.

Myriad contributions were offered by Valentina Vega, Grínor Rojo, Enrique Sandoval, Marta Miranda, Jorge Rodríguez, Cristina Lopetegui, Maruja Pinochet, Mónica Rumoroso, Elsa Álvarez de Balanda, Eduardo Araya, José Aguirre, Betty Díaz, Lorena Jara, Adriana Espinoza, Charlie Dorris, Karin Konstantynowicz, Mari Mana, Carmen Schmidt and Hildegard Schmidt.

The following family members, friends and colleagues read the novel at different stages of development and contributed helpful observations: Alejandra Aguirre, Carmen Aguirre, Litsa Chatsivasileu, Alan Creighton-Kelly, Mónica Escudero, Ted Everton, Hugh Hazelton, Cynthia Flood, Fernanda Giménez, Gabriel Meza, Marta Miranda, Grínor Rojo, Mónica Rumoroso, Enrique Sandoval, Anna South, Carol Stos, Iris Tupholme, Valentina Vega and Jessica Woollard.

Lydia Kwa and Nancy Richler provided crucial support. They also read most versions of the book and offered invaluable feedback

Fellow members of the SDM Writers Group lent encouragement and reassurance.

Rose Gaete was instrumental in helping me to reshape the novel at a time when I felt "stuck" and disheartened.

Ted Everton and David and Ryan Hamar granted me permission to use the name of their Vancouver hockey team: West Coast Guerillas.

All the culinary concoctions mentioned in *Retribution* come from my late mother's kitchen and recipe notebooks. Her dress-making, watercolours and pottery also inspired much of Soledad's creative activities.

My editor, Jennifer Day, pushed me gently but firmly into maximizing the book's potential during the final stages of revisions. I was fortunate to work with a professional with such a keen, sensitive eye.

Sarah Wayne and Brendan Ouellette of Three O'Clock Press worked tirelessly to produce a publication of optimum quality and to ensure that *Retribution* will be read as widely as possible.

Over the years that it took to write the novel, the Latin American Studies Program of Simon Fraser University afforded me many teaching opportunities. Similarly, the Department of French, Hispanic and Italian Studies of the University of British Columbia offered me a position as Writer in Residence and Adjunct Professor in 2009. These educational endeavours helped me as a writer and also nourished my passion for teaching.

Grants from the Canada Council of the Arts and the British Columbia Arts Council allowed me to dedicate prolonged periods of uninterrupted time to *Retribution*.

My deepest gratitude goes to my family.

The spirits of my late father, late mother and late brother Nelson kept me company and comforted me during difficult, pain-laden times. Their lives and deaths also motivated me to continue writing.

My visits to my brother Choche's and sister-in-law Kitty's home were the key to keeping my Southern Chilean soul strong and healthy.

I'm the mother of three remarkable human beings—my best teachers in the difficulties and contradictions of leading a life that intertwines motherhood and political activism. I'm forever grateful for their trust, loyalty, honesty, generosity and love.

I'm also blessed to be the *abuelita*—grandmother—of two beautiful boys. Their mere existence fills my days with wonder and joy.

Last, but not least, I thank Alan Creighton-Kelly, my partner in life, for his love and unwavering support to this project. He is the man *alongside* this small woman.

About the author

Carmen Rodríguez was born in Chile and moved to Vancouver, Canada following the military coup of 1973 in her native country. She has worked as instructor and professor across a range of disciplines—from literature and cultural studies to creative writing and literacy education—in both Spanish and English. She has also served as correspondent for Radio Canada International, and was a founding member of *Aquelarre*, a Latin American women's bilingual magazine.

Her previous work includes *Guerra Prolongada /Protracted War* (Women's Press, 1992), a volume of poetry, and the award-winning collection of short stories *and a body to remember with /De cuerpo entero* (Arsenal Pulp Press/Editorial Los Andes, 1997). She was also the director and writer of Educating for Change, a video and handbook for instructors of aboriginal literacy learners. *Retribution* is her first novel.